A
Harlequin
Romance

1395

TERMINUS TEHRAN

by

ROUMELIA LANE

HARLEQUIN BOOKS

WINNIPEG ● CANADA

First published in 1969 by Mills & Boon Limited,
50 Grafton Way, Fitzroy Square, London, England.

SBN 373-01395-7

© Roumelia Lane 1969

Harlequin Canadian edition published May, 1970
Harlequin U.S. edition published August, 1970

Printed in Canada

1395

CHAPTER ONE

CLAIRE backed her car into the dimly-lit parking space, stepped out wearily, and fumbled for the key to her flat. As usual, that unique piece of shaped metal was missing again. It wasn't until she was halfway up the second flight of stairs in the tall Georgian house that she found the latch key buried under a jumble of oddments in the pocket of her driving coat. Gazing at it with a slightly malicious gleam, she thrust it towards its lock before it could elude her again.

It was then that she saw the line of light under the door. Puzzled, Claire found her hands fumbling. Who on earth...?

She was saved the trouble of struggling with the key, for as she leaned against the door it fell away from her, and as she looked up, the surprise on her face gave way to a glow of pleasure.

'Mike!'

Before she could say anything else the slim figure in baggy trousers and sweater had swept her up in a hug and she was whirled into the room.

'Do you realise,' she said laughingly extricating herself to come to land on the slightly faded carpet, 'it's almost six months since I heard from you! What kind of a brother are you anyway?'

'One that doesn't go much on letter-writing,' he grinned.

As Claire pulled off her coat and swished the shoulder-length hair, slightly paler than his own, he bent to switch on another bar of the electric fire.

'Your landlady let me in,' he pointed out. 'I came yesterday, but she told me you weren't due back until tonight.'

Claire nodded and dropped into a chair. 'I've been driving all day down from Scotland.'

'For fun?' Mike looked at her, widening his grin.

'No!' She tilted him an injured look. 'For work.'

'What's the job now, then?'

'I'm with a motoring magazine.'

5

'You mean, you write?'

'Kind of. I try to put the woman's point of view over for women drivers.'

'Well,' Mike came back to rock over her, 'seeing as you're not a woman yet, I don't ...'

'Hey!' Claire kicked her foot out goodnaturedly to jab him on the shin.

'Okay, no ribbing,' he laughed, and then looking down at her, 'You like the job?'

'I did,' Claire flopped back, smiling wryly, 'until I got to know the British Isles inside out!' Looking to where he had gone to stretch up beside the panelled fireplace, she asked, 'What about you? The last time you wrote, you were chopping trees down in Canada. And the time before that, I think you mentioned a ranch in California.' She tilted a fair eyebrow up to him in quizzical good humour. 'No danger of you settling down to a steady job, I suppose?'

'They're steady for as long as they interest me.' Mike's mouth drooped lopsidedly. 'At the moment I'm trying my hand at truck-driving.'

'Truck-driving!' Claire gave him a sideways look. 'Well, at least it's different,' she smiled.

'It's different all right,' he grinned. 'My route takes in seven countries across Europe and Asia, and I carry anything from helicopter spares to booze for the various Embassies.'

'Trust you to land a job like that!' Claire's eyes widened laughingly. 'Where do you start out from?'

'The company warehouse is in Warren Street, off Tottenham Court Road.'

She gave him a slightly admonishing look. 'You mean to say you've actually been working from London and you've never bothered to look me up?'

'I've only done a couple of runs,' Mike shrugged sheepishly. 'Anyway, I get two weeks off between each one, so we'll be running into one another quite a bit from now on.'

'Considering you're the only family I've got, I think that will be rather nice,' Claire smiled, rising from her chair. 'Now what about a meal? I've eaten myself, but ...'

'Not for me,' Mike shook his head. 'A cup of tea would go down well, though.' As she went off into the small kitchenette he followed her, and lifting the lid of the flowered teapot he said humorously, 'You'll have to show me how it's done, Claire. You know it's the one thing I miss on this London to Tehran run, a really good cup of ...'

'Tehran?' Claire lit the gas under the kettle and swung round, blowing out the match.

Mike looked up from the teapot and nodded at her surprise. 'That's the truck run. London to Tehran.'

Claire caught his enquiring look and sighed lightly. 'Of course you didn't know that Robin went out there.'

'Robin in Tehran?' Mike looked at her and then thrusting his hands in his pockets started to stroll. 'I thought you two would have been married by this time.'

Claire stared at the murmuring kettle. 'We ... we didn't want to rush things.'

'Rush things?' She heard her brother's mildly incredulous laugh. 'It must be all of a year now since he put that ring on your finger. I thought long engagements were out of fashion?'

'He's been abroad almost all of that time,' Claire shrugged. 'He heard of this firm who wanted someone for their export offices out there and ... well, he rather liked the idea.'

'How's he making out?' Mike asked.

'I'm not really sure. He's almost as bad at letter-writing as you are.' Claire poured the boiling water carefully into the teapot and placing the lid on added, 'I haven't heard from him in almost four months.'

'That's a long time for a chap contemplating marriage.' Mike waited until she had set out the tray, and then he carried it into the adjoining room.

Following him, Claire nodded, drawing in her lower lip. 'I must say I'm worried. He might be ill, or have had an accident or something.'

'I doubt it, If I know Robin he's ...' Frowning, Mike lowered the tray on the small table by the fire and came up to say somewhat briskly, 'How would it be if I paid him a call on my next trip?'

'That would be marvellous, but...'

'But what?'

Claire was staring hard at him. She lowered herself into her chair trance-like and said dreamily, 'I've just had an idea.' For a few seconds her gaze went off into space, and

7

then she was jerking to the edge of her seat to say eagerly, 'Mike, tell me about this job of yours.'

'My sweet, I've just told you,' Mike said, pouring his own tea. Seeing his sister's avid green gaze he sat down with a patient sigh to elaborate. 'Well, there's me and this sixty-foot truck and ...'

'No, not that.' Claire jumped a little nearer to the edge of her chair. 'I mean, who runs the company? How big is it?'

'Euranian Transport?' Mike shrugged. 'About eight trucks. I believe Greg Millard started out a couple of years back with one and then ...'

'Greg Millard? Is he the ...?'

'The boss,' Mike grinned, lifting his cup and setting it down.

'What's he like?'

'Oh, thirty-fiveish. Ex-Army. Major or colonel or something. Likes to keep things moving.'

'Would he go for the idea of a bit of free publicity, do you think?'

Mike pulled in a breath at the question, and considered. 'Well, he was shrewd enough to see the advantages of a direct-haul service against the long sea and rail route, and more important the cheapness compared to air freight. I don't see him turning down anything that will help his business.'

Claire absorbed all this glowingly, and watching her, Mike asked with a dubious grin, 'What have you got on your mind, my poppet? I seem to recall that your ideas have an uncanny knack of going haywire.'

Claire was looking at him, but not apparently listening. She asked in a faraway voice, 'You have a co-driver on your trips, I take it?'

'That's right.'

'Well,' she got up and whirled round, smiling to herself, 'I think I'm going to take his place.'

'Claire!' Mike got to his feet and moved towards her with a heavy solicitous air. 'Didn't you say you've just driven down from Scotland? Well, obviously the journey has been too much for you. Now a good night's sleep,' he put his hands on her shoulders humorously, 'and you'll be fine.'

'I feel terrific.' Claire spun laughingly. 'I'm going to see Robin.'

8

'In *my* truck?' Mike folded his arms disbelievingly. As Claire whirled again he asked dryly, 'And how are you going to explain it to the boss?'

'The magazine will take care of that,' she returned lightly. 'They'll ask his permission for me to do a feature on the journey from London to Tehran.'

'I get it.' Mike watched her, nodding slowly. 'A kind of working-your-own-passage scheme?' Rocking on his heels, he asked, 'And do you think your bosses are going to go for the idea of you sampling the three thousand and seventy odd miles in a truck?'

'Bound to. It'll make a fab story, especially from a woman's angle. And it's tailor-made for me with my own brother sitting in the driving seat.'

'And that way,' said Mike, pulling at his chin thoughtfully, 'Greg Millard gets his publicity. The magazine gets its feature, and you get to see Robin?' He gave her his slow boyish grin. 'I've got to hand it to you, Claire. You're a bright kid.'

She stepped up to him, the green eyes big and serious now. 'All joking aside, Mike, if I can arrange it, would you object to me coming along?'

'Not a bit.' He dropped a brotherly arm around her. 'Make up for my neglect over these past months. I wish you luck in trying to pull it off, but if you don't mind me saying so,' he crooked a smile at her, 'it all sounds a shade fantastic to me.'

'That's what the magazine world thrives on.' Claire turned a dancing green gaze upwards. 'You might be the adventurous type, Mike, but you haven't a clue when it comes to adventure in print. And anyway,' she gave him an impish look, 'why should you men have all the fun?'

Sloping his grin, he strolled to pick up his coat from a chair and nodding towards the fireplace said, 'I've put my address and phone number on that slip of paper under the clock. Give me a tinkle if you have any luck.'

'I'll come over.' Claire clasped her hands happily. 'You'll be able to help me with the documents and visas and things that I'll need for the journey.'

Mike moved out on to the landing and sighed lightly. 'Ah, the confidence of youth!'

9

Laughingly Claire stepped up to drop a kiss on his cheek.

'Goodnight, you doddering twenty-five-year-old, you!' she twinkled as he made his way down the stairs.

Dreamily she turned in and closed the door. Let Mike think what he liked. She felt in her bones that it was a good idea.

If *she* was enthusiastic, Tom Gerard, the features editor of *Ride*, was rapturous.

'It's a gem of a notion,' he beamed the next morning, slapping his hands across his desk and making the litter of papers flutter upwards in a worse confusion. 'Should be good for more than one feature.' He groped impatiently through the mess and then snapped at Claire, 'get the feller on the phone. Let's hear if he's a willing customer.'

Excitedly Claire rummaged out the phone from under the morning paper and dialled the number she had written down from the phone book. After only a couple of purring tones she heard a crisp voice state, 'Euranian Transport. Greg Millard speaking.'

As she opened her mouth to reply the editor whipped the phone from her and snapped, 'Here, let me talk to him.'

He lay back in his swivel chair, and staring up at the ceiling through thick-lensed glasses began with his usual line of introduction, comment on the weather, and friendly chit-chat. As Claire paced she heard him edge in breezily, 'We've heard about your truck service, Mr. Millard. I must say it's just the stuff we're looking for for *Ride*. How would you feel about us doing a feature on the next trip?'

He rambled on about inconsequential things after that, and Claire gathered that the man at the other end wasn't much of a talker. But what he *had* said must have been favourable, for Tom Gerard was nodding at her, and beaming down at the mouthpiece, as though he hoped his smile could travel along the wire as well as his voice.

After a final spate of hearty chatter he clapped the receiver down and swung in his chair towards Claire. 'Right.' He pointed a finger at her almost accusingly. 'You're in, girl. You've got two weeks to get any jabs you might need, and tie it up with visa people. I'll push things along for you where I can, but apart from that, you're on your own. Good truck

10

riding.'

He turned back to the jumble of papers on his desk and Claire floated out into the street. Just think! Two weeks from now, and she would be on her way. Admittedly the excitement over the prospective journey outshone a little the realisation that she would soon be seeing Robin again. but once she was actually travelling in the truck she would probably think of nothing else but him.

The days flew quickly by as she hurried from one government building to another obtaining the necessary documents that would get her across the various borders on the route. Mike had been through it all before he started his job, so he was able to give her a lot of useful tips. Just the same it was a time-consuming occupation.

Then there was a question of what clothes to take. She had several gay trouser suits that she used for her job as a driver for the magazine, but as Mike had pointed out, truck life was a little different. In the end she settled for jeans and sweaters, masses of underwear, and a few really good clothes for when she arrived in Tehran.

With so much to do, she sometimes doubted if she would be ready in time, but suddenly all the tasks were completed, and the day before they were due to start out she was able to drive off to her brother's flat and announce sweepingly that she was all set and raring to go.

'You know,' she said, pacing his littered living room with a happy thoughtfulness, 'I think perhaps I ought to go and see this Greg Millard of yours. He might want to give me some last-minute instructions, and I suppose it's common courtesy to go and introduce myself.'

Mike, spruce in nylon shirt, nodded absently as he carefully smoothed out the knot of his tie in the mirror. Watching him, Claire suggested, 'If you're calling in today, I could come along too and then...'

'Uhuh!' Mike was shaking his head. 'Not me,' he grinned, shrugging into his suit jacket. 'You forget, dear sister, that I'm on holiday, and I always make a point of staying strictly away from my place of employment until about five minutes before the grind starts.'

'Hmmm! I see,' Claire smiled goodhumouredly. 'Well, I'll just have to go on my own, then. I've got some last-minute

11

shopping to do this morning, so I'll probably go this afternoon. You'll be in about five, I take it?' she asked, casting a cryptic twinkle over his gleaming hair and finely pressed suit.

'Probably,' he replied, lowering his smile.

As the February day drizzled towards late afternoon Claire washed and changed and applied a fresh touch of make-up, ready for her meeting with Mike's boss. Probably this Greg Millard person would want to show her over his warehouse and give her a running commentary on how he would like her to slant the feature on his firm, so she had better look presentable.

In her mini-sports car she drove skilfully through the London traffic and on towards Warren Street. The Euranian Transport sign hung across the top of the entrance of a huge open yard, and boldly Claire swung in and parked her car alongside a tremendous red monster of a truck. Good heavens, were they as big as that? Stepping out, she gazed along the length in awe, and then seeing a youth nearby, thoughtfully checking a list, she asked politely, 'Could you tell me where I might find Mr. Greg Millard, please?'

The boy scowled over his list and flicking his pencil up said briefly, 'That's him over there near the office.'

Claire followed the direction of the pencil with her gaze and then moved smilingly forward. She approached, experiencing a tiny flicker of irritation, for the man by the glass-windowed office looked straight past her to snap out some instructions across the yard and then went back to the papers in his hand.

Well, he couldn't fail to miss seeing her in the scarlet trouser suit she was wearing, and she was used to masculine glances of appraisal over her pale shoulder-length hair and slender long-legged figure.

Something else that annoyed her was her own silly quick catch of breath at the sight of Greg Millard. He wasn't handsome, but there was a lean lined hardness about the face that somehow made one want to keep on looking. There was no mistaking the military set of those wide shoulders, although the tall lean-hipped frame was casually attired in open gaberdine lumber jacket and light-coloured slacks.

Swallowing her hurt pride at his indifference, Claire

stepped up to say brightly, 'Mr. Greg Millard, I believe? Tom Gerard of *Ride* magazine spoke to you on the phone about me.'

A pair of pale cold eyes swept over her and then returned to the sheaf of papers in his hand. Claire clenched her fingers at her sides but kept her smile to explain breezily, 'I'm to do the feature on the truck journey to Tehran.'

As Greg Millard raised his head she thought, Aha! That's going to make him pay attention. He would be all ears now he knew that she was to do his publicity for him. She waited expectantly for the effusive apologies, the smiles and the invitations to tour the premises, and then her jaw dropped slightly as the narrowed gaze went past her. She heard the curt voice calling out, 'Better get a move on with the loading, Roger. The other truck will be in shortly.' The glance was brought back to the sheaf of papers for a second, then the big figure turned and stepped inside the office.

Well, of all the rude, ill-mannered ... Controlling her rapid breathing, Claire followed him to snap thinly, 'I suppose you have heard of our magazine?'

She was rewarded with a brief nod from the dark head that bent over a cluttered desk and then the clipped reply, 'They said they were sending someone to cover the Tehran run, but I'd no idea it was a female, let alone a slip of a kid.'

What a *nice* person! Straightening her mouth and drawing herself up to her full five feet five inches, Claire said coldly, 'Mr. Millard, I've been driving since I was old enough to hold a licence, and I know everything there is to know about anything on four wheels.'

It was a bit of a tall statement, but ... well, he deserved it! She tossed her head to add, 'And Mr. Gerard doesn't think I'm ...'

'Been abroad?' He flicked a glance upwards.

'Well, no, but I'm going to do a Spanish tour this summer and ...'

He didn't seem to be listening. But then perhaps he didn't do any listening to females! Watching him run his finger thoughtfully along the line of a map she jerked with forced lightness, 'You're living twenty years behind the times, Mr. Millard. Girls are into everything these days.'

'Not in my trucks they're not.'

As his words and their meaning slowly made themselves felt Claire stepped forward to demand angrily, 'Are you trying to say that after all the trouble we've gone to, you're backing out of the idea, simply because I'm . . .'

'Everything's fine with me,' the big shoulders lifted in a lazy shrug, 'just so long as they put a guy on the job. The inside of a truck is no place for a woman.'

'Well, *I* don't see anything wrong with it,' Claire argued defiantly, 'and especially as my own . . .' The sudden thought made her slight frame relax considerably. Of course! He didn't know about Mike. No wonder he was going on! Taking a relieved breath, she said on a light laugh, 'Silly of me! I forgot to tell you. Mike Davey, the Tehran truck driver—he's my brother.'

'So?'

She met the cold stare and clamped her mouth shut again. So that wasn't going to make any difference either!

As she stood there quietly seething, he stretched up from the map, brushed past her in the doorway and said mildly over his shoulder, 'Tell Gerard, if he can get someone lined up in time, the truck leaves tomorrow night at nine.'

Hatingly Claire watched him move off, then flung herself into her car. She slammed on the starter and screeched noisily out of the yard, a satisfied gleam showing in the green eyes as the wheels of her sports car brushed uncomfortably close to the big striding figure.

Back in Mike's flat it was some considerable time before her fury abated. Pacing the living-room floor, she fumed for the twentieth time, '*That man!* He's the most loathsome creature I've ever met in my life! All that ridiculous twaddle about *his* truck being no place for a woman!'

Mike shrugged sympathetically from where he had a transistor to bits on the table. 'He could be right, Claire,' he said gently. 'The going's pretty rugged at this time of the year, and across Turkey it can be hell.'

'I could have put up with it,' Claire retorted to the furniture. 'I've dug myself out of snowdrifts bigger than *him*, and I bet I can take a lot more than *he* can too, tucked up in his cosy little office.'

Mike winced. 'Did you tell him that?' he asked.

'I didn't get the chance,' she quivered. 'He was too busy letting me know that *I* didn't stand an earthly.'

Watching her, Mike mused, 'I gather he wasn't having any of the old fluttering of the eyelids bit?'

'Huh!' Claire tossed her head scathingly. 'I doubt if he even *saw* me! I might as well have been a ... a fly on the wall, for all the notice he took of me!'

Nodding, Mike said soothingly, 'Never mind. Come and sit your piqued little self down and ...'

'I am *not* piqued!' Claire snapped out quite truthfully. 'I couldn't care less what he thinks of me, and if I were a man I'd ...'

She stopped in her tracks and fingered the small jutting chin thoughtfully. The frown on her face slowly gave way to a preoccupied smile.

The sudden silence in the room made Mike look up from the screw he was fixing into place. He put down the screwdriver, watching his sister suspiciously. 'Claire? You've got that look in your eye ... Claire!'

'What?' She blinked up and laughed jerkily. 'Oh, sorry! I was just thinking. If I were a man ...'

'But you're not.' Mike got to his feet. 'You're a soft sweet adorable girl. Slightly fiery at the moment, but ...'

'But if I could *look* like a man?' Claire broke in eagerly. 'Just for one night. The night that your truck starts out from the depot.'

'Now, Claire ...' Reading her thoughts, Mike took a quick step forward. He was met by her laughter.

'Don't you see?' The green eyes sparkled. 'It's all so disgustingly simple! The only time that anybody is going to see who's going with you to Tehran is at nine o'clock tomorrow night when you drive the truck out of the depot. After that you could be sitting next to a chimpanzee for all Greg Millard will know.'

Her meaning becoming clear, Mike threw his fair head back and said with a dry laugh, 'And I thought *I* was the wild one of the family! Are you trying to tell me you would ...?'

'I've got an old pair of corduroy slacks,' Claire rushed on, 'and a chunky polo-necked sweater. And I can tuck my hair into a cap. If you've got a spare driving coat you can lend

15

me, the padded shoulders will give me a bit of height.'

Mike nodded vaguely and then asked slowly, 'Isn't the boss going to think it's nothing short of a miracle that someone else is ready to step into your shoes with only a day's notice?'

'Why should he?' Claire shook her head. 'Magazines have all sorts of cards up their sleeves when a deadline is involved. He'll know that.'

As Mike nodded again, she reached up quickly to drop him a grateful kiss on the cheek, then hurried over to the phone set in a wall alcove.

'You've got to admit,' she said happily over her shoulder, 'it would be crazy to miss seeing Robin just for the sake of those few minutes in the dark tomorrow night.'

She didn't add that she was going to enjoy seeing Greg Millard's face when she arrived back from Tehran.

Picking up the phone, she dialled Euranian Transport and watched Mike's incredulous grin as she said evenly, 'Oh, Mr. Millard. You remember me from *Ride* magazine. Well, I just thought I'd let you know we've found someone else to do the trip to Tehran. He'll be along, as you said, at nine tomorrow night.' She smiled impishly over the mouthpiece towards Mike and then was brought back to it to stammer, 'His name? Oh, it's er ... Dave. That's it. David ... er ... St. Claire.' She clamped the receiver down. 'Phew, I nearly forgot to find myself a name!'

Mike had gone to where one of his coats was draped over a chair. He came over with it, and held it, and as Claire struggled to find herself in the mound of navy blue he stuck out a hand to grin, 'Hi, Dave!' Laughingly she thrust her own out of the over long sleeve and when they had waltzed around hilariously she looked up to ascertain delightedly, 'You're really going along with me, Mike?' He shrugged with a philosophical grin. 'In for a penny ...' As his humorous gaze trailed over her, Claire looked down at the oversize coat.

'Thank heavens I've still got time to alter this,' she smiled. 'Nothing permanent. I'll just stitch up the sleeves and maybe nip in the waist a bit. It will certainly give me the masculine look I'll be needing. Come to think of it,' she looked at him, 'how shall we go about me getting into the truck tomorrow night?'

Mike considered. 'I'll have to be at the depot all day to make sure that everything's loaded okay. The best thing is for you not to come along too early. Make it about five to nine. And if you don't see me straight away, don't hang about. Get into the truck quick. It will be the one directly to the left of the entrance.'

'Won't it be locked?'

'Not at that time. I'll probably be there myself anyway, but just in case Greg wants to give me any last-minute instructions, your best bet is to step straight up into the truck. Okay?'

As Claire nodded, Mike turned his gaze to the photograph of a smiling girl propped up near the clock, and murmured in different tones, 'and it's time I was getting changed.'

'All right, I'm going,' Claire said with a knowing twinkle. She picked up the driving coat and folded it over her arm, then turning at the door winked conspiratorially. 'See you tomorrow night, then.'

Mike nodded. 'And don't forget, no earlier than five to nine. We leave at nine, so nothing much can go wrong in five minutes.'

Nothing would, Claire was confident. She spent the next morning sewing and laying out her masculine get-up for the evening's performance. In the afternoon she went to the cinema to try to keep a stopper on her steadily mounting excitement.

What the film was about she had no idea. The only pictures she saw were of herself and Mike up in the cab of the truck, rolling along some continental highway and having the time of their life. Instead of the cinema having a soothing effect, she left it with her heart positively leaping in her throat.

The idea of cooking a meal for herself in this state was out of the question, so she stopped off at a restaurant and picked her way through three courses. It was after seven when she got back to her flat, and in less than an hour now she could start thinking about getting ready. She was just climbing the stairs when Mrs. Bell, the landlady, came out of her room to call up, 'Your brother rang several times this afternoon, Miss Davey. He seemed most put out at not being able to talk to

17

you.'

'I've been to the pictures,' Claire smiled. 'Did he leave a message?'

'Yes. Yes, I think I've got something here.' She delved into her apron pocket and pulling out a small slip of paper read over the top of her glasses, 'You're not to go out tonight and he will get in touch with you.'

Claire looked blank and walked slowly down the stairs again. 'That can't be right,' she blinked. 'Are you sure you . . .?'

'I wrote it down with my own hand.' Mrs. Bell passed the slip of paper to her. 'I thought it was funny myself, you due to go away and everything, but . . .' She shrugged and smiled, then turned back into her own room.

Claire climbed the stairs, her eyes fixed on the few words of print in front of her. She felt numb with surprise. What was Mike talking about? 'Don't go out tonight.' Of course she had to go out. She was going to Tehran with him, wasn't she?

Up in her room she paced, read, and re-read the note. Then she sat down and drummed her fingers on the table, trying to think of a reason for Mike's sudden change of tune. Why had he decided to back out of taking her with him? It wouldn't be concern for his job. Claire was sure of that. Mike had never been one to worry about holding a job down. No, it wasn't that.

But it *could* be. . . . She jumped up and started to pace again. It could be brotherly concern for her. Of course! That was it! He had said himself that the journey was a rough one at this time of year. Now he was having second thoughts about taking her along. Well, she squared her shoulders smilingly, he needn't worry; he was going to find out that she was every bit as tough as he was.

Blithely she ran downstairs and told Mrs. Bell that she would be leaving for abroad tonight as planned, then came back and washed and started to pull on the clothes she had laid out on the bed. The effect was better than she had expected. Most of her figure was lost in the sweater and well-worn corduroys. Suitable shoes, that she had forgotten about, and were going to pose a problem, turned up in the shape of a pair of old crêpe-soled brogues that she had long

18

since discarded. With her hair tucked up under a soft peaked cap, left over from her scooter days, and the collar of Mike's driving coat turned up about the tell-tale column of white throat, she hardly recognised herself.

With an amused gleam she swept off the cap and coat, and folding the cap into a pocket, draped the coat over her arm. Wouldn't do to be seen leaving Mrs. Bell's respectable ladies' establishment looking like that!

She picked up her suitcase, made sure her writing equipment, travel documents, and small but powerful transistor, in case Mike hadn't mended his, were all safely tucked away in her briefcase, then went downstairs and out to her car.

It was early yet, barely ten past eight, but she felt too keyed up to hang about. Besides, she might need time to convince Mike that she was capable of making the trip. Driving down the maze of dimly lit streets, she chose a garage along a dark side turning just facing Euranian Transport's entrance. There she gave instructions for the car to be returned to the magazine offices while she was abroad. Walking now with her suitcase and briefcase in hand, she stopped off in a doorway, pulled into Mike's driving coat, coiled her hair up feverishly under the cap, then strolled jauntily down the street towards Euranian Transport.

She could see the big red truck just inside the entrance. There was another one, some distance away, but Mike had been explicit in his instructions and Claire was in no doubt which to make for.

There were one or two men dotted about the yard, and several small lights burning, but not enough to be too revealing, thank goodness. She hesitated for the fraction of a second at the gateway to snatch a steadying breath, then strode purposefully towards Mike's truck. She had an awful moment when it occurred to her that the door might be locked, it being only just eight-thirty, but the handle gave easily in her hand and the square of red metal swung towards her, the weight of it almost knocking her flat. She was just muttering a silent prayer for a step-ladder to get her into her seat way up there somewhere, when her heart suddenly catapulted into her throat.

The office door just across from her had opened, and silhouetted against the dim light from within was the unmistakable bulk of Greg Millard. She saw the chiselled features as the dark head turned sharply in her direction, then he was enquiring, 'David St. Claire?'

Quaking she raised and lowered her head in some kind of nod and after a heart-stopping moment, the dark head inclined in a brief nod back. Still holding her breath, Claire flicked what she hoped looked like a jaunty man-to-man greeting, then tossed her suitcase up lustily into her seat. Not knowing how she managed with what little strength she had left, she somehow found footholds and handholds for her trembling limbs, hoisted herself clumsily up and fell almost face forward on to the leather seat. Making a show of pushing her suitcase nonchalantly to one side, she draped back against the seat, ignored her thudding heart, and pulled the door to with a flourish.

Phew! She wrestled with her strangled breaths down beneath the collar of her coat. Not for anything would she want to go through *that* again. Not with those flinty eyes watching every move she made.

The pounding of her heart eased off as the big figure strode away, and gradually as a silence settled over her dark little world of the cab, Claire began to expand in a feeling of rosy wellbeing. She had made it! She was here in the truck all set for the trek to Tehran. Mike would be along in about twenty minutes and he wasn't likely to make any fuss at this stage. He was fairly easy-going, thank goodness, and once he saw her sitting there he would be quite happy to slip back into his original frame of mind.

With a satisfied air she pushed her case and briefcase under the seat and examined the shadowy interior of the cab. She picked out several of Mike's small possessions, including another picture of the same girl that smiled out from beside the clock in his flat. Dropping back, she breathed a carefree sigh. She had never been in any doubt that this was her brother's truck, but it was nice to feel a hundred per cent sure.

She found a pair of Mike's fingerless mittens and thankfully pulled them on over her pale hands. There was no need now of course to worry about her appearance, having successfully made it past Greg Millard, but there was no heat yet in the cab, and as she was so snug everywhere else in her heavy clothes, she might as well have warm hands too.

Thrusting the gloved hands into her pockets and tucking her chin into the big collar again, she settled down to wait. No doubt Mike would be on the very last minute, so why not get comfortable? The silence of the cab, the warmth of her clothing, and the blissful feeling of accomplishment, all conspired to soothe her into a deliciously relaxed state. One she felt she had earned after all the hectic hours of planning.

She didn't realise she had dozed until the feeling that someone had dropped into the seat along from her made her eyelids fly open. She was aware of a dim shape leaning over the wheel and pushing various levers, then she breathed easy. Thank heavens Mike had arrived at last. She must remind herself to hug him at the first available moment, for not making a fuss over her presence.

The engine rumbled into life, and there were hearty shouts of farewell from the men in the yard, then the broad column of headlights sprang on and forged out into the darkness beyond the gate.

Feeling the truck moving slowly forward, Claire was almost singing a song beneath her breath. But she would have to contain herself a little longer yet. Once they were out on to the road, she could let her hair down. Literally! The laughter bubbled up in her throat irrepressibly as the truck was skilfully manoeuvred out of the depot entrance. She was just on the point of whipping off her cap, with a wild shout of jubilation, when her eyes, above the tall coat collar, became riveted on a figure caught for a fraction of a second in the beam of the headlights. The stricken face turned up to hers as she was transported by froze her laughter into a strangled gasp.

What was going on? Was she still dozing and dreaming or something? How could Mike be out there, when he was supposed to be up here beside her driving his . . .

A slow horrified realisation started to creep over her as she became aware, for the first time, of the excessive height and bulk of the figure sitting next to her.

She didn't want to believe it; couldn't believe it, but . . . Sliding her eyes slowly to the side to take in granite profile and flinty eye, the awful truth hit her.

The man coolly manoeuvring her through the London

21

traffic on the first stage of the journey to Tehran was none other than Greg Millard!

CHAPTER TWO

CLAIRE sat paralysed in her seat, the prickle of perspiration cooling at her temples as views of gaily lit shops and crowds and tall buildings gave way to wide suburban roads, then narrow winding ones. She listened in fascinated horror as the deep-toned voice explained lazily over the throb of the engine,

'If you're wondering what happened to the guy you were supposed to be making this trip with, I've put him on the Scandinavian run. Mike's only done the Tehran trek a couple of times, and he might find it tricky at this time of the year without a co-driver. I figured the magazine wouldn't want to lose one of its feature writers en route.'

The dry humour and friendliness of the man so expertly swinging the wheel only served to make Claire sink lower behind her coat collar. Whereas before she had been congratulating herself on the sheer cleverness of getting past Greg Millard, now she was cursing her success. If only he had been a little bit suspicious! Just a little bit. It would have been so much easier to turn to him now and admit the hoax, and laugh the whole thing off as a joke. As it was, he had no reason to believe that he wasn't talking to this David St. Claire person she had concocted, and heaven help her when he found out the truth! In fact, from what she remembered of those few tight-lipped minutes in his office yesterday, she didn't dare picture his reaction at their second meeting. In here!

Grimacing in the dark, she bit hard on her lower lip. Why, oh, why hadn't she waited to see Mike? She could guess what had happened. He had been told today that he wouldn't be making the trip. That was why he had been trying frantically to reach her on the phone. The minute he had got some free time, he had rushed over to her flat to explain, and she like a fool had set out early and missed him.

He must have just got back to the depot as the truck was pulling out.

Poor Mike! He had looked just as aghast as she had been when their eyes had met. He had probably thought that she wouldn't go through with it. Well, she had and ... oh dear, what a fix she had landed herself in! Getting out of it didn't bear thinking about.

She stole another glance at the sharply etched profile and gulped. She would have to own up, of course. It was obvious she couldn't go bowling merrily along in a truck she had no business to be in, with the boss at the wheel.

Pulling in a silent breath, she braced herself. Well, here we go! No sense in putting off the awful moment any longer. She came up out of the collar turned to him, and with an avalanche of words at the ready opened her mouth. Just as she was about to speak Greg Millard said in faintly authoritative tones, his eyes staying with the narrow ribbon of road, 'I should try for a spot of shut-eye, if I were you, Dave. It's a good couple of hours to the ferry at Felixstowe and there's nothing to see in the dark.'

Claire ducked back into her coat, grateful for the respite. Coward that she was, two hours of feigning sleep seemed distinctly preferable to a second clash with the boss of Euranian Transport. Perhaps she could just slip away and disappear at Felixstowe, or at the worst, turn tail and run the minute she had confessed. Anything was better than facing him here, across a few inches of space.

Yes, it was definitely the best idea to wait, she told herself. And wiser too. He might run off the road if she told him now!

For the first time since the truck had started out she began to relax. Nothing could be gained by sitting on tenterhooks for the next two hours and as long as she lay back and said nothing she was safe. She could spend the time working out what she would do at Felixstowe. Of course it would have been much more exciting if she could have got as far as Holland or somewhere like that, but ...

Though she was draped back apparently asleep, Claire couldn't suppress a slight tensing of her frame as the thought came to her. It *was* only a thought, but supposing ... just supposing she didn't say anything at Felixstowe? It was an

23

overnight crossing to Rotterdam, and if she could get away with the crazy impersonation this close to Greg Millard, surely there could be nothing to it on the ferry? After all, she reasoned, she was going to know his wrath anyway, so what difference would it make whether it was on this side of the North Sea or the other?

The idea had something she told herself, smiling thoughtfully beneath the peak of her cap, so why not give it a whirl?

With every uneventful mile that passed beneath the wheels of the truck, she became more sure of herself, and as her confidence grew so did her ambitions. Come to think of it, she mused, why say anything at all, even on the other side of the sea?

She opened her eyes and twinkled up at the roof of the cab, knowing that if Mike could see her now he would say with that suspicious gleam of his, 'Claire, you're up to something!'

And what was she up to? Nothing really except ... she sneaked a glance from beneath her lashes at the man at the wheel. It might be rather fun to see how far she could get before he found out. It would be light at Rotterdam, of course, but her disguise was fairly effective, and she could always make a pretext of scribbling furiously if he made any attempt at conversation. That way, there was no telling how long she would be able to keep it up. Why, she might even....

Swallowing, she schooled herself into curbing her excitement. Maybe the idea was gathering mammoth proportions, but wasn't it reasonable to suppose that the further she could get along the road to Tehran the less likely Greg Millard was going to want to turn back? He was a business man with goods to deliver, also he had to think of the publicity that the magazine feature was going to give his firm. The value he put on that was bound to outweigh his stuffy outmoded prejudices against females in the end, so....

She closed her eyes again, trying to quieten her thudding heart. It was a mad scheme, of course, but hadn't the whole thing been mad so far? Why stop now? Why not push her chances to the limit? She had done half the journey to the coast already. Who could say how far she might get if her luck held? All she had to do was stay mute and act masculine, and let the rest take care of itself.

Completely calm now, with only the merest tingle of excitement coursing through her, Claire settled down to await events. She almost fell asleep at one stage, so content in the knowledge was she that it was going to be comparatively easy, and wholly satisfying, to outwit the man who had coldly referred to her as a 'Slip of a kid.'

And then something happened that made it look as though all her carefully laid plans were about to be toppled in one go.

A slight change in the rhythm of the engine made her languidly open her eyes. They jerked wider as she saw a neon-lighted roadside café come up alongside her window. Before she had time to gather her scattered wits, they were pulling in and Greg Millard was turning to say pleasantly, 'Coffee, Dave? We've got time for a few minutes' break.'

Claire was seized with an uncontrollable bout of panic. She hadn't expected to stop until they reached the ferry. How was she going to escape the man's scrutiny under the glaring lights of the café? Some of their glow spread over her now as she lay hunched up beneath the driving coat, and for the life of her she couldn't come up to croak out a comment.

Her paralytic state, however, turned out to be the thing that saved her, for apparently assuming that his travelling companion was sound asleep, the transport boss jumped lightly down from his seat and closed the door softly behind him. She watched him stride away towards the lighted building and breathed a long low sigh of relief. When he had disappeared from view she struggled with the door on her side, and almost fell out to the ground. If ever the opportunity for escape had offered itself, it was now. But Claire knew she wouldn't run. The spice of intrigue was far too tempting to want to give it up at this stage, even though she was liable to come out of it all a nervous wreck.

She went on her own tour of the sprawling buildings alongside the road, then made her way back to the truck. Coming up to her side, her knees almost buckled at the sight of the big figure moving in from the opposite direction. She opened her door and scrabbled up, thankful for the shadows.

As Greg Millard swung himself up to meet her in the cab

she heard him say goodhumouredly, 'Decided to stretch your legs after all?'

Thankfully the roar of the engine drowned much of her throaty reply, and after that all the man's concentration was needed to get the truck back on the road. While this operation was in progress, Claire was racking her brains for what to do next. She obviously couldn't fake sleep any more, and it would be just crazy to pretend to make notes in the dark. Yet if she sat upright, conversation was bound to follow.

When the truck was cruising along the road again she had an idea. She stretched her arms and grunted a yawn, marvelling at her own nerve, then reached for the transistor radio from her briefcase. It was only small, but it packed a noisy punch, and switching it on she breathed a relieved sigh as the sound of trumpets, drums, and castanets echoed to the four corners of the cab. Holding it in her hand so that she could jiggle it to keep the sound blaring, she thrust her trousered legs out in front and settled back with ostentatious contentment.

They didn't stop any more after that, thank heaven, although Claire's heart leapt into her mouth once or twice when the truck slowed down. There was nothing to see in the dark except the white line of the road and the occasional mist-shrouded lamp. Just the same she kept her gaze fixed out there. Brave as she was, she couldn't bring herself to turn her head and try to find out what Greg Millard was thinking. Lucky for her he was a man with a lot of truck on his mind, and she was spared any comment as he followed the roads towards the coast.

When at last they came into Felixstowe and then the ferry terminal, Claire didn't know whether to be relieved or more worried. True, she had made it this far without much trouble, but that was because the transport boss had been fully occupied with his driving. The ferry was a different matter. There would be nothing to divert his attention from her once they were on board; a fact that she had recklessly glossed over in her calculations, but viewed with increasing alarm now, as they took their place behind a convoy of vehicles.

As the procession moved forward she tried to soothe herself with the knowledge that at least she had a single cabin booked, and it shouldn't be too difficult to slip away to it. Presumably Greg Millard would be taking over the cabin that had been booked for Mike.

She could see the truck inspection yard up ahead and held her breath as their turn came to move in, then she heard the man beside her instructing above the din of the radio, 'Take your place in the queue over there, Dave. I'll see you on board.'

Not if I can help it you won't! Claire thought, making a dive for her luggage and clutching hastily for the door. She almost dropped the transistor in her haste to get out, but had the presence of mind to slip the strap over her wrist, before jumping all the way down to the ground with a jolt. She managed to slam the door shut weakly behind her and then the truck was moving slowly forward.

Never before had she been so grateful for the dark as she pulled off her peaked cap and let the pale hair fall over the shoulders of the unbuttoned driving coat. She gave the customs officer a sweet smile, and had her passport stamped without the merest flicker of an eyelid at her quaint garb.

It wasn't so easy to stuff her hair back under the cap with so many people about. She had to wait until she was on board and making her way down a deserted passenger deck before she could accomplish the task. Even then she had a horrible fear that Greg Millard would come striding round the corner before the last wisp was put away.

Nothing had ever looked more inviting than the number of her cabin coming up on the left. Long before she reached it, her free arm was stretching out eagerly towards it. At last she was turning the handle of the door and after a quick look to the right and left, she slipped quickly inside.

Phew! Talk about cloak and dagger stuff! There was getting to be more of it by the minute. She leaned back thankfully against the door, and pulled in a mischievous smile. If only she had someone to enjoy it with!

Her suitcase out of the way, she placed her briefcase on a small table near the wall. The transistor was still hanging on her wrist, and she realised with a twinkle that it was still switched on. Her rather erratic form of travel after leaving the truck had somewhat silenced it, but it came up loud and clear in the small confines of the cabin. She placed it on the table and, aching for a rest from its din, fumbled for the switch. She was just about to flick it off when the door opened, and without so much as a nod Greg Millard stepped in.

Claire had to lean against the table for support, but she had enough presence of mind to appear engrossed in the task of unzipping her writing case. She thanked her lucky stars that the radio was still bouncing. The racket might deter the man from whatever purpose he had come for. She could hear him moving about the cabin, probably looking over the interior. Though why should it concern him...?

She had managed to get hold of a pencil and pad, but there was no need to put on an act of busily writing. Her shaking hand did that of its own accord. The high brassy sounds of a dance orchestra were blaring out from the minute radio. Claire froze, aware that Greg Millard was standing only a few feet away. She heard him say in contrasting gravel tones against the din, 'Beats me how you think with that thing on, let alone write.'

She shrugged her shoulders, hoping it would look like a good-natured reply, and after a while he moved away again. He moved away, but there was no relaxing her pose while he was still in her cabin, and he seemed in no hurry to leave. Counting the seconds, she waited. When she could stand the strain no longer she turned her head in the direction that he had moved and ... horror of horrors! Not only had he taken off his coat and loosened his tie, but she noticed for the first time that there were two bunks in the cabin!

She watched aghast as he pulled off the tie and loosened the buttons on his shirt, then flung her glance away.

Help! Nothing like this had come into her scheme of things. She hadn't even considered the possibility that he might move in to the cabin booked originally under her name, thinking that two were unnecessary.

Now what was she going to do? Her panic-stricken senses held her rooted, but she knew the game was up. Oh yes, quite definitely! It had been fun. But there was a limit to how far she could go.

Taking a strangled breath, she swung round and babbled, 'Mr. Millard... Stop! I want to ... I mean ... I've got a confession to make.'

28

She waited for the bomb blast, but none came. Her fractured sentence had been lost in the gush of water, as Greg Millard bent over the washbasin.

Oh, heavens! Now she was going to have to say it all again, and she would never find the nerve. She steadied herself while the big figure sluiced under the taps, then he was patting himself dry to say through the towel, 'I'm not happy with the line-up of the truck. I think I'll bed down in one of the bunks in the cab tonight, just to keep an eye on things.'

Claire could hardly believe her ears, or her good luck. Here she was all ready to admit the hoax, and now there was going to be no need. Travelling at a safe distance from the truck boss was going to make getting across to Holland a relatively simple matter.

She was so busy gloating over the blessed turn of events that she forgot she had temporarily abandoned her masculine pose. Turned full face, and well up from her coat collar, her heart started to race as she saw Greg Millard's narrowed gaze roam over her.

What could he see? There was no telling. Though there was only one small wall light on in the cabin, it might be enough to give her away.

With bated breath she held his gaze. He threw his tie and sheepskin-lined driving coat over his arm and came closer. Too close.

Feeling hot under the rim of her cap, she affected a casual turn back to the table. The pencil was there at her finger tips. She picked it up, then let go of it as though it were hot when she saw the stones of her engagement ring winking up through the woollen mitten.

Had he seen? He must have done.

Bracing herself, she looked up to find the flinty blue eyes still on her face. He said with a slight frown, 'Looks like the staff of *Ride* are all teenagers. How old are you, Dave?'

'Nineteen.' What else could she do but answer? She saw the dark head nod then he was saying mildly, 'Not much of an age for a tough assignment like this. Reckon you'll make out all right?'

'I think so.'

He nodded again and then shrugged, 'Well, how about supper?'

It was becoming an effort talking in low tones and she had no desire to set foot outside the cabin tonight. She shook her head and held up a bar of chocolate from her pocket. Thankfully her excuse was accepted, for he moved off towards the door, knotting his tie. She heard him say as he went out, 'We dock at Rotterdam about eight. Suit yourself about breakfast, but be in the cab ten minutes before we move off. Goodnight, Dave.'

She lifted a mittened hand in polite salute, then rushed up to lock the door as it was closed. That was what she should have done in the first place, of course, but it was a good job she hadn't now. It might have aroused suspicion. And come to think of it, she gave herself a pleased hug, hadn't she come off rather well, from her first real encounter with the transport boss? At least she didn't have to play a husky, expansive man of the world type. He saw her as a shy, rather reticent youth, and that part suited her just fine.

She waltzed in front of the mirror, smiled, and gave a satisfied pat to her peaked cap, then went to switch off the confounded radio and munch on her chocolate.

Perhaps her mistake was in not having a proper meal, or maybe going to bed on the chocolate. Whatever the cause, the effect was terrible! She spent half the night telling herself it was the bunk, and not her, rocking from side to side, and the other half pacing a giddily spinning floor. The dim light of dawn saw her crawling thankfully over to the washbasin, and by daylight she was washed and dressed and marvelling on her pale green complexion in the mirror. She went to open the cabin door to let the sea breezes revive her, but the sight of that heaving swollen mass sent her groping inside again.

Some minutes later she heard a firm footstep on the deck, and then Greg Millard was stepping quickly inside. He took one look around the cabin, saw that everything was packed, then swung away to the door again to say curtly,

'We're on a tight schedule, Dave. Ignore it and you're liable to get left behind.'

Ignore it! Claire grabbed her luggage and stumbled after him crossly. She had been far too occupied in putting herself together again to give him or his dratted schedule a thought. He was striding away miles ahead, and willing her legs not to buckle under her she struggled to keep him in sight. Everybody on deck was hurrying along and nobody cared in the least that she was battling at death's door. She cast a jaundiced eye over the view of leaden skies, spidery cranes, and fat tugs and tankers, and fervently wished she was back in her mews flat.

Trailing after the big suede-coated figure, she eventually came to the deck where rows and rows of freight vehicles were all revving up ready to move off. The big red Euranian Transport truck stood out from all the rest. Greg Millard was already swinging the wheel and moving ahead when she arrived. She was bracing herself ready for the suicidal climb up into the moving cab, when the voice from inside barked, 'No sense in coming aboard now. I'll pick you up when you've been through the customs.'

Charming man! Claire watched him go with an acid smile. He drags her halfway across the boat and then tells her she can walk ashore. Vaguely she knew she was better off clearing the customs without his eagle eye in the background, but the way she was feeling at the moment she didn't much care whether she continued with the masquerade or not.

Palely she drifted in with the people leaving the boat, not bothering to do anything about her bizarre appearance. Perhaps the lackadaisical attitude gave an impression of cocky confidence, for she cruised through the formalities of landing without mishap. The passport official eyed her odd outfit with a tolerant grin and a twinkle that said nothing surprised him these days.

She saw the truck with Greg Millard at the wheel, parked a short distance away. Moving languidly towards it she was unable to feel any concern for the fact that it was broad daylight and she was on full view.

As she came up to the cab she fully expected the transport boss to jump down and confront her with the truth. But he didn't. He was having a clipped conversation with another freight driver a few yards away, and seemed only just aware of her arrival. As she threw her luggage up and fell into the seat herself, he flicked the engine into life impatiently and moved forward towards the gate.

'Bad weather ahead, Dave,' he scowled. 'Snow on the roads and more to come, by the look of it. We're going to have our work cut out making Elten on time.'

31

Elten, according to Claire's memory of the route, was on the border with Germany. The prospect of travelling the entire width of Holland and goodness knows how much more after that, because she could roll into a decent bed, filled her with morbid dejection. She slumped down in her seat and gazed lifelessly on a scene of retreating ships' funnels, grey-looking wharves and terminals. Later they came upon tall new blocks built almost entirely in glass, then gabled houses and a bustle of traffic.

The snow, floating icy flakes that clung to the windscreen like clippings of tissue paper, started just as they were coming on to the autobahn. Mike had told her about the wide motor highways that made travelling across Europe fairly easy. She was impressed at the amount of traffic humming by, but not at the speed with which each set of spinning wheels zipped over the icy surface.

Happily the truck was too heavy for any such high kicks, and she watched as Greg Millard steered into the lane carrying moderately paced goods vehicles. She was surprised, though, how their own speed picked up once they were out on to the open road. Obviously the man at the wheel believed in making every second count.

The land spread away on all sides, flat and green and dotted with farms, neat picket fences, and windmills. Trees were faintly flecked with green, and if it hadn't been for the heavy skies and patches of snow she could almost have imagined it as a spring scene; which of course it would be in four or five weeks' time.

The traffic thinned out as the truck ate up the miles. Apart from two half-moons of glass, swept monotonously by the wipers, the windscreen was packed tight with snow. Claire was beginning to feel miserably aware of the intense cold. She could have sworn that things had been more comfortable on the drive to Felixstowe. The temperature had been low when they started out, but she didn't recall feeling as cold as this.

Instead of her heavy clothes being a comfort now, they hung about her, doing nothing at all for the shrunken, shivering frame within.

Greg Millard must have noticed her blue nose from the corner of his eye, for he drawled over the wheel, 'Heating linkage is jammed, I'm afraid. Happens sometimes in new trucks.' He shrugged cheerfully inside his sheepskin-lined coat. 'We'll be pulling in for a meal in maybe two or three hours from now. I'll see about getting it fixed then.'

Two or three hours! Claire could barely keep her teeth from chattering. She would be frozen to the seat by then! It was all right for *him*, sitting there so smug. And he had probably eaten a decent breakfast too. She could do with a little inner warmth herself. Food! The mere thought of it made her realise just how hungry she was. Her stomach had come back to the fold, and nothing would have pleased her more at this moment than to welcome it with a hot tasty meal.

She swallowed longingly and slid a dejected glance towards the lean profile over the wheel. Two or three hours, he had said, but he couldn't mean it, could he? What about the mid-morning break? Coffee or something. Mmmm! Hot steaming coffee! What wouldn't she give for a cup? She couldn't see Mike neglecting his comforts when he was doing a trip like this. But of course it wasn't her fun-loving brother up here beside her. Oh no! She had managed to get herself landed with none other than the big boss himself, and by the look of that clamped jaw, *he* had no intention of wasting time on unnecessary stops.

The only one they made through the morning was for fuel, and he was engrossed with that long enough for her to creak down from her seat at her side, stiffly explore the adjoining facilities and then clamber back up again.

As lunchtime approached, she began to take an avid interest in the roadside restaurants that kept coming up. Each one was gaily lit and painted attractively. They all looked gorgeously cosy in the grey mist of swirling snow. Dragging her gaze back from every one that sped by, she wondered longingly when Greg Millard was finally going to bring himself to pull into one.

The prospects of being found out now seemed relatively unimportant, compared with the thoughts of being defrosted and fed.

She waited and watched, and each sign they passed seemed to offer more in the way of food than the previous one. Not all the lettering was in English, of course, but the

33

mouth-watering pictures were enough to go by. Occasionally she caught the odd rosy glow of an interior, and was induced to move a little to the edge of her seat, and at one point she actually got an inside view of tables and chairs and round smiling faces, as the truck took a neat turn off to an adjoining feed road.

It couldn't be long now. As they forged along the narrow strip she clutched at the door handle, ready to pile out at the first sign of a welcome ahead. They were travelling at reduced speed and it occurred to her that the man at the wheel must have somewhere special in mind. He wouldn't have turned off from the main route of the motorway otherwise, would he?

She strained eagerly to see through the snowflakes, feeling better than she had done all morning. She might have known he would have his own favourite stopping-off place, a regular port of call that was almost as good as a second home to him. Well, that was even better than she had hoped. There was nothing she needed more right now than a second home. Scrumptious home cooking, Dutch style, of course, and the chance to thaw out in the delicious warmth of a blazing log fire. Oh, the sheer bliss of it all!

She was already fumbling to unbutton her coat in a tremble of anticipation as the truck came to a stop. Her frozen finger-tips fiddled under her collar ... then lowered slowly at the sight before her.

The road had circled out on to an open tract of ground that was bare and stony under the film of snow, and dotted with icy puddles. There was a couple of deserted-looking buildings off to one side and beyond a belt of swaying pines, were wailing their discontent at the weather.

Claire gazed around stupidly, hardly aware that the transport boss had swung open his door and jumped down. She watched as he thrust his hands into his pockets and hunched his shoulders smilingly over the view.

'I gathered we'd have the place to ourselves,' he commented drily. 'The land around here is packed with trailers and tents in the summer. Right now though, I reckon, is no time for a picnic.'

A camping site!

Claire spiralled down inside her coat, gulping back a self-

34

pitying moan. All those lovely, luscious, cosy eating houses they had passed and *he* had to pick on a freezing, deserted camp site!

He was pulling out of his driving coat. As though he sensed some of his travelling companion's frustrations, he said, throwing his coat into the seat and pushing up his sleeves, 'The Dutch like to linger over their meals. We haven't got the time. We'll rustle up a quick snack and then get moving.'

Rustle up! Claire didn't feel she could sit swaying in the cab any longer. She pushed open the door on her side and dropped out, landing luckily but painfully on her feet. Thousands of tiny pins and needles shot through the frozen blocks as they came into sudden contact with the hard earth.

She was still wincing some time later when Greg Millard lifted his head from under the bonnet of the truck and came round to pull a tool box out from under the side. He didn't look up, but she thought she sensed a slight impatience in his tones as he pointed out, 'There's canned food in the back, Dave. I'll be with you as soon as I've fixed the heater.'

In the back? He must mean in the back of the cab. There were bunks there, so presumably a cupboard. She struggled her way inside again, banging her head as she went, and biting her lips crossly at the pain. And how did one get into the back? All she could see was the long padded seat, and a sliding door in the centre behind.

She prodded and fumbled with a separate section at the back of the seat, like an arm slotted away ready to pull down. Really! A person was expected to know everything around her. To her surprise the arm pulled down to make a step up to the door behind.

It was amazing just what *was* in the small space behind the cab. Besides the bunks, there was a window at either side, a slim wall cupboard, a formica-topped table designed to pull down from another wall, and a small stove. A sliding door at the rear of the room revealed a tiny washroom.

Though everything had been cleverly designed to take up the minimum of space, it was all surprisingly adequate. She could see now how a two-man crew could keep moving practically the whole of the time with the amenities they had on hand.

35

She was gazing up at the side of the wall to where two flat polythene containers were strapped when the big figure showed in the doorway.

'I should fill both tanks while you're at it.' He nodded through the window, towards the trees. 'Tap's over there at the start of the path.'

There he was, giving his orders again! Miserably aware of her cold and fatigue, she had to bite on her trembling lip to refrain from letting drop a choice remark. When he had disappeared, she reached the containers down and battled to get them out of the small space of the sliding door. It was all she could do to ease past her seat with one in each hand, and to stop herself overbalancing on the climb down she had to let one go.

The transport boss came to pick it up from where it had clattered to the ground.

'Take it easy, Dave,' he clipped, 'these are pretty important pieces of equipment.'

And what about the crew? she fumed silently. Apparently *they* didn't count. She trudged off, cursing the Euranian Transport Company, or to be more explicit its owner.

Mike would never have stopped at a place like this. If he had been driving the truck, they would be sitting in some kind of civilised comfort by now, eating a decent meal. She found the tap, a short walk away and up a slight incline. Barely expecting it to start in the freezing cold, she jerked it sharply round. It started all right—in a torrent that gushed out over her shoes and hands and anywhere but into the openings of the containers. Fighting a surge of temper, she held grimly on to one, filled it, and then stumbled away.

If he wanted any more he could jolly well come and fetch it himself!

She wasn't sure whether her legs gave way under the weight of the brimming tank, or whether her wet shoes on the icy path had something to do with it. All she remembered was turning from the tap, and then the ground was hitting her squarely in the stomach and the sharp gravel clawing at her cheek. Winded and without the strength to get up, she lay there, clenching her teeth against the tears, and fuming at the sound of the water merrily glug-glug-glugging from the neck of the container.

She was hazily aware of another sound, but couldn't bring herself to investigate until a hand dropped heavily on her shoulder. And then it was too late. She was pulled roughly to her feet and Greg Millard was saying in exasperated tones:

'For heaven's sake, Dave! Can't you do anything right? I should have thought filling a couple of water bottles would be a relatively simple ... What the ...?'

As he swung her round, the peaked cap, knocked askew by her fall, slipped a little more to one side. She was aware that several strands of pale silken hair had crept out to trail wispily in the wind. But who cared? Her face stung with pain, and her wet mittened hands were slowly freezing over, and it was all his fault anyway.

As she raised her head defiantly, the tears that she had been so carefully in control of suddenly brimmed over. She saw a face carved out of granite just above hers. Narrowed blue eyes raked her, and then the rest of her hair was tumbling about her as he whipped the cap off with one sharp oath. After a full thirty seconds to take the sight of her in, he made no attempt to stand back but hung over her to demand menacingly through clamped teeth, 'What in hell's name are *you* doing here?'

'Fulfilling my duties as your co-driver, of course, although I can't say I ...'

Her feeble attempts at flippancy was short-lived, for his arms shot out and he jerked her towards him. She had to suffer another lengthy going-over by those piercing blue eyes and then he was saying in little more than a growling whisper, 'Are you trying to tell me you've been with the truck since London?'

The blue eyes began to smoulder as she nodded. She swallowed and then rushed on with, 'Well, of course I have. And why not? Nobody else objected to my making this trip except you, and how did I know you were going to change places with Mike?'

'But you sat it out anyway.' His fingers gripped deep into her shoulders. 'Of all the scheming little ...!'

'It wasn't like that at all,' Claire squirmed, jutting her chin. 'I was merely trying to prove to you that women are every bit as good at this kind of thing as you men seem to think you are, and ...' As soon as the words were out she

37

knew she had said the wrong thing.

She saw the gleam of mocking contempt as the blue eyes trailed relentlessly over her grazed and grubby appearance and tear-wet lashes. He crooked a dark eyebrow and drawled with a hateful smile, 'Oh, you've proved *that* all right!'

Claire blinked back the tears furiously and dragged herself away. 'You couldn't resist that, could you?' she snapped shakily. 'But then I don't suppose a tossing boat bothers *you* at all. And I've no doubt that having slept all night, you ate a decent breakfast this morning, which is more than I did.'

'Serves you right for trying to pull a stunt like this.'

'Well, don't worry! If I'd known you were going to drive all day and freeze me to death into the bargain ...'

Flinging herself blindly away, Claire forgot, until it was too late, to choose her steps carefully. As the ground spun away from her for the second time, she felt a firm grip on her arm and Greg Millard was saying drily, 'Go and get cleaned up—and try to do it standing on your feet.' He turned her towards the nearest of the two buildings started her off, then turned back to collect the water tanks.

The camp facilities were good. Inside the neat timbered hut Claire found washbasins and mirrors and everything to help her try to make her appearance less wretched. Wincing a grimace at her reflection, she peeled off the wet mittens and her coat and proceeded to wash away the dirt and the mud. The water was painfully cold but soothing on her grazed cheek. She used endless paper towels trying to blot up scratches into something less hideous, but had to give up in the end.

She had no make-up and no comb, and emerging some time later she felt that the effort had hardly been worth while, but at least her hands and face were clean and she had got rid of the horrible wet clinging mittens.

There was a delicious aroma emanating from the truck as she approached. She saw a pair of wide shoulders moving around in the back of the cab and hovered about uncertainly outside. The transport boss jutted his head out through the space of the sliding door and said evenly,

'Come on up.'

He draped down into the driving seat and watched her as she pulled herself in. With his gaze fixed on her face he

38

reached for the first aid box clipped under the dashboard. With him sitting there, there was nothing else to do but sit down too. She looked silently on as he poured some colourless liquid on to a knot of cotton wool, but when he turned to her lifting his hand she drew back with a hasty, 'Oh, it doesn't matter, really! I'm sure I . . .'

'Hold still!' he ordered, dabbing her cheek matter-of-factly and continuing to do so as she screwed her face up with pain. Once the stinging had subsided she had to admit that the graze felt better, but she kept her gaze rigidly to the front as he replaced the things in the first aid box and clipped it shut.

He nodded towards the back compartment.

'Get the food while it's hot, you'll feel better. I'll get on with the heater.'

Claire turned meekly in through the door. He must have eaten, for there was a cup half filled with coffee on the table, and what looked like the outer cellophane wrapping of packed sandwiches. She found a small pan of stew simmering on the stove. The picture on the empty can certainly looked appetising. The coffee pot was keeping hot too, and there was a tin of steamed pudding opened ready to turn out.

She didn't waste time investigating any further. Searching out a plastic plate and spoon from the cupboard and another cup, she settled down to savour the meal.

Nothing had ever tasted so wonderful! But then she had never been quite so near to starving before. Well, not really starving. Making short work of the food, she smiled to herself, draining the last of the delectable coffee. Actually, she had only missed supper and breakfast, and looking back on it all now, it didn't seem so terrible.

A dreamy sense of wellbeing washed over her as she sat on the bunk and leaned back against the wall. Her eyelids felt heavy. She let them flicker slowly to a close. They sprang open a few seconds later, when the transport boss stooped in through the door and moved around, hunching his frame in the confined space. Picking up a coil of wire from a ledge, he looked at her briefly and said on his way out,

'Might as well get between the blankets. I don't know how long this is going to take.'

Claire had no intention of accepting his suggestion at first. Then the warmth of the coffee and the food began to wear off, and she decided it might be wiser to curl up in the blankets for a while. It would only be for a few minutes, and there was no sense in sitting up freezing, was there? She would just put her head on the pillow for a moment and watch the snowflakes floating down past the window and . . . .

It seemed that she had only closed her eyes for a second, but when she opened them she knew it must have been for considerably longer. The sky was a darker shade of grey and much of the light had gone from the tiny compartment. There was a lovely overall warmth about the air and stretching luxuriously, she felt reluctant to get up. She lay for some moments listening to the silence and then, because it *was* so silent, she rose quickly and moved towards the door. Going round to her seat, she rooted her toilet bag from out of her case, then poked her tousled head outside. Greg Millard was leaning against the mudguard of the truck pulling lazily on a cigarette. As he turned to look up she heard herself saying foolishly, 'I'm . . . sorry, I must have dropped off to sleep.'

He stubbed his cigarette out, and she climbed down, giving him a tentative smile as she landed. 'I'll just freshen up. I'll only be a minute.'

She heard him starting up the engine as she walked towards the camp building. When she came out the truck was waiting a few yards away. She climbed up into her seat and pulled the door to sweepingly behind her. As the truck moved forward out of the camp site she asked cheerfully, gazing around with interest. 'Which road do we take next?'

'The one back to Rotterdam,' he clipped.

Claire flung herself round to him. 'But . . . but that must be more than a three-hour drive the other way?'

'You should be in time to make the evening crossing.'

She slumped in her seat, still watching him. 'You mean you're taking me back to the ferry?'

'What else did you expect?' He gripped the wheel, swinging it occasionally to follow the bends in the road.

Claire pressed her lips into a line. 'Well, I thought you might at least have given me a chance.'

He made no comment, but continued to watch the road to

40

the end, and then waited his opportunity to move in on to the main highway. As they edged out on to it and back in the direction they had come, she snapped coldly, 'I can see you're not going to overlook your stupid prejudices!'

She watched moodily for a while as the road zipped under the front of the truck and then decided to try a different approach.

'Look,' she offered brightly, 'why waste time going back? It must be a nuisance for you. Why don't we just turn round at the first chance we get? I don't mind how fast you go to make up the schedule.'

Not the flicker of an eyelid.

A couple of miles further on she tried again. 'I really am a good traveller, you know,' and then softly, 'please! Couldn't you give me a try?'

Curving him a smile, she waited ... and waited. The only sound was the steady hum of the engine as it ate up the miles back to Rotterdam. There wasn't so much as a crack in that granite profile above the wheel.

Claire flopped back angrily in her seat. She might just as well save her breath. *He* had no intention of wasting any, by the look of it. She sat staring miserably ahead, watching as snow-clad fields, farmsteads, and windmills continued to sail by in the wrong direction. This wasn't how she had planned at all. But then she hadn't reckoned on Greg Millard being built out of rock. And who could argue ... or plead ... with a rock?

They had been travelling for some time down a deserted secondary road. It was as the truck slowed almost to stop to negotiate a tight turning off on to another one that she straightened slightly in her seat. An idea leapt into her mind. It spread in a telltale gleam to her eyes and she lowered them quickly, in case she should give herself away. After a few moments she swivelled a sideways glance to the grim presence in the driving seat. Maybe she couldn't hope to chip through that rocky surface, but there might be a way of skirting round it.

She waited her chance with bated breath, and a feeling that she had come too far to give up now without some kind of a fight. Her hand crept up surreptitiously towards the handle of the door. As the truck slowed down for another

41

corner she felt its cold steel in the palm of her hand. Greg Millard had his eye trained on the line of the truck through his nearside mirror. As he turned the wheel, Claire saw the grass verge come up close on her side. She hung on until it looked almost stationary and then flung open the door and jumped.

She was surprised to find the ground not in the least steady beneath her feet. The momentum of her flight sent her stumbling giddily forward for several yards. When she finally pulled up to a sickening stop, the truck was slamming to a halt beside her.

In the grey evening light she could just about see the taut face above the wheel. The voice, biting out, was icier than the wind whistling around her ears.

'What the *hell* do you think you're doing?'

Claire faced up to the driving seat and folded her arms over her heaving bosom. When she could find the breath she said staunchly,

'I'm not going to let you take me back to Rotterdam.'

There! That would settle it! He couldn't leave her stranded out here miles from anywhere, and she wouldn't get back into the truck until he promised to take her with him.

She waited expectantly as he rose from his seat and then he was bending.

'Suit yourself,' he clipped, swinging her luggage out and jumping down to drop it neatly at her feet. 'There's a town about two miles down the road. You can catch a train for the port from there.'

'But ... but ... I haven't got the fare,' Claire stammered faintly. It was crazy but true. She hadn't dared approach the magazine for expenses for fear of upsetting things at the last minute, and all her salary, apart from a few shillings in her purse, had gone on preparations for the trip. She pulled herself up to say jerkily, 'I expected to be travelling with Mike in the truck. I just never gave money of my own a thought.'

'That's your problem.'

As he waited she turned a hateful glance upwards and jerked, 'Well, don't worry. I'll get round it somehow.' She shot a bleak glance over the deserted countryside and then bent to shut her briefcase inside her suitcase. 'Goodbye, Mr.

Millard.' She tried to put on an acid smile. 'It hasn't been nice knowing you. And no thanks for your help in stopping me from making the trip to Tehran.'

She put up a hand to hide the tears of defeat that threatened and tried to push past him. He didn't move immediately out of her path as she had expected. She found him blocking it with calm deliberation. The piercing blue eyes lowered over her searchingly. Up against them, Claire had a feeling he was going back in his mind over her tenacity to stay with the truck. She pretended to smooth the strands of hair away from her face as though they were a nuisance, and saw his gaze stray towards the ring on her finger.

After several seconds had elapsed he asked evenly, 'What's so important about getting to Tehran?'

It shocked Claire a little to find that she had to gaze at the ring herself to be reminded of the reason and then she was saying coldly, 'My fiancé works out there. I haven't heard from him in months.'

'So he's lazy with a pen,' Greg Millard shrugged. 'You've only to contact his firm. They'll give you details of him.'

'That's not the same as seeing him myself, is it?' she said shortly. 'But you wouldn't understand that, would you? You've probably never had a loving thought in your life.'

A tiny spark kindling in the hooded blue eyes told her that this wasn't a man you could talk to as you liked. She heard herself adding rather more earnestly, 'I'll never be able to save up the fare to go all that way, but this assignment was going to be the perfect answer. I could keep my job, yet still get to see Robin.'

There was a silence and then the transport boss was asking, 'Anyone looking out for you at home?'

'There's only me and Mike.' Claire lifted her chin.

After another long silence he flung a hand up through his hair and growled to the night, 'The weather looks like being as rough as it can be, the going likewise. I've got to get this load across seven countries in one piece, *all I need* is a lovesick schoolgirl on my hands.'

'Well, believe me,' Claire flared, 'I can't wait to get off them! So if you'll kindly step out of the way ...'

He did as she asked and somewhat shakily she moved off. She managed to say as she went, 'The idiotic thing is, I could have written the feature on your precious trucking business every bit as well as a man, and I bet none of the people reading it would have minded either.'

Stumbling away up the road, she kept tear-starred eyes fixed firmly ahead. She heard the slam of the truck door and then it was starting up. As it passed alongside her she tilted her chin in icy unconcern, and carried on.

About a yard ahead of her the truck stopped. As she came level Greg Millard barked,

'Get in!'

Claire turned and stared up through the open window. The dejected look in her eyes started to fade behind a warm excited glow as she asked on a breath, 'You mean ... you're going to take me with you?'

The blue eyes flickered over her and then he rose to clip testily, 'For pity's sake get a move on! We're blocking the road.'

He grabbed her case and slung it roughly under the seat, then took his place behind the wheel again. Claire climbed up and closed the door quickly as they moved off. She gazed meekly ahead, much of her old dejection returning. It would have been nice to think he had changed his mind because he considered her worth helping, but of course it wasn't like that at all. Her parting comment had reminded him that without her along to do the feature, his firm would be losing valuable publicity. And he would put up with anything to get that. Even her!

She had known that from the beginning, hadn't she? So why feel this tiny stab of regret?

CHAPTER THREE

THE countryside had been swallowed up in a pit of darkness. Traces of the recent snow were caught in the beam of the headlights that spilled out over the road, but the only indication that there was anything beyond was the occasional blob of yellow light as a farmstead or a cottage spun by.

Hands clasped in her lap, Claire stole a sideways glance at

the man at the wheel. She wished he would say something. Perhaps he was fully occupied with steering the truck along the dimly lit road. She liked to think it was that, although there was still no comment when they were in among the bright lights and speeding along the motorway. Out in the darkness the blobs of light had taken to gathering in clusters, suggesting hamlets or villages. Most of the time the road by-passed the built up areas, but occasionally the truck would rumble through a town, and Claire would be on the edge of her seat, craning to get a look at the houses and people before they were sucked away again into the night.

Around eight o'clock the sign for Elten showed up clearly among many others at the roadside. Approaching the village, she gazed ahead eagerly. Now that they were really underway she found it all rather exciting. Elten was on the border with Germany, and these days you couldn't just wander where you liked. There would be guards at the crossing to examine their papers and to check that everything was in order.

She cast her mind back diffidently over the various pieces of paper in her briefcase, hoping she had got all the right ones. Wouldn't it be awful if she had gone to all this trouble to stay with the truck only to find that there was something lacking in her documents?

It wasn't likely, though, she reassured herself happily. Mike knew all about these things and he had checked over everything with her. Her thoughts lingered for a moment on her brother driving somewhere in another country. Did he ever wonder what she was up to? She could smile now at the memory of him gaping up at her as she had ridden by in the truck last night, but it hadn't been funny at the time.

Expecting to continue straight on to the frontier, she was a little surprised to find that the truck had turned off to the village. A few minutes later the brakes were going on in the forecourt of a garage. Could be a stop for fuel, Claire supposed. She waited for the man at the wheel to give some indication of what he had in mind. After he had checked the various knobs and switches and levers, he opened his door.

'You'll need your case,' he told her, jumping down with his own holdall in his hand. 'We're staying the night in Elten.'

Slamming the door, he was striding away before Claire had had time to grasp his words. She staggered down, splaying over the weight of her case, and pushing the cab door to, struggled after him. It wasn't a pleasant thought, being left alone in a strange country in the dark. She needn't have worried, though, for the suede-coated figure swung off at the first turning up a narrow cobbled street and into the doorway of a gaily lit inn. She just had time to see gabled roofs, black against the sky, leaning into each other up the length of the street, and then the light of the inn shut out the view. Inside she waited in docile silence until the transport boss had signed a book at the desk and then he was handing her a key.

'Someone will take you to your room,' he informed her. 'We'll leave about seven in the morning. Be ready.'

Claire looked up to him before he turned away to say, 'I ... I thought you more or less kept moving on these trips. I mean ... well, the schedule won't stand up to overnight stops, will it?'

'Take what you can while it's here,' he said crisply, moving off. He left his holdall at the desk and went back outside again. She watched him go, pulling in her lip. It had been a silly comment on her part anyway. He couldn't be expected to drive day and night. She was the only crewmate he had and no doubt he was cursing the fact.

A plump smiling girl came and picked up her case as though it were a paper bag. She took the key too, and speaking in almost perfect English she had introduced herself and given a full layout of the inn by the time they reached a corner door on the second floor. Inside Claire saw a small comfortable room with Dutch-style furniture and ornaments.

'The dining room is closed for the night,' the girl stated apologetically, 'but I am to bring you up a tray.'

Claire smiled her thanks as the girl went out.

The meal, when it arrived, consisted of bread, thickly buttered, thin wafers of cheese, slices of sausage, and chocolate. There was coffee in a lidded beaker. She ate strolling around the room and trying to find an English station on the radio near the bed, then seeing that it was only nine o'clock she decided to have a look round downstairs.

It was nice to linger on the landings taking in the various

46

Dutch touches as she went. Delft pottery on high shelves and decorated wooden clogs hanging on the walls. The pungent smell of wax polish and old beams mingled with the spicy aroma of local cooking.

Downstairs there was a low-ceilinged bar beyond the reception desk. Strolling in, Claire considered changing some of her money into guilders to buy a drink. It would be an excuse to sit for a while in the pleasant glow of oak beams and firelight, instead of going straight back to her room.

She was just about to go out again when she caught the smiling glance of a young man sitting not far away at a table.

'*Goeden Avand.*'

Taking this to be some form of greeting since he had inclined his head, Claire smiled back and murmured a tentative, 'Hello.'

'You do not know the name of the drink you want?' He half rose questioningly.

'No, it isn't that,' Claire explained. 'I was just wondering about changing some English money.'

The man spread an arm towards his table.

'I will get you something.'

'Oh no! Really!' Claire looked slightly aghast but he was beside her lifting his hand.

'Please!' He bowed shyly and went to the bar.

Sitting on the wooden bench that skirted the room, she let her gaze wander around. There were not many people about. Two men sat separately, musing over their drinks, and down at the far end, a jovial bald-headed man was wrestling with the tap of a barrel. Down at the far end too, Claire noticed for the first time Greg Millard minus the suede driving coat, draped back with a glass in front of him. She didn't know whether he had seen her or not. If he had, he gave no indication, but simply continued the conversation he was having with two elderly men.

The young man came back and put a glass down on the table in front of her, stating,

'*Citreonjenever.*' When she looked blank he smiled, 'Gin ... with lemon.' He took the seat beside her and sipping a little from his own glass enquired politely, 'You are on holiday in Holland?'

47

'No,' Claire shook her head, smiling, 'I'm doing a trip in a freight truck.'

He lifted a silver-blond eyebrow, then trailing a humorous but not unkindly gaze over her heavy polo-necked sweater, corduroy slacks, and clumsy shoes, he grinned, 'As you English say, that figures!'

'No, the Americans, I think,' Claire laughed lightly, sampling her drink. After a silence the young man crinkled his brow to query, 'Excuse me. Freight truck?'

'I'm getting material for a feature I'm writing,' Claire explained, realising with a guilty pang that she had not put a word on paper yet.

'Ahah!' The crinkled brow smoothed out. 'And the big Englishman sitting at the end of the room. He is your driver?'

'Yes,' Claire affirmed, not following the young man's gaze. She saw it return slowly to her face and the light-coloured eyes were dancing mischievously as he murmured, 'And does he beat you?'

She lifted a hand quickly to her grazed cheek.

'I tripped,' she smiled, lowering her gaze to her drink.

Frans was from Hilversum. He was studying to be an engineer and part of his training was at a factory nearby. After some time spent talking with him, four of his friends came in; two men with their girls. They made a pleasant group and Claire finally gave up marvelling at the perfect English spoken, when she learned that it was taught as a second language in Dutch schools. She wondered what methods they used, for they made a far better job of it than she did with her G.C.E. French.

Towards ten, Frans left, shaking her gravely by the hand, and the foursome more or less retired into themselves. Claire still had much of her drink left. She sipped at it meditatively, occasionally letting her glance stray down the room.

Greg Millard was pulling on a cigarette. He leaned forward every now and again to add a word to the conversation that was going on. She didn't see how he could have missed noticing her, but he had given no sign of recognition. No use fooling herself that he would, Claire thought. He might have to take her along with him, but he didn't have to like her. She leaned back with apparent unconcern. The room was pleasantly warm, the fire in the hearth leaping from glowing red logs. She had everything in the way of comfort that she had been longing for all day, yet somehow, now, she wasn't in the mood to enjoy it.

Dutch life got under way very early in the morning. There were sounds of the village swinging into the day's work by six o'clock. By seven, Claire was taking a last look at her reflection in the mirror before vacating her room. She brushed her hair for the hundredth time, admiring the way it fell silkily on to her shoulders.

She had packed the bulky sweater in favour of a soft fleecy turtleneck in pale green. She spent several seconds picking imaginary bits off it, and a few more to stand back and linger over the effect, then she tossed the driving coat carelessly over her arm, picked up her case, and tripped out of the room.

There was no sign of the transport boss downstairs, so she hurried to the desk to hand in her key. The clerk was nodding her a pleasant farewell, so there was nothing for it but to make her way out to the truck.

The sky had that pearly grey sheen of winter's first light, and the breaths of the people hurrying by, froze on the biting air. Invigorated by the cold and the feel of foreign places, Claire stepped out, absorbing the sights and sounds around her. Her case seemed to float in her hands this morning.

There was no mistaking the way to the garage. The route they had taken last night was easy enough to remember.

The truck looked like a big benevolent uncle winking its windscreens at her in the morning light, and beaming a wide radiator smile. Not so its owner. He stood thumping his gloved hands together, frowning over the tyres and paint-work of the truck as she approached, and giving no sign that he had seen her until she was practically stepping on his toes.

'Isn't it a gorgeous morning?' she said on a quick breath and a smile.

With a brief glance over her, he reached out a hand for the coat over her arm and opening it, held it towards her. 'You'll freeze to death without this,' he clipped, 'and the hair looks better under the cap.'

Claire thrust her arms into the coat, feeling her smile slip. The cap was stuffed into one of the side pockets. She ignored it for a second, then turning away, dragged it out and clamped it on her head, coiling her hair up in one thick twist beneath it. Without so much as a nod of approval as they met again inside the cab, he merely positioned her case under the seat and swung the truck into action.

Claire didn't nurse her irritation for long. There was far too much to interest her beyond the windscreen she told herself, for her to care what went on this side of it. Of course it would have been nicer if Greg Millard had been the friendly type. Someone she could chat to. But at least he was letting her make the trip, and one couldn't have everything, could one? She blinked a wistful gaze over the scenery and then settled down to make the most of the ride.

The crossing at the border was so quick and effortless she hardly knew they were moving into another country. The transport boss had taken charge of her briefcase, and one of the guards flicked through her passport, turning a bemused smile over her and then the truck, then the men were checking other things. In no time, the truck was cruising unhampered along the autobahn.

At first Claire was alert and intrigued at the two-lane one-way highway with its speeding traffic, but she soon became bored with the scene, especially as it seemed to go on and on with nothing to break the monotony. The only towns she saw were silhouetted picturesquely but distantly on the skyline. There were the fuel stations, of course, with small cafés adjoining, and meticulously clean rest-rooms, situated every thirty or forty miles. She knew about these because Greg Millard had pulled in once or twice, when the parking sign gave permission. Sipping her coffee, she had enjoyed the view then of deep forests and rolling countryside.

When they were off on their way again after one of these stops, and seeing that there was nothing new to catch her eye outside, Claire turned her attention to the inside of the cab. There was a road map lying open on the dashboard, and reaching for it she couldn't suppress a small thrill at the sight of the journey plotted out across Europe.

Forgetting that there had been a complete lack of conversation so far, she enquired eagerly of the transport boss,

'Will we get across Germany in one day, do you think?'

'Hard to say.' He kept his eyes on the road.

Following his gaze, Claire asked dreamily, 'Where do you suppose we'll get to?'

'If we're lucky we might make Munich by nightfall.'

'If we're lucky?' Claire turned, twinkling slightly to comment, 'You talk as though this were a ship, and I were some kind of jinx.'

'Not exactly a jinx.' He didn't move his gaze from the road, but she saw the spark of something there, she wasn't sure what. Something like the sun glinting briefly on icy pools.

She turned her attention back to the map and chattered, 'It's all terribly exciting, isn't it? Driving all this way across two continents. But then,' at the expressionless profile over the wheel, 'I suppose you've done it dozens of times.'

'Dozens,' he remarked lazily.

'Before you got your fleet of trucks.' She didn't know why it should irritate her that he was so successful, but she heard herself adding sweetly, 'Congratulations.'

'I didn't get them carrying females around,' he replied drily, flicking the wheel.

Claire looked down at the map to carp, 'We're back on that tack again, are we?'

'I guess we will be until we reach Tehran.'

His tones now were as difficult to fathom as that look had been, but for some unaccountable reason Claire felt pleasantly disposed again. She concentrated on the map for a while, trailing her finger along the route they had taken and on to where they would go. As familiar names cropped up she couldn't resist saying them out loud.

'There's Cologne and Bonn and ... oh, could we stop at Frankfurt? I've always wanted to see ...'

'The sooner you get it into your head,' the transport boss watched a vehicle pass him on an adjoining lane and then continued in somewhat wintry tones, 'that we're not on a pleasure trip, the better. Transporting freight is a serious business.' He brought his gaze in from the road for the first time to add, 'And we've got to get to that boy-friend of yours in Tehran. Remember?'

'I know. And I think of him all the time,' Claire said

hastily. 'But we can't get there non-stop, can we? And anyway, Frankfurt is on the way.'

'And if you look a little closer at the map you'll see that our road goes nowhere near it.'

She *had* seen, but she had chosen to ignore it. Now as he pointed it out she set her mouth in a small straight line and sighed. There seemed no point in further conversation. It was obviously an effort on his part anyway, so why should she bother? She turned her attention to the view, amusing herself with fanciful notions of fairy-tale castles hidden among the trees, and peasants in picturesque costumes working in the fields.

She had long since resigned herself to the never-ending strip of road and its unchanging scenery. Therefore it came as something of a surprise when, some considerable time later, the truck turned off on to another highway and continued towards a built-up area. Her surprise increased when she saw a sign clearly announcing the town of Frankfurt, but now, with half-timbered houses and quaint cobbled streets to gaze on, she didn't feel inclined to spoil things by asking what they were doing here.

Further on into the town, the transport boss chose as before a garage with a large forecourt to pull into. When the brakes were on Claire waited to see what was going to happen next, and then as he swung his door open and jumped down, she thought she might as well do the same. As she came round to his side he said, without looking up from the papers he was leafing through in his wallet, 'I've got a couple of things to attend to on the truck. I'll see you back here in about an hour.' As Claire gazed about her with a slightly lost air he raised his head to state, 'This is Frankfurt.' When she didn't react he pointed out with a certain crispness, 'I believe you said there was something here you wanted to see.'

Had she said that? Lifting her eyes to meet, unexpectedly, a pair of light blue ones, Claire found she couldn't think straight. If she had said it, she probably hadn't meant anything specific, just the town itself.

'Yes, I ... er ... was thinking about the shops,' she said. hoping she didn't sound too vague.

He nodded along the road from where they stood. 'Keep

going. You'll come to them.'

She pulled off the peaked cap and shook her hair loose, then rolling the cap into her pocket, she set off a little uncertainly in the direction he had nodded. This was actually Frankfurt, so she had better make the most of it. Given the chance, of course.

The way it looked, the first kerb on the corner was as far as she was going to get. The traffic was hurtling by from all directions, and each time she put a tentative foot out to cross a barrage of horns warned her to take it in again. About to try for the third time, she felt a firm grip on her arm and Greg Millard was saying in faintly irritated tones, 'Hang on, I'll come with you.'

She saw him turn back and lock the doors of the truck, then he was taking her arm and guiding her over the road at a different point from where she had tried to cross. After walking for a while, he stopped a passing taxi and asked for 'the Kaiserstrasse'. Not long after that, they were stepping out among shops and bustle and beautiful old buildings. As Claire gazed around, unable to take it all in, Greg Millard lifted wide shoulders in the big driving coat and said with lazy tolerance, 'It's all yours.'

Claire gave a soft laugh and moving off suggested eagerly, 'Shall we try this street first?'

'They're *Strasses* here, not streets,' he drawled, taking her arm as she almost collided with two heavily loaded shoppers.

At first it was difficult to appreciate all the beautiful things on show, so conscious was she of the big figure strolling and stopping where she stopped, but eventually her shyness left her and then she couldn't keep back the exclamations of delight and wonder at the displays.

There were Bavarian music boxes, peasant dolls, and drinking mugs made in everything from wood to porcelain. Black Forest cuckoo clocks hung around the walls in many windows, and wax art candles looked like priceless jade carvings of Chinese figurines.

They strolled along *Strasses* and *Platzes*. It must have been fully an hour since their tour had started, although Claire didn't want to spoil it by looking at her watch. When the transport boss took her arm, she thought it was a sign that they were going back to the truck, but instead she found herself being guided into a downstairs wine restaurant. It was rather like a cellar with stone archways and pillars, but there was nothing grim about it. The clothes on the tables were snowy white, and dark polished cherubs looked down from whitewashed walls. Thankfully everyone was heavily dressed against the cold, so Claire didn't feel out of place in her stout shoes and slacks. Slipping off her coat, though, she was glad she had put on the soft pale green sweater.

The transport boss ordered for her as he had got into the habit of doing in the cafés along the route. He wore a maroon pullover in heavy knit, and if anything it accentuated the width of his shoulders and dark craggy looks. She saw there were tiny creases around his eyes when he smiled, which was often when he was talking to anyone else but her. His teeth were even and white.

The food when it came was delicious and plentiful, though she didn't wonder at the outsize waistlines of some of the diners if they always ate in such quantities. The conversation from the tables was guttural and sprinkled with *unds* and *ja's*.

Claire had been prattling on to herself most of the time in the shops, so she found it pleasant to sit and listen to everyone else for a change. When the meal was over she felt reluctant to leave the cosiness of the restaurant and lingered over the showcases in the entrance. She could have stood there dreaming over the colourful wine labels indefinitely, but then the transport boss was coming up behind her to state evenly,

'Time to get going, Dave, if we're going to make Munich by tonight.'

Claire nodded, not knowing why she should feel that some of the pleasure had gone out of the interlude. Perhaps it was a sneaking disappointment that Greg Millard didn't really see her as 'her' at all. Her hair might be smooth on her shoulders, the triangle of sweater palely feminine at her throat, but to him she was just another crewmate. And that was all she had been throughout the shop window gazing and the meal.

The sky had hardened to a dull metal grey when they got back to the truck. There was a bitterly cold wind blowing, and Claire was glad to settle herself into the cab and relax in the warmth that slowly started to circulate once they were on their way again.

As the truck raced to eat up the miles on the autobahn, she felt a delicious drowsiness stealing over her, but she fought it as she would anything that would give Greg Millard the chance to point out that she was weaker than he was. She had to smile inwardly at her own mixed feelings. A little while back she had resented him seeing her as a hardened crewmate, now she was striving to give the impression of being one. But it was only because he had been so sure that she wouldn't be able to stand up to the journey.

Once it was dark and there was nothing to see outside, it became more and more difficult to stay awake, but she kept cardboard eyelids up somehow and watched the never-ending succession of lights roll by. On and on they went. Claire was sure that they were riding to the ends of the earth. Her body seemed moulded in its slumped position against the seat, her legs bent rods in front of her. Each time the truck pulled in for refreshments she was amazed to find she could still walk. The second time she didn't have to crawl out like a cat, for the transport boss was there to take her lightly round the waist and swing her down. That made a nice change anyway, she told herself, looking quickly the other way as she landed.

She had been waiting so long for Munich to show itself, it sprung up on her without her even realising it in the end. The road seemed to be laying itself down ahead in the same old monotonous way, then suddenly there were buildings and more buildings and then brightly lit streets, with wine taverns and shops. The size of the city was considerable. They seemed to be riding through it for hours, then eventually the blocks were thinning out. As the lights dropped low again, Greg Millard said above the wheel, 'We'll pull in at Riechentstee. It's a small village just beyond Munich. To-morrow we'll only have about thirty-five miles to go to the Austrian border.'

'Tomorrow?' Claire straightened her aching back. 'It must be that now, isn't it?'

'Not quite,' he gave her the flickering of a smile. 'Tired?'

'No more than usual,' Claire lied, striving to look the picture of scintillating freshness.

There was no telling what the village looked like, for

everywhere was pitch black now. Not that Claire cared anyway. She had had her fill of outdoor scenery for one day. It was the indoor kind she was interested in at the moment. The sight of a steaming bathtub, for instance, a huge feather bed with three or four pillows and about the same amount of eiderdowns.

Better not get too optimistic, though. In fact, better not be optimistic at all! She had an awful feeling it was going to be the camp site all over again when the truck pulled into a deserted parking lot. Then Greg Millard was climbing down and nodding away into the darkness to say, 'There's a motel on the other road.'

Thank heavens for that! She realised she was in no position to expect anything, but no doubt he would present her with the bill at the end. He swung out her case and his holdall, and moved off. Claire hurried from her seat, and groped gingerly along hoping that nothing would come up and hit her out of the dark. Something did loom up in her path, but it was only the big figure of the transport boss turning back. He came alongside her and lifted the holdall slightly to say, 'Take hold of my arm. It's not far.'

He didn't sound too impatient, thank heaven. She linked up with the suede-coated arm, grateful to have something to hang on to in the inky blackness. Walking along in this silent world of night, sensing him matching his steps to hers, she was suddenly seized with an overwhelming desire to giggle. Neither of them could possibly have foreseen a moment like this, when they were glaring at each other that day in his office.

The humorous mood fled as quickly as it had appeared, and then she knew something like a heady pleasure tinged with wistfulness. It was rather a nice arm to cling to. What a pity the owner had a metal-encased heart, just like his trucks! They might have become good friends. Only friends, of course, for there was Robin in Tehran. Funny to think, though, that the nearer she got to her fiancé, the further he seemed to fade into the distance.

She saw a light ahead winking palely through the frosty air. It turned out to be a small office with an elderly man in attendance. He looked up from his paper as they entered and after an exchange of sentences in German, he handed the transport boss two keys from the rows of hooks on the wall. Claire followed him out, wondering where they were off to next. She didn't have to wonder for long. A few minutes later he was pushing a key into the lock of a door that looked like one of many in a line. As he switched on the light, she saw a small, rather austere room with a bare polished floor and the minimum of furniture. The mattress on the bed looked wafer thin under its folkweave cover, and the pillow showed itself in a slight imperceptible rise at the end. Still, it was all beautifully done out, and intensely modern and feather beds were old-fashioned anyway.

The transport boss took her case inside and went to switch on the electric fire. Drawn by the red glow of the bars, Claire shuffled over to it and started to undo the buttons of her heavy driving coat. As she slipped out of it, she felt it being taken off her shoulders, then Greg Millard was dropping the key into her hand to say lazily, 'Don't forget to lock up before you turn in.' He hung her coat up, swung her case on to the bed and came to stand by the fire to ask, 'Anything else you want?'

Claire raised her head, shrugging off her disappointment with a worn smile. 'I had visions of a gorgeous hot bath, but...'

'Coming up!' The tight mouth relaxed slightly as he strode to an adjoining door. Seconds later there was the bliss-ful sound of running water. He came back into the room to say drily, 'Don't fall asleep before you get there. It's filling up fast.'

'I'm not all that sleepy.' Claire tossed her head, feeling her hair tumble about her as she pulled off the peaked cap.

The transport boss eyed her searchingly, then commented with the ghost of a grin, 'I shouldn't worry too much. You're standing up to the treatment quite well.'

Claire felt a rush of pleasure at his words, but to keep herself in check she tilted her chin to say lightly, 'What did you expect? That I would get a fit of the vapours every three or four miles?'

'Something like that.' He sloped a smile over her. She held his gaze to point out humorously, 'We girls have come on quite a bit since grandma's days, you know. Although there are still a lot of men around who insist on seeing us as just a

57

household attachment, the little lady who should stay cosseted at home.'

'It's more in keeping with the way they look, I guess,' he shrugged.

She wanted to ask him how they looked, or rather how *she* looked, but her courage deserted her at the last moment.

The silence stretched, then he was thrusting his hands into his pockets to say briskly,

'I'd better go and lock up the truck, and you'd better get to those taps, before you have to swim through.' He strode across the room and opening the door turned to point out, 'My room's next door on the left, if you're wondering.' He gave her a brief nod, 'Goodnight.'

'Goodnight ... Mr. Millard.'

She watched the door close and stared at it for some time, then she turned her gaze over the room; the glowing fire, her coat on a hanger, her case lifted on to the bed with its catches open. She turned to look at the door again, tilting her head on one side with a questioning half smile.

Metal-encased heart? Well, maybe not quite metal, mmm?

The bed turned out to be surprisingly comfortable, so comfortable in fact that Claire just slept and slept. It was eight-thirty when she awoke. She looked aghast at her watch and tumbled hastily out of bed. The transport boss hadn't mentioned any starting out time last night, but that was probably because he had forgotten to. She washed rapidly and pulled into the corduroy slacks. The heavy polo-necked sweater was the first on hand and there was no time to worry about fashion this morning. She buttoned up the driving coat, flung everything else into her case, then drew the curtains to brush her hair quickly at the mirror.

The first thing she saw when she looked out of the window was the truck, parked some yards away near the main building. One of the doors was open and Greg Millard was dusting a side mirror. Claire relaxed considerably. She couldn't be all that late or he would be banging on her door by this time. She watched the tall figure for a while before applying herself to the task of brushing her hair. Coming up against the reflection in the mirror, she couldn't help noticing a strange new sparkle in her eyes, a certain glow about her complexion. Even the graze on her cheek seemed part of her this morning. It was only the ice cold water she had washed in, of course, and the good night's sleep she had had.

As she tossed the smooth hair back on her shoulders, the wide mouth smiled back at her as though nursing some secret of its own. She went outside, leaving her case by the door until she found out where to return the key. Her outfit was not exactly the height of elegance and yet she felt as though she had a gossamer gown floating about her, as she stepped out lightly towards the truck.

The transport boss turned as she approached. Apart from being clean-shaven, and the dark hair in place as though freshly combed, he looked exactly as he had done last night standing by the fire. She thought his eyes rested over-long on her smile, then he was turning away to say curtly, 'I wondered when you were going to show up. Maybe I should get you an alarm clock.'

The harsh voice was like a draught of cold air, colder than that biting about her ears. When she had got over the blast of it, he turned back from wiping the rim of a window to ask in the same temperature, 'Had breakfast?'

Claire shook her head, holding up the key.

'I was wondering where to take this?'

'Drop it in at the office at the end.' He pointed. 'You'll see a restaurant there too. Get yourself fixed up with something to eat.'

'But ... but I don't speak German.'

'You'll get by.'

Claire went off to deliver the key, feeling herself plummet to earth with a bang. Who would have thought the man seemed almost human last night? Human! She pulled her lips into a grimace. If there had been any softening in that granite exterior she must have dreamt it.

Everyone in the restaurant seemed to be expecting her, and she was served with coffee and rolls without having to open her mouth. She ate with one eye on her watch and resisting the desire to linger over a second cup of coffee hurried outside.

Her case had gone from the doorway where she had left it, so she turned in the direction of the truck. As she made her way slowly towards it, a tiny thread in her heart pulled tighter.

Well, well! This wasn't the Greg Millard *she* knew! He was smiling down at a wavy-haired girl who was standing close enough to be almost touching him. Something she said brought a deep-throated laugh from the big frame. The girl's own laughter tinkled out gaily to meet it, as she gazed up at him.

Claire didn't know whether to swing away or just pretend that the two were invisible, but the transport boss saw her as he looked up. He straightened and nodded towards her with the tail end of his smile to enlighten the girl lazily, 'My crew-mate.'

The girl looked at Claire from head to toe, with curious amusement, saying as she did so, 'I'm very pleased to meet you.' Her English was as neat and precise as her petite figure.

Smiling a greeting she somehow didn't feel, Claire heard Greg Millard put in, 'This is Nina. Her parents run the motel.'

After a noticeable pause the girl lapsed back into her own tongue, apparently taking up where she left off, and seeing that her case was in the truck Claire climbed up to join it. Sitting there listening to the tinkling laughter, she cursed herself for not taking that second cup of coffee.

When the transport boss finally took his place behind the wheel, she couldn't resist saying sweetly,

'Don't tear yourself away for me.'

She saw a flicker of humour in the blue eyes as he swung the truck into gear, then he was clamping his jaw and looking straight ahead. All set for the usual happy-go-lucky drive, Claire thought. Seeing the girl waving outside the motel, she slumped back. That must have made his day anyway!

As the truck picked up speed she found she didn't want to turn her gaze to the front just yet. She couldn't stare openly, of course, but pretending to rest her head back she could watch the slim hands deftly swinging the wheel; notice how the dark hair curled slightly at the back of his neck. There was a rim of light checked shirt showing above the collar of the big driving coat, a mustard tie knotted under the jutting jaw. All in all she supposed there might be something attractive about him; in a rugged hard-bitten way, of course, and especially with the gleam of white smile she had seen back there.

Not that he was ever likely to use that on *her*!

Dragging her eyes away from the set profile, she turned her attention outside. If he wanted to be grim about things, she didn't have to get like that herself, did she? And the view was a pleasure at least; pastel blue skies and forests of snow-gowned fir trees. For the first few miles she kept the glow of it to herself, but when the truck started to weave through the Bavarian mountains, it was impossible to keep her delight bottled up. She enthused non-stop over the great craggy peaks and the sugar-frosted chalets nestling below in the valleys.

There were no chatty rejoinders to her bubbling comments, although the transport boss did use his voice lazily once or twice, to tell her to stay in her seat as they swung round a corner, and to sit back when he wanted to see through her window.

They reached the German Customs fairly quickly, but getting through took some time. There was much poring over forms and checking lists and when this was done the uniformed officials seemed in no hurry to say goodbye to the big figure in the suede jacket. Watching from the cab, Claire noticed the relaxed air of the transport boss as he talked; one hand thrust into his trouser pocket, his head inclined slightly to take in a guttural sentence, and the occasional blur of his white smile as one of the men made a hearty joke.

When it looked as though the Austrian Customs were going to take as long, if not longer, Claire toyed with the idea of making some notes on the trip so far, but somehow she couldn't bring herself to concentrate with the tall figure standing just up ahead. She decided instead to get out of the truck and stretch her legs. It was bitingly cold away from the comfort of her seat, but the view more than made up for it.

As she gazed up, a young official detached himself from the customs group and strolled to stand by her side. He was friendly in a shy boyish kind of way, but she couldn't understand a word he said to her. With a shrug and a grin, he offered her a cigarette, and when she smilingly refused he resorted to pointing out the different mountain peaks to her, reciting names she could never hope to pronounce.

After a few minutes the transport boss came up behind her to say crisply, 'It's time we were moving!'

Irritated by something she couldn't quite define in his manner, Claire heard herself saying airily, 'Well, who's waiting for whom?' His only answer was to take her by the arm and lead her back to the truck. She was vaguely surprised to have his assistance as she climbed up.

Once they were on the road again, and especially now they were in Austria, she picked the map up eagerly. Following the route with her finger, she asked, 'Where do you think we'll stop next?'

'Salzburg,' was the brief reply.

The shine of happy surprise showing in her eyes, Claire turned in her seat 'As soon as that?'

The transport boss flickered a gaze over her to comment, 'I've got a call to make there.'

Hardly caring what his mood was, Claire said laughingly, 'I'm awfully glad you have.'

Well, who wouldn't want to see Salzburg? she mused, sliding to the edge of her seat. She had seen pictures of it, of course, and heard of its music festival, but she hadn't dared to hope that they would stop off there.

It wasn't long before signs were announcing the city of Salzburg and soon after they were passing through the outer suburbs. As the transport boss swung the truck skilfully along the narrowing roads Claire kept her gaze fixed beyond the panoramic windscreen, not wanting to miss anything of the beautiful medieval buildings and tall houses.

They turned off before the centre of the town and climbing a hill were at once in the countryside again. At first Claire thought she was in for a disappointment until the truck pulled into a large forecourt where one or two cars were parked. Then she sat completely entranced by the setting. The wooden built hotel was decorated in typical Austrian fashion with gaily painted panels and window boxes. It was tall with timbered balconies, and deep overhanging eaves, and behind it snow-dappled slopes rose clear to the heavens, glinting where the sun picked them out against an eggshell blue sky.

It was the sunshine and the view that made Claire hum

happily beneath her breath as she climbed down. There was no snow underfoot here, in fact she could almost say there was a touch of spring in the air.

Greg Millard had already jumped down and slammed his door, and Claire was just on her way round to meet him when a girl with arms outstretched, and flying cornsilk plaits, raced out of the door of the hotel, and beat her to it.

'Grey ... gorr ... reee!' Ecstatically the girl threw herself against the suede-coated figure and Claire watched as open arms caught the girl close and swung her round. She set her mouth slightly at the lowered dark head and deep laugh. It was positively sickening the way he unbent with other people. Especially *female* other people.

'I thought it was Mike to coming this time.' The girl gazed up into the blue eyes in laughing bewilderment.

With a shrug the transport boss let her go. 'I'm taking Mike's place on this trip, Rossita,' he said, and then waving at Claire, 'This is Mike's sister. She's travelling with me.'

'That's nice.' A wide if somewhat cool smile lowered over Claire, then Greg Millard was adding, 'She's going out to her fiancé in Tehran.'

'That's *nice*!' With the accent on the second word this time, the girl took a step forward, deep dimples rushing in to melt the ice around her smile.

Claire smiled back, but she had never been so concious of her clumsy clothing than she was at this moment, standing opposite the sparkling prettily dressed girl, with the big suede-coated figure looking on. She was glad at least that the peaked cap was rolled up and stuffed down the back of her seat. She resolved there and then to get rid of it at the first opportunity.

With a happy sigh the Austrian girl turned to lead the way towards the hotel, and Greg Millard came alongside Claire to explain lazily, 'Rossita helps in the hotel. She's the ...'

'I know,' Claire said sweetly, nodding her head slowly and deliberately, 'the daughter of the owners.'

'Niece, actually,' he corrected with a faint smile. They were almost on the point of entering the doorway when a husky, thick-set young man, with rolled up shirt sleeves and a cap of white blond hair, pushed his way out. He nodded and grinned around, then stood over Claire with an interested light in his eyes. The girl turned back to explain tolerantly,

'Is my brother Klaus.'

'That's nice,' Claire murmured succinctly, smiling up into the handsome face, then swinging her gaze innocently towards the transport boss. She deliberately held on to the metallic twinkle, before turning back to the husky young man and allowing him to lead her inside.

They sat in the beautifully decorated bar, Claire eyeing the tourists with interest, and Klaus eagerly plying her with drinks and his barely understandable English. Greg Millard had gone off through another door and probably wouldn't show himself until they were ready to leave.

When he reappeared some time later she rose, expecting to be told to get back to the truck, but instead he took her arm and with a somewhat austere nod at Klaus, led her through into a room filled with tables.

'Might as well eat here,' he drawled, guiding her down the room. Oh, might as well! Claire thought acidly, spotting the smiling figure of Klaus's sister hanging prettily over one of the tables. The girl skipped backwards and forwards once they were seated adding extra little touches to the table. She placed Austrian dishes proudly before them with dancing-eyed pleasure, but Claire had a feeling it wasn't *her* smile of appreciation that Rossita was looking for, so she kept her gaze on the view. With windows stretching the length of the dining room, there was enough there to keep her occupied for the whole of the meal.

When it was over Rossita showed her where to tidy up. Later she met the transport boss outside, and followed him over to the truck. He didn't climb up as she had expected, but reached under the dashboard for a small parcel and locked the door again.

'I've got a delivery to make,' he explained evenly, and then looking at his watch, 'I'll be back here in an hour ready to roll. Make sure you're here.'

Claire watched him stride away, lifting her shoulders and letting them drop disconsolately. He might have taken her with him. What could she do on her own for a whole hour? Klaus was busy lifting crates out of a van, and there was no one else she could spend her time with.

She drew in a sigh, staring around. She could always walk of course ... or come to think of it, wasn't there a mountain railway not far from here? She had seen a card advertising it in the bar, and the tourists had been discussing it. She hurried over to Klaus now to find out more.

'Ah!' He smiled knowingly as she carefully explained her interest in the railway. 'Up is very good fine view. See Salzburg.'

'Oh, it sounds marvellous!' Claire followed his gaze excitedly to the slopes above the hotel. 'But how long does the trip take?'

He shrugged swinging a crate into the doorway, and checking his list. 'About of tventy minots,' he said, scribbling.

Twenty minutes! Well, that was perfect. That was only forty minutes altogether. She would have time to snatch a quick look at the view at the top before coming down again. She thanked Klaus and moved off, digging her hand into her pocket for her purse. It shouldn't take much to buy a ticket, and she could change to Austrian coinage in the hotel. She quickly made the transaction and then hurried off, following the sign pointing to the railway.

It was only a minute's walk, and following the example of a group of laughing holidaymakers, she bought a ticket and took a seat in the tiny carriage facing a window. There was that mutual undercurrent of excitement that was always apparent when a party of people were about to do something they had never done before, and Claire had to admit that she was contributing her share, if only by not being able to sit still.

She couldn't wait for the train to start. When it did, it jerked everybody back in their seats, and a ripple of delighted titters passed down the carriage. Claire sat glued to the window. There wouldn't be anything to see straight away, of course, for it was a gradual ascent, but she wanted to be ready when they started up the steeper incline and the valley began to spread out below.

This didn't come as soon as she expected, and after a while she began to wonder when the train was going to pick up speed. It clicked merrily over the lines at little more than trotting pace and though it was tilted now to take in the slope, there still seemed an awfully long way to go.

She tried to feel unconcerned, but found herself stealing a worried glance at her watch. Fifteen minutes gone already, and she could only just see a few roof tops below! The train was going to have to sprout wings to get to the top in five minutes.

Biting back her worry, she turned to two middle-aged ladies, who were sitting just across and chattering amiably to one another in English.

'Excuse me,' she interrupted politely, and then seeing that they were smiling at her she asked, 'Have you any idea how long this ride takes?'

'About an hour, I think,' one said pleasantly. The other one put in with a proud wriggle of plump shoulders, 'You'll find it well worth it, my dear. I've done the trip once before and it's quite a fascinating experience.'

'Thank you.' Claire turned to fling her panic-stricken gaze over the view.

An hour each way! What on earth was she going to do? She had expected to cut it fine by a minute or two, but an hour!

It was no good blaming Klaus. With his limited English it was probably 'Tventy minots' for everything, and her own common sense ought to have told her it would take longer than that.

Well, she couldn't jump off the train, so there was nothing for it but to make the best of the ride. She would think what to do when she arrived. Trying to relax, she made a concerted effort to enjoy the trip along with everyone else.

As they climbed, it was impossible not to be enchanted by views of the city spreading out below and the fortress high on a wooded hill, but towards the top Claire felt as though she was dragging the train the last few yards herself. When it stopped she was out in a moment, but the queue for the downward line made her heart sink. She couldn't possibly take her turn in that! Gazing about her she saw a pipe-smoking young man swathed in woollen cap and scarf and hard-wearing gaberdine. Judging by the badges stitched on his rucksack he knew his way around. She approached and plunged straight into conversation.

'I haven't time to wait for the train. Please, could you tell me if there's another way down?'

The man bit on his pipe authoritatively and then took it out to jab it over her shoulder. 'There's a road just beyond the start of the lines over there. It will get you down fairly quick. It's a shorter route.'

Claire thanked him and hurried off. That was something anyway. At least she would be moving instead of hanging about for the train. As soon as she was on the road she could tell why it was a shorter route. It was steep and winding and made up of endless blind corners. She doubted if many cars came up here, except in the summer, when the surface would be dry and safe.

Now that she was actually on her way back to the hotel she didn't feel too bad. She was bound to make it quicker than the train, and Greg Millard would probably end up by keeping her waiting anyway. She stepped out, enjoying the silence around her. This was a world apart from the one down below. There was the occasional happy twitter of a bird as it swooped across the road and sometimes the faint sound of bells in the distance, but somehow the peace was all-embracing and nothing could invade it.

The blissful mood stayed with Claire for some time, but as the road continued to wind down and round endlessly, her old worries started to creep in again. She was going to be very late. What was the use of pretending differently? Greg Millard would have got back to the truck ages ago. She could see him now, striding around and looking grim-faced at his watch. What if he decided that the feature she was going to write on the trip wasn't all that important after all? That it wasn't worth losing time for? Nothing, she was sure, would give him greater pleasure than to swing the truck into action and leave her behind. And if he did...? There was something like a small ache at the back of her throat. It wasn't so much not getting to Robin in Tehran as...

Without knowing it she suddenly broke into a run. With her hair flying out behind and the wind whipping colour into her cheeks, she ran as she had never ran before. So fast, in fact, that turning the next bend and streaking straight towards a big suede-coated figure, she found it impossible to stop.

CHAPTER FOUR

PUTTING everything she had into pulling up, she saved herself only inches from the wide chest, but it wasn't quite soon enough for the transport boss had taken another step forward. As he steadied her against him she gazed up half laughing to blurt awkwardly, 'I ... I thought you'd go without me!'

She had never been quite so close to those lean, lined features before. Something in the blue eyes made her feel acutely conscious of the silence all around, and her own quick breaths.

After what seemed an endless moment he lowered his arms to say on a slightly irritated note, 'What gave you the crazy idea of coming up here?'

A curious buoyant feeling made Claire swing her gaze around and return lightly, 'What's crazy about this?'

He tilted an eyebrow at the view of distant mountains, and Salzburg, with the river curving through it below, and drawled, 'I'm a working man myself.'

'Couldn't you forget it for once?' Claire laughed, skipping beside him, and getting her own fill of the scenery now that there was no hurry.

'I think not.' The transport boss tossed her an oblique look and added with a taut grin, 'Not on this trip.'

It was just his way of making idle conversation, of course, but Claire didn't want to suppress a vague feeling of pleasure that fluttered inside her. To make some conversation of her own she asked, 'Did Klaus tell you where I'd gone?'

Greg Millard nodded.' I guessed you'd start worrying when you got to the top.'

She looked at him and then along the road to twinkle, 'I might have come back down on the train.'

He lifted his shoulders with the suggestion of a smile.

'I'm getting to know the way your mind works.'

'Is that good?' She lifted her eyes innocently and found the light blue ones hanging on to them for some considerable time, then the transport boss was swinging his gaze to the front to say briskly, 'Let's get back to the truck.'

They were coming down fast now, almost on a level with the town. Claire could see the hotel in the distance, and the truck looking slightly incongruous in the pretty setting. A car came without warning round the bend in the road and Greg Millard curved an arm about her shoulders to draw her in. She noticed that his mouth had relaxed again, and ventured to chatter happily, 'Do you think we'll get far through Austria today? Or rather what's left of the day?'

'Hard to say,' he replied easily, dropping his arm away. 'There's snow ahead. More than we've seen so far. We'll just have to hope for the best.'

Rossita and Klaus were there to meet them at the truck, the latter happily unaware of the misleading information he had given her. Someone ought to tell him about his 'Tventy minots', Claire smiled to herself later when he was helping her up into the truck. His hands lingered about her waist, and as she turned to look down at him, he said seriously in his laboured English, 'I am hope you to let me show all of Salzburg one day.'

The transport boss thrust her brusquely into her seat and clipped, 'That's hardly likely, Klaus. There's a fiancé in Tehran, remember?'

The young man tilted his head and grinned and Claire smiled down at him after her door was slammed shut. She preferred to keep her gaze that way, anyway, rather than watch the way Rossita was saying her goodbyes; reaching up on tip-toe to brush her lips against a lean cheek.

Claire waved to Klaus as they pulled away, and spared one for Rossita now that she was fading nicely into the distance.

While she had been freshening up in the hotel, the heater in the cab had been doing its work, now as the truck took to the open road and sped along there was a cosiness about the small interior, even, she might venture to say, a pleasant intimacy. The truck radio had been switched on and was playing softly, and occasionally Greg Millard would whistle a low accompaniment to the music beneath his breath. Tired after her adventure, Claire was content to relax back against her seat, silently absorbing the view, though for most of the afternoon the mountains and lakes and woodlands were enough to keep her turning her head as they paraded by.

They stopped for a late tea at a white-fronted roadhouse,

then the snow started to show itself in earnest when they left the main highway and took a steep winding route. Whereas before it had been mere slush on the roads, now it was banked up high at the sides and sometimes packed hard under the wheels. She could see why the transport boss had pulled in to attach the wheel chains. There were other motorists trundling gingerly upwards, so Claire didn't feel too concerned, but when the wheels of the truck churned up a shower of ice as they drunkenly negotiated a bend, she gazed down slightly horrified at the world hundreds of feet below. She relaxed again as soon as she saw Greg Millard's reassuring smile and heard his lazy, 'The hazards of winter travel.' The firm hands skilfully swinging the wheel were enough to disperse any lingering worries she might have had.

The sky had been darkening into dusk when they had started out after the meal, but the pass they were travelling along now was so narrow it was impossible to see anything above. Probably the stars were pricking through by this time. The traffic had thinned out considerably, most of it siphoning off on to local routes, but occasionally a hardy little car would come honking up behind, asking to pass. Claire didn't know where they were, but she had a feeling they had covered a fair distance since Salzburg.

After a while they came out on to the open road again, to a small snowy plateau, and here set back in the cleft of the mountain, all lit up and looking like the setting for a Christmas card, was a tiny chalet inn. Claire gazed on in delight as it trailed by the windscreen, then turned to the transport boss to see if he had considered it worth sparing a glance. He had, and he was still looking, but he seemed mainly concerned with the cluster of cars crowded into the small parking area. Turning to follow the road again, he said, as though thinking aloud, 'I'm not so sure I like the look of that.'

Claire was puzzled. In the last of the light she recognised the cars as those that had passed them earlier on up the road but beyond that she had no idea what he meant. He turned to her and nodded ahead, 'There's a narrower pass not far from here, and if it's what I think it is ...

He clicked on the headlights and hung over the wheel, and Claire found herself straining hard ahead too, for what, she

70

didn't quite know. Nor did she want to ask when such all-out concentration seemed to be needed. When a large sign loomed up in the middle of the road, she was still no wiser with the foreign lettering, until Greg Millard threw on the brakes and pulled a deep breath to state, 'It's what I suspected. There's an obstruction up ahead. We'll have to turn back.'

Very sensibly the sign had been so placed to give enough width in the road to execute the feat, but it was some minutes before the cumbersome truck had turned and then Claire was asking, slightly wide-eyed, 'What will we do?'

'I'll make enquiries at the inn.' He kept his gaze ahead. 'See how long the hold-up's likely to last. We'll have to take it from there.'

'Isn't there another way through?' she asked.

'Not for us. Not without going practically all the way back. By that time the pass will probably be cleared.'

He pulled the truck in off the road and brought it to rest at the far side of the inn, against a sheer sweep of rock. It was about the only spare space in the small area of level ground, and looking at the huddle of cars, Claire wondered what would happen if anyone else came along. She had her question answered when the transport boss came round to open her door.

'They'll have got the obstruction notices out along the route by this time,' he explained lazily, taking her by the waist and swinging her down. 'No one else will come up unless they know they can get through.'

Which was maybe as well, Claire mused, preceding him into the inn and finding it packed tight with laughing drinking men. Goodhumouredly, the transport boss channelled a way through with his free arm and brought her forward with him in the curve of the other.

It was difficult to tell who was in charge of the tiny establishment, there were so many people hurrying backwards and forwards behind the bar. But there was a blackboard with some writing scrawled across it, propped up for all to see, and the transport boss, still holding her against him in the crush, seemed to get to know what he wanted from this. After studying it for a few minutes he held on to his chin to say slowly, 'Looks as though they don't expect to have the road cleared before morning. Apparently it's quite a heavy fall of snow.'

Claire looked up to him to see what his next move would be, not particularly caring whether he hurried or not. After turning a glance over the crowded room, he grinned down at her to shrug, 'Might as well make the best of it like everybody else.'

Claire had noticed that nobody seemed particularly perturbed at the hold-up. Now as she followed the big frame down the room, she had a feeling that most of the men welcomed the break. Tankards were being raised above beaming faces, and the conversation almost drowned the music playing somewhere in the background.

At the end of the room, Claire soaked up the warmth of a blazing log fire, then felt the transport boss drawing her forward, as a red-faced man with a carved tasselled pipe and leather lapels on his jacket offered her his seat. She slid in between the table and the wall at the end of the bench, smiling her thanks. It looked as though the suede-coated figure was going to have to stand towering at her side, but then there was another shuffle along the seat and she found she had a space next to her.

'I'll sit that side,' Greg Millard helped her out, nodding his thanks to the smiling young man, the next up the line. 'You'll get the warmth from the fire at the end.' He ordered from the aproned man with the tray, then settled back to light up a cigarette.

Claire rested her arms on the table, soaking up the friendly cosiness of the small room. The ceiling was low and the walls of panelled wood polished and dotted with black knots. Skirting the room just under the ceiling, alcoved shelves were decorated with old clocks and Austrian dolls and all manner of beautifully shaped drinking vessels. The wall benches and long tables were heavy and solidly made and everything reflected the mellow golden glow of the fire and the lamps. A tankard, or did they call them steins in Austria? was placed before her and laughing lightly she turned to find that Greg Millard had one too. Without knowing why she clinked hers gently against his as they raised them. She rather wished she had done something like that a lot earlier on in the trip, for he actually gave her one of his rare, well, for her at least,

72

white smiles.

It was hard to say which had the most intoxicating effect, that smile or the deep red wine in her tankard, but as the night wore on something brought a pink glow to her cheeks and a gay light to her eyes. Perhaps it was the feeling that both she and the transport boss were a part of the general air of enjoyment of the room.

The men with their big features and stained red cheeks seemed to accept it too. She noticed with a kind of guilty pleasure how their smiles trailed over the ring on her finger and up towards the dark man at her side. As the rollicking brass and flute sound of Bavarian music came into its own, some of the men formed into groups to sing, often in marvellous harmony, sometimes in comic pantomime. Claire wondered what they were. Salesmen? Representatives? Stranded perhaps while they were doing their jobs— It was difficult to say, for the transport boss didn't enter into conversation with any of them. Either he didn't know enough of the language, or he didn't particularly want to talk. He sat back, pulling on his cigarette and shaking his head when the jolly white-aproned man kept coming to replenish Claire's tankard, or lowering her a half smile when she turned her laughter up to him at a particularly amusing incident.

It must have been very late when he leaned forward to say to her above the din, 'I'm going out to see how the truck's set for the night.'

'Oh, can I come?' Claire turned to ask eagerly.

He sloped her a grin. 'It's probably freezing out there.'

'I don't mind. I'm used to it by now.'

She rose as he rose and fastened up the buttons of her driving coat. There was no need to plough a way down the room this time, for the men stood obligingly to one side as she moved. She lowered her eyes so as not to see the knowing twinkles that followed her and the big figure coming up close behind.

Out near the bar, the transport boss stopped a jovial but harassed-looking man, who was probably the innkeeper. They spoke together for several seconds, most of which the man spent shrugging his speckle-suited shoulders and lifting his hands and his eyebrows in a gesture of frustrated apology. The transport boss nodded and shrugged a smile

73

and moved towards the door.

Outside the air was crisp and biting after the cosiness of the inn. Claire told herself it was the sudden contrast that was making her teeth chatter. In any case, the moonlit night, with its frosty glitter of stars above majestic silver peaks, was well worth a little discomfort.

The transport boss looked down at her to say with a slightly taut smile, 'I told you you'd be cold.'

'I'll be all right in a minute,' Claire shook a laugh. 'Just give me time to get acclimatised.'

'Well, you'd better do it against me. I don't want you turning into ice before we get back.' He put an arm around her and drew her close to his side, and meeting the smile she turned up he added lazily, 'Not that there's much danger of that.'

Walking was precarious on the snow-packed uneven ground. The black shapes of the cars were like crouching animals waiting for the night to end. Only the truck, stretching back against the upsweep of rock, looked impassive and uncaring at its forced immobility. The transport boss looked along its lines and then up to the sloping grey rise above.

Following his gaze, Claire said worriedly, 'You don't think the snow will fall on it, do you?'

'I shouldn't think so.' He shook his head slowly. 'Probably packed hard in this temperature. Just the same,' he looked thoughtful, 'I don't like the idea of you sleeping out here on your own.'

'*Neither do I!*' Claire swung her glance up to him quickly and questioningly. She was glad of his arm about her now in the dark. After a moment she turned her glance towards the inn to murmur, 'Surely there's . . .'

He pulled in a slow breath, shaking his head.

'There isn't a bed left in the place. I've just asked.'

'What are *you* going to do?' Close to him like this she could see the gleam of his teeth as he talked. The light blue eyes were as dark as the night now in the finely chiselled features. He shrugged as she waited for his reply, then he inhaled to say, 'Go back to the seat near the fire. What else?'

She looked at the truck in the eerie shadows and said quietly, 'It sounds infinitely more inviting than that.'

'Maybe not as comfortable.' He looked down at her for

some considerable time, then turned back towards the lighted windows. 'But just in case that snow does fall I'd better have you inside with me.'

There were signs that things were quieting down when they got back indoors. Many of the men had disappeared, presumably to the beds they had been lucky enough to book. The rest were either draped back in their seats or talking in subdued tones over the remains of their drinks. It was wonderful to feel the warmth again, and as they moved down the room, Claire noticed that the fire had been banked high with logs obviously to provide all-night comfort for those with no beds.

She unfastened the buttons of her coat, then felt it being drawn from her shoulders as Greg Millard pointed out in deep tones, 'You can't relax in this.'

He hung his coat alongside hers, then took his place between the table and the wall. Claire slid in afterwards and pushing up the sleeves of her oatmeal sweater she rested her arms on the table and said cheerfully, 'I feel wide awake. I probably won't sleep at all.'

She sat gazing dreamily at the fire, hardly aware that the hot glow was having a hypnotic effect on her eyelids. It must have been halfway through the night, when someone crept in to restoke the blaze, that she stirred and found herself resting against a wide chest. She was vaguely aware that her hair was brushing a lean jaw and that her waist was supported by a muscular arm, but the position was altogether too likeable to want to go into detail.

Of course there was nothing interior sprung about the solid backrest, but as a truckdriver's mate who was she to grumble? They called it living rough, didn't they? She inhaled a contented sigh, and nursing a smile drifted back off to sleep again. There was nothing rough about being held like this!

She awoke to the sound of the revving of car engines and sat up to find the room almost empty. The fire was a huge red glow, and the small windows a dazzle of snow-reflected light. As she watched first one and then another car pull away up the road, she heard the transport boss say behind her, 'Thought I'd let the bulk of them get away before we made a move.'

Claire nodded and stretched dreamily. Watching her, he sloped a smile to ask, 'Stiff?'

'A little,' she nodded, noticing the dark stubble of beard on his chin and thick lock of hair hanging over one eyebrow.

'A hot bath and a good breakfast and you'll feel almost as good as new,' he grinned, taking her arm and helping her out from her seat.

Such luxuries were easily obtainable now that the inn no longer suffered from overcrowding, and Claire found she could linger over both without feeling in any way hurried. Certainly Greg Millard seemed in no hurry as they sat at a table overlooking the valley. He pulled lazily on his cigarette, and exchanged an occasional word with the innkeeper, who saw to their needs in a fussy ebullient kind of way. Watching the heavy-jowled man, Claire had an idea he was already regretting the fact that she and the transport boss were the last two still at the inn. Though he had looked harassed enough last night, she mused, a blocked up road up here couldn't be anything but good for business. Later when they rose to leave, his face crumpled slightly, but he bowed them pleasantly and politely through the door.

There were signs that workmen had been toiling all night to clear the road, for rolling by now were lorries with huge lights in the back and work implements. Greg Millard kept the truck ticking over at the roadside, and while they waited for the procession to pass, Claire pored over the map. After running her finger along the last stretch of motorway they had completed she had to look up in cheerful exasperation. 'I haven't a clue where we are. There's Salzburg, but ....'

He leaned over close to study the map. 'Here we are.' She watched the finger of the firm brown hand run over the line. 'We're coming up to Graz here and then it's Maribor just over the border.'

'Yugoslavia?' Claire looked up. 'Will we get there today?'

'About three o'clock if all goes well.'

She tilted her head to one side and laughed, 'It's funny, but it doesn't feel any different, does it, when you go into another country?'

'Only in the pocket,' Greg Millard said drily, swinging the truck out on to the road. 'For a bus this size, tolls are not small.'

'But you make a living?' she twinkled.

'I make a living,' he grinned, settling down to the business of driving.

The road was narrow and winding at first through lake and mountain scenery, then they proceeded through a succession of river valleys flanked by steep pine-covered hills.

Graz turned out to be a sizeable town with lots of old buildings, but the roads were congested and not for lingering in and the transport boss took the truck straight through, favouring a lunch stop at a motel along the main highway. Through the afternoon, villages were constantly cropping up along the route, but they were so tiny the truck left them behind in seconds. Claire reckoned they must have made good time, for it was only ten to three when they came up to signs announcing the frontier.

There were the usual formalities at the Austrian Customs and then it was on to the Yugoslav barrier. The truck went off to be weighed again and Claire wondered if everything was proceeding just as trouble-free here. She had a feeling it wasn't. There was much shaking of heads among the officials, and more as they looked over the truck. The transport boss went into a huddle with two men of superior rank, but the headshaking continued and Claire paced about, trying to work out what was wrong. She had arrived at no satisfactory conclusion when the transport boss came over to take her arm. 'We've got a slight hold-up,' he explained mildly. 'They only okay so many trucks of this size on their roads in one day, and apparently the full quota's gone through.'

'Is *that* all?' Claire breathed a sigh of relief. 'I was beginning to think it was something really serious.' She watched as he thrust his hands into his pockets and asked, 'When can we go?'

'One minute past midnight.'

Claire drew in a breath. 'That's a long wait.'

'There's nothing we can do.' He took her arm and led her to the truck, then as they met again inside the cab he added with a thoughtful grin, 'Not round here at any rate.' When they were cruising back along the road again he looked at her to ask, 'How much did you see when you went up the mountain railway yesterday?'

'Not much,' Claire smiled. 'I was too busy finding out the fastest way down.' She watched as he swung the truck on to a different road and asked in a quick breath, 'You don't mean we might...?'

'I doubt if there's anything in that line around here,' he said lazily, swinging the wheel, 'but there's a holiday village a few miles off the main route. We can see what they've got to offer.'

Claire turned to give him a glowing gaze, but made herself say politely, 'Won't you find going there a terrible waste of your time?'

'We can't stay cooling our heels in the Customs for nine hours,' he replied in deep casual tones. 'We've got to get through them somehow.'

Claire had no intention of grumbling. All those hours to while away in a winter resort! The thought didn't seem in any way painful.

Some thirty minutes later they came out on the fringe of a lavender-misted valley. Blue columns of smoke were rising from the tiny dwellings nestled in the bowl, and multi-coloured fly-like objects skimmed over the surrounding white slopes. As they approached Claire saw several fair-sized hotels set conveniently near the ski areas; one had a pearl grey well populated ice rink stretching the full length of its frontage. Taking the gentle curving road downwards, the transport boss pulled the truck in at the bottom and brought it to rest beneath a line of snow-encrusted pines.

'We'll walk from here,' he said, jumping down from the cab and slamming his door.

Claire stooped, poised in the doorway taking in the scene of chalet houses laced with tangles of wild creepers. Ahead were rows of minute shops under stone archways and every road seemed to be made of bubbling cobblestones.

'Okay?'

Automatically she brought her smile down and found herself meeting the quizzical white one of the transport boss. He swung her lightly down and locked the door, then stood back to examine the position of the truck. After looking along both sides he seemed satisfied and taking her arm moved off towards the village.

In spite of its obvious popularity as a small resort Claire was struck by its peace. Sleigh bells and the gentle swish of skis were the only sounds to be heard. The odd jubilant shout was lifted bodily by the breeze and swept quickly away as though considered out of tune with the music of the place. They walked along narrow streets that weaved and curled under swinging signs. Out beyond the village, bullock-drawn sleighs were gliding along the snow-packed lane, and ski parties were making for the chair-lifts. As Claire watched fascinated at the patterns being snaked out in the snow on the slopes, Greg Millard asked lazily,

'Ever done any skiing?'

'Never,' Claire smiled. 'But it looks fun.'

'It is if you stay on your feet,' he grinned, then looking down at her, 'Like to try?'

'What, now?' she laughed up at him. 'Do you think I dare?'

'I don't see why not.' He was already leading her forward. 'The nursery slopes are not all that frightening.'

Well, it was something different, Claire had to admit, but swinging her way upwards in a chair-lift she couldn't help wondering how she was going to fare. The skis draped across her knees looked tremendous. They looked even bigger when the transport boss strapped them on for her at the top. He wore his like a professional, and moved in them with lazy ease, and perhaps it was his relaxed air that gave Claire the confidence she needed. Listening to his instructions, she was able to strut clumsily by his side, digging the sticks in to steady herself and hoping she looked as though she knew what it was all about.

'You're doing fine,' the transport boss smiled, and nodded ahead. 'We'll try the slope beyond the trees.'

Claire was glad he had decided on somewhere away from the crowd. If she was going to make a fool of herself she would rather do it in private!

As it turned out she didn't feel too bad wobbling down the gentle inclines he chose for her. There was far too much to think about, for one thing. For another, once you got the feel of it, it was quite invigorating. After several runs down the tiny slope, she graduated to a fair-sized one, and ended up laughing at the bottom, but still miraculously on her feet.

Greg Millard skimmed down to drop his white smile over her as he slewed to a halt at her side.

'We won't need to take the chair-lift down if you go on at this rate,' he said deeply, resting a blue gaze on her animated features.

'Oh, let's go down this way,' Claire begged, 'I'm sure I can get to the bottom.'

'You might,' he nodded in agreement, 'but don't be in too much of a hurry. Take it in short runs.'

Claire did as he suggested, taking the small slopes he pointed out to her and bringing herself to a stop every now and again. But after a while she began to feel less and less inclined to interrupt the smooth flowing motion she was beginning to develop. Surely, she reasoned, if she kept going she would become more adept at it. Stopping every few seconds had been all right at first, but now she had learned to stay on her feet and the way down seemed to slope hardly at all.

After the next gentle incline she kept herself going, then carefully took in another and yet another. At first the feeling was one of gay exultation as the wind whipped past her cheeks and her skis whistled over the snow, but then, without any warning, the ground fell away from her in a sickening dip. As she gathered speed she knew a slight feeling of terror. How did one stop at this speed?

There was no time to find out. Her skis followed the steep incline with deadly precision and Claire felt as though she was dropping down the side of the world. She wanted to fall back, move her legs, anything to put an end to the jet-stream she found herself in, but the skis had other ideas. And she was fastened securely to them.

She didn't consciously recall any sudden determination to prove herself the boss. Perhaps it was a hidden mound that foxed the skis? Whatever it was in the next second she found herself leaving the ground and then falling backwards to land with a soft thud in a tangle of crossed skis, flying hair, and flailing arms.

It was such bliss to find herself stationary again, she just lay where she was staring thoughtfully at the benevolent blue sky. Greg Millard seemed to swoop over the hill and have his skis off beside her in one swift movement.

'Are you all right?' He knelt to give her a searching gaze.

'I'm fine,' she smiled up weakly, aware that the snow was mingled with her hair.

'No bones broken?' he twinkled.

'Not a one,' she laughed softly. There was a moment when the blue eyes seemed to hold her as the blue sky had done, only in a different kind of way, then he was unstrapping her skis and helping her to her feet to say mildly, 'Well, you're not going to get another chance to break your neck. We'll call that it for today.'

Claire was in no position to argue. She was too busy trying to stand without leaning too noticeably against the wide chest. Thankfully the transport boss didn't seem in too big a hurry to pick up the skis. When he did, he came to put the other arm about her waist to help her through the snow.

One of the hotels near the chair-lift had an open-air bar built around banks of snow, and when he had handed in the skis Greg Millard bought two drinks. He put one into her hand and lifted one himself.

'Puts life back into the limbs after a tumble,' he nodded, then trailing a gaze over her glowing cheeks and sparkling eyes he added drily, 'I'm not sure which one of us needs the drink!'

'I feel marvellous,' Claire laughed, looking up towards the slopes. 'I wouldn't have missed it for anything.'

Bringing her gaze back to meet a deep blue one, she was sure the transport boss had been about to make a reply. In the icy air, her misted breath mingled with his as they stood close at the bar. She was struck by the wind-whipped colour in the lean features, the contrast of dark hair and white smile against the blue-white of the snow. If he had been about to say something, it was lost as he threw his drink back in one swallow and placed the glass down carefully on the bar.

When Claire had finished her own drink he took her arm to say easily, 'We've got time for a meal and a quick look at the night life of the place, before we head back for the truck.'

The sun was already sliding down the valley as they walked. By the time they had eaten in a luxurious little inn with beamed ceiling and high-backed chairs, the mountains were pink and silver against a navy blue sky.

If the village had been a haven of peace during the afternoon it made up for it in the evening. Gay Tyrolean music drifted out from the cafés, and the tiny tourist shops were a tinkle of bells as the doors were constantly opened and closed. Hotels advertising beer-hall song and dances were pulsing with noise, and gusts of laughter wafted along the street as groups strolled by.

When they turned away from the gaiety to the quieter outskirts of the village, Claire said on a happy sigh, 'I love Austria. I'm going to come back often.'

'Often?' The transport boss thrust his hands deep into his pockets to drop her a tolerant smile.

'Well, there's so much to see.' She looked up as they walked. 'All those dozens of villages and towns we've passed. And anyway, I like travel. I'm going to do lots of it!'

The furrows of snow along the road became difficult to negotiate and as he draped a negligent arm about her shoulder she smiled to say introspectively, 'Just think, there's me. I've hardly seen anything at all of the world, and yet I've read about these rich people who are so jaded with travel and everything familiar that the holiday agencies have to keep racking their brains to come up with something new. The latest, I think, is package tours to the Antarctic. Just for a change!'

She laughed softly, and as they made their way towards the dark shape of the truck, the transport boss gazed down at her to drawl, 'You reckon it will be a long time before you resort to that?'

'I won't ever.' She shook her head. 'I'll never get tired of the ordinary sights.' Seeing his tilted eyebrow, she asked with interest, 'Do you like travelling?'

'I can take it or leave it,' he shrugged.

Looking up to where alpine hotels swung like lanterns in the darkness and the silver tipped mountains ranged majestic against a starlit sky, Claire sighed lightly, 'Imagine being able to take or leave this!'

'We all come to it in time,' he smiled.

She thought he had reached up to take the handle of the truck door and leaned back against it to tax him with, 'And you think *I* will?'

'No. I think you will always be like the kid who's seeing

82

her birthday cake for the first time.'

Claire felt the blush of self-consciousness, but she laughed it off with, 'Was I like that this afternoon? I'm afraid I couldn't help but enjoy myself.'

'No crime.'

She realised he wasn't moving but leaning too and caught against him and the door, her laughter seemed to flutter back into her throat. Not for anything did she want to move. And she had this curious idea that the feeling was mutual.

In the darkness he traced the blurred graze on her cheek with her finger. 'Hurt?'

Claire shook her head. 'It's almost healed.' She was glad she spoke the truth. Somehow she wanted nothing less than perfection for this dark blue gaze on her now.

A sound that she finally recognised as her own exploding heartbeats urged her to keep on looking up. She saw a mouth that was crooked and somehow taut come down close. It seemed to draw all the breath from her as it hung there just above her lips, then she heard a soft curse and felt the door being jerked open at her back.

'We've got three hours to catch up on some sleep before we head for the Customs,' he said tersely. 'You'd better get in.'

He almost threw her up into her seat and slammed the door before she could turn. Striding round and coming up into his own seat, he pulled the sliding door back, reached in for a blanket and pillow and nodded her curtly through.

Claire moved in towards the bunks feeling her case being thrust in after her. As she started to undo her coat the transport boss snapped, 'Stay as you are. You'll have to get out at the Customs!'

The door was pushed home in one swift movement, and Claire groped her way to a bunk and stretched out to gaze at the stars.

They hadn't had much rest last night at the inn, and supporting her on the seat for most of the time, Greg Millard must have fared even worse than she had. Perhaps that was why he had seemed short-tempered just now. Lack of sleep always made people tetchy, she mused, thinking of the slammed doors. Funny, though, it didn't seem to have affected her that way. If anything she felt slightly exhilarated.

83

CHAPTER FIVE

IT was some time before she could bring herself to kick off her shoes and curl up under the blankets. When she did, sleep came quickly. Somewhere in the haziness of it, she was aware of the truck rolling into motion and humming over the roads. She recalled the tap on the wood panel above her head and remembered being helped sleepily down from the cab, but the cold night air and bustle at the Customs had little effect on her dazed state. After being assisted back up into the cab again, she crawled thankfully away to her bunk, hardly aware that there had been an interruption. On the edge of sleep, she felt the truck lurch into action again, and drifted off, sighing pleasurably at the soothing motion of the wheels on the road.

It was the lack of this, or any kind of movement, that woke her some hours later. The sky through the tiny windows was the dull matt grey of dawn. There was a stillness outside that suggested the open countryside. Tracing her mind back drowsily, Claire had a feeling that the truck had been stationary for some time. Probably the transport boss had driven for a while in Yugoslavia and then pulled in to sleep for the rest of the night.

She heard a footstep outside and then the hum of an electric razor. The sounds brought a happy light to Claire's eyes. She lay listening for a while, then jumped up to open her suitcase with a flourish. Now what to wear? She rummaged for a while and moved into the small wash-room. The water was icy cold but just right for washing away the sleep. Refreshed, she pulled into a pair of pale jeans, well worn, but neat and trim-fitting and doing justice to her long legs and slim hips. Discarding the heavy shoes for a lighter pair, she tied the laces and slipped into a soft rib-knitted sweater in white.

Her make-up bag, buried under her clothes in the case and so far unused, she dug out and blissfully applied a light dusting of powder and a brush of lipstick. Wonderful to feel whole again! Hair brushed and gleaming, she pulled the sliding door back and moved up into the cab.

There was no sign of the transport boss, but she could hear him moving about at the rear of the truck. As she started to climb down he called out, 'Bring the small screwdriver near the steering wheel, Dave!'

Claire reached back inside the cab, then jumped down and moved towards the rear of the truck. Turning at the end, she stepped up with the screwdriver and a smile to say lightly,

'The name's Claire.'

Blue eyes roamed her face, trailed down the length of her and came up under a scowl to clip, 'As far as I'm concerned it's Dave. Where's the screwdriver?'

'It's here.' Claire pushed it under his nose. She added with a shrug of impatience, 'I don't see why you can't forget that silly impersonation of mine. After all, it was . . .'

'That's how you joined up with this truck and that's how it's going to stay until we get to Tehran.' He bent to tighten something on one of the rear lights and then straightening, looked at her again, and inhaled to say testily, 'Get rid of that hair.'

'I can't.' She faced him with the sparkle of defiance. 'I've lost my cap.'

Not exactly lost, she had to admit, but still stuffed nicely out of sight behind the seat. As she turned big green eyes upwards, he set his jaw and pushed round her to clip, 'Well, just stay out of my way!'

Claire obliged by wandering around and looking at the scenery. The truck was parked at the side of a rough dirt road that wound out of sight both ways, over ground that was rock-strewn and hilly and dotted with odd patches of snow. Not far away a stream sputtered down from an over-hanging of rock and fell into a small pool below. Judging by the transport boss's spruce appearance he had taken advantage of the running water laid on.

Standing around, she soon began to feel the cold and went back to the truck for additional clothing. She ignored the clumsy driving coat lying on the bunk, and chose instead a hip-hugging blue anorak with a straight plain front and a small zip at the throat, which she left open to show the white neck of her jumper. Although much lighter than her driving coat it was warm and had a hood for bad weather. With this falling back on to her shoulders she moved up into the doorway, ready to have another wander around. She had barely got her head out when the transport boss swung up at the other side. He spent a few seconds removing the pillow and blanket into the room behind, then with a curt, 'It's time we were rolling,' he draped down into his seat and jerked the engine into life.

Claire just had time to pull her own door to and flop down as the truck lumbered forward and swung out on to the road. A good thing she hadn't left anything behind, she thought a little crossly, watching the stream and the parking site disappear in a cloud of dust.

The realisation that they were actually travelling through Yugoslavia caught up with her when they passed a scattering of black-garmented peasants working in nearby fields, and clusters of white-walled villages sprinkled at the base of the hills. That unquenchable excitement for new places bubbling within her again, Claire leaned forward to snatch up the map. She ran her finger along the route, humming a tune beneath her breath, and then stopped with a delighted, 'Oh, we pass Zagreb! I had a friend who went there once. She told me . . .'

The truck lurched into a rut in the road and righting it, the transport boss said, grim-faced, 'And *I've* told you, this is not a holiday tour.'

'I was only going to say . . . about Zagreb . . .' she faltered, straightening her lips slightly. 'And it *is* on the way to Belgrade.'

'We're not going to Belgrade that way,' he clipped, swinging the wheel round a horse-drawn cart. 'I'm taking the northern route. It's quicker.' And then on an intake of breath, 'And we could do with a bit of speed on this trip.'

'Meaning, of course,' Claire said moodily, 'that *I'm* slowing you down?'

The grim mouth twisted into something that couldn't be called a smile. He gazed ahead to say sourly, 'Let's just say I'm in a hurry to get to Tehran.'

Claire turned her eyes dejectedly to the front. She hadn't wanted to face it, but she knew why he was bad-tempered. In return for taking her to Tehran he was supposed to be getting a feature publicising his trucking business. And she hadn't written one word yet, and they had already crossed three countries. After the happy interlude in Austria, she had completely lost sight of the fact that she had come on this trip to do a job. But obviously *he* hadn't. His thoughts were strictly on business, which was natural enough, she supposed, only ... well, she wished ...

Flinging a glance round to him, she let it rest on the granite profile for a second, then heaving a sigh, took her gaze on to her writing case resting in the rack behind the seat. He was right, of course. She would have to start writing something for him some time. It might as well be now. She pulled the plastic writing case down and unzipped it on her knee, where the pad of stark white paper stared up uninvitingly. Lifting a thoughtful gaze to the windscreen, she felt the blue eyes swing round to her and then lower to the pad and pencil on her knee. She couldn't understand why the truck suddenly veered into the side of the road, and she comprehended even less when the writing case was flicked to on her knee and swung up towards the open window. As the transport boss tossed the lot into a clump of nearby bushes, Claire rose on a gasp to wail,

'What are you *doing*?'

'You'll have to forget the fairy tales,' he smiled thinly. 'We're moving from now on, and as there will be no stopping off at cushy hotels, your time will be taken up with the chores.'

'What chores?' she snapped, looking vainly after her writing materials over his shoulder.

'You can start by cleaning up the mess you've made in the back,' he flicked his head, 'and then you can see what you can line up for a meal.'

'I didn't sign on as a domestic.' Claire set her mouth and stayed in her seat.

'You signed on to work your passage,' he clipped, 'and *I'll* decide how you do it. Now get moving!'

She would have liked to ignore him, but something in his tones made her drag up from her seat and push moodily through into the compartment behind. Correction about her lack of writing being the cause of his bad temper, she thought miserably. It was just that he had decided he couldn't stand the sight of her.

A little shamefacedly she saw what he meant by 'the mess

in the back'. She had left her clothes and possessions scattered over the bunks and the floor. And worse still, a sight that she had blithely ignored earlier on, but which stared back at her now, was the congealed stew pan on the stove, the plates and coffee cup that she had used that first day in Holland.

Drawing in a sigh, she slipped off her anorak, pushed up her sleeves, and set to work. There was a certain satisfaction in making the tiny compartment spruce and shining again. She cleaned the stove and rubbed the formica table top until it shone, munching chocolate biscuits from the tin as she worked. The bunks looked neat and uncluttered with the blankets tucked tight around the mattresses and turned back over the pillows. And the rubber mat on the floor was fresher for a sponge over with soap and water.

She could feel the wheels of the truck humming over the road as she moved about, and guessed they were going at a tidy speed. Probably this was how truck drivers really covered the distance, she mused. Occasionally through the tiny side windows she caught a glimpse of rolling hills and a distant minaret, and once during the morning the sun lifted the lid of the clouds and beamed through in a slash of fiery gold. Apart from a fuel stop at a roadside filling station mid-morning, Claire doubted whether the truck touched on civilisation at all. If anything the terrain seemed to get wilder as they sped on.

In the slim wall cupboard she found an assortment of tinned foods, and settled for soup, corned beef with plain biscuits, and tinned fruit. There was tea and sugar and powdered milk, and everything was fairly easy to prepare, although she did wonder how she would have fared if they hadn't been travelling on a particularly good road.

She set out two of everything on the small table, then put her head out to the cab to state cheerfully, 'It's ready when you are!'

The dark head nodded, and she watched as he slowed the truck down and brought it to rest on a tract of open ground at the side of the road. She turned inside, expecting him to follow her, but instead he ordered curtly, 'You can bring mine out here.'

She looked at him, or at least at the jaw jutting towards

the windscreen, and stammered, 'But it's soup ... and I don't know whether you ...'

'I'll cope,' he said tersely. 'There isn't room for two of us back there.'

Well, with his size it might be a little cramped, but not unpleasantly so, Claire thought, drooping, but doing as he asked. She ate her own meal in solitary silence, thinking of that first afternoon on the camp site in Holland, when he had come in for something with which to fix the heater. He hadn't seemed to notice a shortage of space then.

After the meal, she washed the plastic cups and dishes dutifully, then freshened up herself. When everything was finished she climbed down to dispose of the bucket of dirty water collected through the morning's chores. The transport boss was smoking a cigarette some distance away. Taking advantage of the break, she hurriedly got rid of the water, dumped the bucket and went to stand on a slight rise to get a look at the view.

It was disappointing really. Nothing but the same rocky slopes and an occasional belt of trees. Still, it *was* Yugoslavia, and the air *had* to be different at least. She took a deep breath, tilted her chin, and let the breath out on a happy sigh. It *was* different, if only more bitingly cold—a fact that she was becoming increasingly aware of in only the white sweater and slim jeans. Still, she could hang on a minute yet. She took another breath and searched for something different in the view. It didn't matter that there wasn't anything. There was something about the wildness here. Smiling to herself, she had almost forgotten about the big suede-coated figure, until she turned and found the blue eyes on her and not on the view.

A scowl flickered into life, seconds after she had met his gaze. He ground his cigarette under his heel and rasped, 'We're not here for the day. Let's get moving.'

'All right, I'm coming!' Claire went to swing the bucket up crossly, and climbed back in her side.

With everything neat and tidy in the back she felt justified in taking her seat beside the wheel again. There was no mistaking the steely reserve of the man next to her, but ignoring the inflexible jaw and ramrod shoulders she concentrated on the soft musical tones of the radio, and kept her eyes open for anything of interest in the view.

They had been climbing steadily for some time, and the forests and tangled heaths seemed merely a dull grey or black against the snow. The road that twisted and turned was good for a while and then very bad, then slightly better again. She saw little or no traffic and wondered if that was why the transport boss had chosen this route. One could certainly move when not hampered by other vehicles. Just the same she would be glad when the scenery was just a little more ...

A loud bang and a sudden shuddering about the cab made her jump and hang on to her seat. She heard a low curse as the man beside her held on to the flying wheel and kept the bucking cab in check, then he was slamming on the brakes and scraping to a stop. He took a deep breath in the silence, turned a glance over Claire sitting huddled in her seat, and then tightening his mouth again barked, 'A fine time to get a puncture!'

The collar of the suede coat turned up against the cold, he climbed down to investigate. Claire turned back inside for her anorak, fastened it warmly about her and stepped down herself. The transport boss was already bent beside the flattened wheel, the tools spread out at his side. After watching him for a while and realising that he had to work without the assistance of a crewmate, Claire bent to handle the tools and asked eagerly, 'Can I help? I know quite a bit about what to do.'

'You can help by staying out of my way,' he said irritably, striding round her to roll in the new wheel. Claire set her mouth and stepped back. She watched him work expertly, then seeing that he had no need of her assistance, turned away. At least it was an opportunity to get a look at the scenery again. Not that there was anything awe-inspiring about skeletal trees and tall black pines, and undergrowth petrified in the snow. She wandered along a path, hopeful of finding a tiny flower, or a bud of blossom. After all, it was nearly spring, and the woods in England would be sprouting colour.

She didn't hear the footsteps behind her, and jumped almost out of her anorak when a hand gripped her arm. She was swung round and the transport boss was demanding roughly, 'Just what do you use for sense? Wandering out here on your own! You're not in a picnic park! This is wolf and bear country.'

Well, there could be no bigger bear than the one she had here! Claire thought, snatching her arm from his grasp and stalking back to the truck. She sat in the cab staring rigidly to the front while he put the tools away and washed his hands in the back. If it hadn't been for the radio playing, weak but soothingly, there was no telling how long she might have sat and fumed.

During the afternoon they stopped at a lonely fuel station, but there was no time allowed for lingering over cups of coffee. Claire was obliged to make those when they were on the road again. Later on the terrain flattened and there were signs of civilisation again as tarmac roads came up under the wheels, and villages moved by in the distance. For the first time Claire was beginning to feel weary of continuous travel. She was relieved when the transport boss pulled the truck off the road and brought it to a halt. She would stretch her legs for a while, have a wash to freshen up, and then see about concocting the evening meal. It occurred to her as she stepped down that there was very little water left in the containers and that she had better keep that for drinking purposes. Anyway, this looked like an old camp site, so there was bound to be water around somewhere.

The transport boss looked as though he had been taking stock of their surroundings. As he came back through the trees, Claire said pleasantly, 'I'm saving the water we've got left for drinks. Is there anywhere I can wash?'

'Straight ahead.' He flicked a glance over his shoulder.

Claire walked a few paces, then stopped dead in her tracks. Her eyes fixed on the object in front of her, she gasped, 'A horse trough!' As she whirled round the transport boss shrugged,

'It's all you'll get till we get to Belgrade.'

'You can't expect me to wash in *that*!' she glared.

'If you had filled the tanks when you had the opportunity,' he pointed out maddeningly, 'you wouldn't have to, would you?'

As he strolled back to the truck Claire hurried up and planted herself in his path. 'You're being deliberately horrible to me!' she accused tremulously.

91

He gazed down at the over-bright green eyes and reached for a cigarette. He made a point of drawing on it deeply before saying irritably, 'I should have put you on that boat at Rotterdam.'

'But you didn't.' Claire blinked the mist from her eyes. 'And you've been regretting it ever since. Well, don't worry,' she choked, '*I* can't wait to get to Tehran either, and if you can't drive day and night then I'll drive too!'

There was a flicker of steely humour in the blue eyes as he drawled, moving away, 'Your place is over the stove.'

'That's what *you've* decided!' Claire flamed to his back. 'Because you think we'll get there quicker with me acting as domestic. Well, I can show you an even quicker way!'

She flung herself into the driving seat, not quite sure how far she intended to go, but the sight of those wide shoulders calmly moving away incensed her to jerk the truck into life and slam her foot on the starter. She would show him that some women were capable of a lot more than just standing over a stove!

The truck was like a monster in her hands, but she had watched often enough to know roughly how to handle it, and within seconds she had it roaring off up the road. Her anger dissolved into satisfied elation as she watched the scenery flash by and thought of the big figure standing back there, unable to do anything for once.

She daren't attempt the turning coming up, but she could go on past the bridge ahead, she smiled wickedly, just to give him a run for his money. As the archway came nearer she decided to slacken speed. No sense in rushing the enjoyment, and it would give him a chance to catch up. Perhaps if she had given more attention to the bridge coming up, and less to the driving mirror, where she couldn't wait to see the suede-coated figure come tearing into view, the disaster might never have happened. But Claire trundled straight ahead, blissfully unaware that the bridge came down to just about where the top of the truck left off.

The only warning she had that anything was wrong was a sudden jarring that jerked her against the wheel, then there was the screech of metal brushing stone and the truck bucked to an abrupt and sickening stop.

It was several seconds before Claire could collect her dazed senses, then she gazed horror-stricken at the sight of the stone archway curving away from either side of the windscreen. Her hands trembling over the handle of the door she climbed down and stood swaying and staring up unbelievingly until a figure loped up alongside the truck.

The transport boss grabbed her roughly by the shoulders, ran a searching blue gaze over her, and let out a pent-up breath to growl against her, 'You idiot! You prize little idiot!'

Maybe she was. Claire didn't much care. All she knew was that Greg's precious truck was scratched and dented and locked under the bridge, and *he* was holding her close as though he thought she would break into pieces.

She could have stayed there leaning against him indefinitely, but the worry of what she had done made her look up big-eyed to ask, 'What on earth are we going to do?'

Her words seemed to stir the man holding her into life. He stepped briskly away and after taking a long and critical look at the truck commented drily, 'You've certainly jammed it good and proper, haven't you?'

'I'm sorry.' Claire lowered her eyes and raised them again to offer, 'I'll be glad to do anything I can to help.'

'Just keep your fingers crossed that nothing comes along this road for the next half hour or so.'

As he unbuttoned his coat and threw it up into the cab she asked anxiously, 'What are you going to do?'

'Let all the tyres down,' he said, setting to work.

Claire stood over him as he bent, and casting a hopeful glance towards the arch of the bridge she asked, 'Do you think it will work?'

'It's the usual practice in a case like this,' he replied, unscrewing the cap of a valve.

'You mean ... it's happened before? I'm not the first one to ... to ...'

'To boob?' he grinned. 'I don't make a point of employing inexperienced drivers, but a couple of them have come up against similar trouble.'

'Well, that certainly makes *me* feel better,' Claire laughed in relief. 'I thought it was the end of the world.'

'Nice to know you can sound so lighthearted about it.' His tones were suddenly rasping. As the air hissed out of the tyres he stretched up to take hold of her roughly, and finding herself caught against him Claire felt as though she had just stepped down groggily from the truck again. The blue eyes lowered over her sternly, almost angrily, then he was saying with the ghost of a tolerant smile,

'Just don't get any more bright ideas about trying to go it alone to Tehran. All right?'

'All right,' Claire smiled up, hardly aware that she had replied in little more than a whisper. Perhaps there was something about the moment she didn't want to spoil; something in the palpitating stillness of night rolling over the countryside. Neither seemed to realise that the air had finished rushing out of the tyres. When it finally dawned on Claire she searched for something to say and prattled, 'Greg! You really must let me do something to help.' As a peculiar glint showed in the blue eyes she laughed up softly, 'Well, you can't expect me to keep on calling you Mr. Millard!'

His arms had dropped away from her, and he was stooping over the next tyre hardly before she knew it. Unscrewing the cap carefully, he drawled, 'Your fiancé might prefer it if you did.'

Claire pulled in a breath. Yes, there was Robin. Funny, she found it difficult to think of him these days. Hurrying to pick up a spanner, she called cheerfully, 'I'll start round the other side, shall I?'

Once all the tyres were down, it wasn't a difficult job backing the truck out from under the bridge. Claire couldn't see much in the dark, but it looked as if most of the damage was on top out of sight. There was the business of inflating the tyres again and then Greg took the turning that Claire had overshot, and kept going until they found a garage with an outside tap. The dust of the last few hours washed away, they took to the road again, but after a few miles Greg brought the truck to a halt beneath a belt of trees.

'We won't make Belgrade tonight,' he said, locking the brakes. 'This will have to do for the next five or six hours. I'll take a look round and make sure we're not trespassing.'

'I'll see about making a meal,' Claire replied, rising from her seat. The weariness that she had been able to dismiss for a while engulfed her as she moved about the small interior at the back. It dragged at her limbs now and made her head throb noisily. It would be better when she had eaten, she told herself, struggling to work efficiently.

The meal did help a little, but most soothing of all was later when she stretched pyjama-clad on the bunk with the blankets wrapped round her and the soft pillow under her head. She thought she would have slept instantly, but the dull ache around her eyes seemed to fight off sleep rather than encourage it. She could hear Greg strolling outside probably smoking his last cigarette. She didn't know how he fared sleeping in the cab, but the seats were well upholstered and no doubt he could stretch out in a fashion.

A long time later she heard him climb up and settle in, and wanting to break the silence she called through the gap in the sliding door, 'Greg, what time is it?'

'Almost one o'clock,' he replied quietly. 'You should have been asleep hours ago.'

'Too much fresh air, I suppose,' she smiled in the darkness. 'Or is that supposed to have the opposite effect?' As the silence stretched she toyed with her thoughts and then called, 'Greg?' At his lazy 'Mmm?' she asked, 'Why have you never married?'

'Give me time,' he seemed to smile, 'I'm only thirty-three!'

'Most men have growing families at that age,' she pointed out lightly.

His reply was a long time coming. When it did it was short and tinged with irritation. 'Let's cut out the cosy chat, shall we, and get some sleep?'

If only she *could* sleep, Claire thought, rearranging her aching body in search of a comfortable position. She closed her eyes and tried not to think of anything, and finally the weight in her head lifted and drowsiness crept in.

If anyone had told her she had slept seven hours she wouldn't have believed them, but that was what her watch said as she put her foot gingerly out of the bunk the next morning. She pulled into a warm dressing gown and shuffled to the washbasin to look in the mirror. Strange that her face could look so normal, when behind it there seemed to be dozens of tiny men at work. Her legs didn't feel too good either, but it would probably pass off when she was moving about, and a hot drink could work wonders.

As she filled the kettle with the last of the water she heard the footsteps outside turn up into the cab, then Greg was stooping in the doorway to say with a lazy smile, 'I looked in earlier, but you were out like a light.'

Claire swung her hair shyly to murmur, 'Am I holding things up? I'll get on with the breakfast.'

'Don't bother with anything fancy,' he said, lingering in the doorway. 'There's a motel on the road to Belgrade with everything laid on from bacon and eggs to hot showers.'

'Sounds heaven!' Claire smiled, thinking mainly of the hot shower.

She was aware of the blue eyes resting on her meditatively, and then Greg was saying with a tinge of humour, 'Had enough of the rough life?'

'I don't mind it.' She tilted her chin and matched the light in his eyes with one of her own, then turned to make the coffee. He watched her measure it out, then said briskly, turning to drop in behind the wheel,

'Get dressed. We can have coffee on the way.'

The motel turned out to be a streamlined affair with all kinds of comforts and amenities, but Claire was willing to overlook everything for the sake of a reviving shower. Greg gave her a ticket and pointed towards a separate block, saying as he did so, 'I'll see you out front in about half an hour. And by the way,' he grinned, 'you're a Zenski.'

'A what?' Claire turned a puzzled glance at him.

'You'll see,' he nodded, 'when you get there.'

Claire did see. There were two doorways, one marked ZENSKI and the other marked MUSKI. Thanks to Greg, she knew enough not to walk into the men's washroom by mistake.

The shower was all she had hoped it would be, but it didn't do much for the peculiar twinges in her limbs. She pulled into her clothes lethargically and went out the way she had come in. Greg was waiting. He had changed and looked devastatingly masculine in heavy polo-necked sweater and slim dark slacks. The suede jacket was open, but he had the collar turned up against the biting cold. Watching her as she approached, he asked with a grin, 'Better?'

'Much,' she smiled, glad that the truck was only just round the corner.

Guiding her towards it, Greg asked, 'Sure you won't change your mind about something to eat? The food's good.'

'No, I'm fine, thanks.'

The seat behind the windscreen was becoming like a second home to her. She sank into it thankfully now, glad that she wouldn't have to move for the next two or three hours. Greg set the truck in motion and they were soon cruising along the road to Belgrade.

To say that the town was the capital of Yugoslavia, Claire couldn't work up much enthusiasm to view it. In the warmth of the cab she felt more induced to doze off rather than gaze at the tall impressive buildings, and people in heavy knee-length overcoats and fur caps. But she daren't give the impression of being anything other than a robust crew mate, so she sat up straight and made bright comments, and asked about the peculiar lettering on the street and shop signs.

'They use the Cyrillic alphabet,' Greg told her, nodding towards the dashboard shelf. 'You'll find a leaflet on it somewhere.' As Claire searched he went on, 'The A is like ours, but their B looks more like a figure six.'

'And D looks like a squashed square with tails on,' she pointed out, finding the page. 'It must be terribly confusing without one of these for a guide.'

'Only if you get lost,' he sloped a smile. 'Which seldom happens in the trucking business.'

And not surprising on these roads, Claire thought, watching now as the truck picked up the motorway again and spun on towards Nis. The sign said two hundred and forty-three kilometres, which was roughly about a hundred and fifty miles. To Claire it seemed twice as much again. She browsed through the map book and made coffee at intervals and a meal when they were half way there. She was rather glad now that she could sit alone at the back, otherwise she might have been forced to eat for appearances' sake. The thought of food repulsed her at the moment.

She made herself take in the views at the roadside stops, and sat and looked out as the truck sped through snow-clad agricultural country and along a river valley. The light of the day was fading slightly as they passed the ancient building of Nis, then the road led them through wild rolling country with fantastic mountain views and eventually to the Yugo-slav and Bulgarian frontier.

Claire braced herself for all manner of things that could go wrong here, but thankfully everything went smoothly and towards evening they were cruising through Bulgaria. There was the ascent of the Dragoman pass about three hundred feet up, although one could hardly tell it in the dark, and a fuel stop after the descent, then as the headlights picked out a snow-ridged strip snaking across open country Greg slack-ened speed and brought the truck to a halt off the road. He put the light on in the cab and draped back to comment, 'Not bad going. We've covered quite a bit of ground today.'

'Have we made good time?' Claire asked conversationally.

'It's an improvement,' he grinned, reaching for cigarettes. It was probably no more than nine o'clock, but she couldn't hold out any longer. She rose as casually as she could and asked, 'Will it be all right if I go to my bunk now?'

He turned a glance to her as she reached the sliding door. 'Tired?' he queried.

She shrugged lightly. 'You said yourself we've covered quite a lot of ground today.'

She hung around in the back, hoping he would go outside for his smoke. The first aid box was just beside the steering wheel. There might be some tablets in there to get rid of her aches and pains. She undressed slowly, had a cool wash and slipped into pyjamas and dressing gown. Greg had finally climbed down. She could hear him strolling some distance away.

Carefully she made her way into the cab and fumbled for the first aid box. In the dim light it was difficult to see anything, but eventually her fingers came up against the cold metal. She considered taking the box back inside with her, but decided against it. She might have trouble trying to put it back undetected later. Better open it here and see what she could find. The clasp was of strong metal and try as she might she couldn't prise it open.

She was struggling with it feverishly when the cab door suddenly opened and Greg was saying lazily, 'If it gets much colder there's liable to be . . .'

Claire saw the blue eyes drop over her and the first aid box in her hand. She said hastily, 'I was just looking to see if you had any aspirins. I ... I've got a slight headache.'

He moved in to give her a searching look. 'I thought you looked all in. Get back to the bunk. I'll see what I can find.'

Claire shuffled back inside and slipped between the blankets, hoping he would forget all about it. She might have known he wouldn't stay out long in the biting cold. Now he had an idea that something was wrong.

She hid her fiery cheeks and feigned sleep as the big figure moved inside, but she heard him pouring a cup of water and opening her eyes saw he had a glass phial in his hand. As he moved towards the bunk she said politely, 'Thank you. I can manage now.'

He gave her the cup, waiting until she had propped herself up on one arm, then stooping to rest the back of his hand against her cheek, he said tersely, 'You're practically going up in flames. Why haven't you said something before this?'

'Because there wasn't anything to say before this,' she snapped, irritated at his probing gaze. 'And anyway,' she trailed off miserably, 'you were always so sure I wouldn't come up to your standards as a crew mate.'

'Even crew mates can feel under the weather sometimes,' he slanted her a smile.

Maybe so, Claire thought. But she wished now that she had waited until she had completed the trip before boasting about how well she could do it.

He tossed two tablets out from the phial. 'Take these. They might help.'

'Thank you.' Claire took the tablets primly and swallowed them down with the water and a grimace.

'Sure it's nothing to do with the argument you had with the bridge?' he asked, watching her.

'I'm sure,' Claire nodded. 'I didn't hurt myself at all.'

'Could be sheer physical exhaustion.'

'Oh, do stop it!' She flung herself back under the blankets. 'I've had as much rest as you. And look at you!'

She heard him go and place the cup down, then he was stooping in the doorway to say evenly, 'We'll see what you're like in the morning.'

Now that he knew, he was determined to keep his eye on her, Claire thought miserably. And if she didn't feel better in the morning ... well, this was a loaded truck, not a clinic, and it was already hopelessly behind schedule. She closed her eyes and prayed that the tablets would do a good job.

CHAPTER SIX

DAYLIGHT was creeping in at the windows when she awoke. The electric shaver was going, and there was even the excited twitter of birds. It was some moments before she could recall her last waking thoughts last night, and then not daring to wait to see how she felt she stumbled out of bed and into the washroom. There was no hiding from the fact that her pyjamas were soaked in perspiration, but a sluice down would put that right, and it might be only the after-effects of the tablets.

Pulling into her clothes, she ignored the fact that the room was swimming, and gritted her teeth over the fastenings on her jeans and sweater, but it was the mirror that finally put an end to her shaky optimism. Brushing her hair, she saw a face drained of colour, and there were deep violent smudges beneath lack-lustre eyes. It was a picture she didn't care to linger over and taking the brush, she moved quickly into the other room. If only the rest of her would behave, she could easily keep her face hidden for the day.

She was trying to instil some strength into her legs when, after a light tap, the sliding door was pulled back and the big figure stooped in to say lazily, 'How goes it?'

Claire tossed her head to put on a show of scintillating health. She found a smile and started off with forced lightness, 'I feel ...' But before she could finish, the room started to whirl and she found herself falling in a mist of spinning objects. As an arm shot out to save her and she was caught against a wide chest, she was forced to admit weakly '... awful!'

'You'd better get back to the bunk,' Greg ordered, guiding her there. 'I'll start up the truck.'

Sinking down dejectedly, she asked, 'What are you going to do?'

He shrugged, 'Well, Bulgaria's not exactly the best place to land up looking for medical treatment, but you obviously need it.'

Feeling the last of her strength ebbing away at his words, Claire looked up to stammer pleadingly, 'Couldn't we ...? I mean I'm sure I ...'

He seemed to be studying her closely, and then he was swinging away to rasp, 'I don't know how long you've been struggling with this thing, but fiancé or no fiancé, you're in no fit state to go on.'

As the truck thundered into life Claire crept between the blankets and pushed her face into the pillow, cursing the aching throb of her head. She must have fallen asleep, for it seemed a hazy unreal world when she opened her eyes. Someone hovered near the bunk, then she heard Greg's voice, strangely distant, even though his face was close to her own.

'We're on our way to Parzarzic. It's quite a ride. Think you can make it?' She must have nodded, for he gave her a grin to quip, 'Spoken like a true crew mate!' He added in even tones, 'It was tougher than I reckoned getting something fixed up, but you should be okay.'

He moved away and Claire closed her eyes. When she opened them again it was dark and there was some kind of commotion going on outside. She could hear voices and the sound of footsteps above the steady ticking of the engine. It seemed to go on for a long time. So long that she drifted off again.

The next thing she knew Greg was saying close to her ear, 'Parzarzic,' and carrying her, blankets and all, through the night towards a lighted doorway.

Claire didn't even bother trying pronouncing the name. It could have been the moon. She was past caring. Perhaps it was the moon! She seemed to gaze for long periods at a time at craggy knobbly shapes and a pale grey stretch of pitted circles. Sometimes a face came between her and the landscape, sometimes it disappeared altogether, but sooner or later it would be back again, and she would be frowning in her brain to try and make out what it was.

Then there was a time when she opened her eyes and saw it with such sharp clarity she wanted to smile. Of course! The ceiling over the bed in which she was lying. Granted it was one with rather more ornamentation than she was used to seeing in England, but it was a ceiling nevertheless.

She dragged her eyes away from the time-worn intricate patterns and pushed herself up to turn her gaze over the rest of the room. There wasn't much to see. Two tall windows with sombre drapes showed a view of grey skies and crooked rooftops. The floor stretching back from the windows was a dull polished wood, and the bed and barest essentials in furniture seemed lost in the vastness of space. As she was turning her gaze round for the second time to see if there was anything she had missed, the door opened and a long-skirted woman walked in. She was big-boned and heavy-featured and all her clothes were black apart from the pale apron tied round her. The sight of the alien figure moving about the gaunt room brought it home to Claire with a sudden sharp shock that she was lying in a bed somewhere in Bulgaria.

Bulgaria! She jerked up, relieved to find that her head was quite steady on her shoulders, and called to the bending figure, 'Excuse me, I ... er ...'

The woman turned with a smile and nodded, ''Otel Konovgrad,' and went back to work.

'Thank you,' Claire acknowledged, biting back her impatience, 'but what I wanted to ask you was ...'

''Otel Konovgrad,' the woman beamed, polishing vigorously. She pounced on to another piece of furniture, swished her duster round and returned to the door, repeating the name once more for good measure as she came.

'Yes, I've got that,' Claire smiled. 'But could you tell me how long I've been here?'

The big shoulders lifted and eyes paler than the sky outside stared blankly towards the bed. Obviously the woman didn't understand a word of English and Claire didn't somehow see herself attempting Bulgarian. She racked her brain for a way to make her question understood, then, seeing her case unlatched on a nearby table, she slipped out of bed, scrabbled for a small handbag diary that she knew was there, and returned flicking the pages until she got near enough to the date.

She showed the woman the dated page, pointed to herself lying in the bed, and then turned the pages slowly. It was a crude attempt to get her question over, but after repeating it a couple of times with added signs, a dawning light showed in the pale eyes. The woman made some kind of exclamation, put up her hand, and after staring at it for some time with considerable thought, she turned the thumb down and pushed four fingers towards the bed.

Four days! Claire gave a disbelieving smile. She ventured to turn two or three of the fingers down, but the woman was adamant. She thrust four fingers at Claire, jerked her chin down to emphasise the point, then with a farewell nod she turned and left.

Claire sank back into the pillows, swallowing her dejection. If it *was* true and she *had* been here four days, then Greg must be miles away by now. He would be speeding through Turkey or even Iran by this time. The thought of the big figure behind the wheel, swinging the truck along the roads without her, brought a rush of tears to her eyes. She would have liked to have gone all the way to Tehran with him. Now it wasn't likely that she would ever see him again. He obviously had no use for the feature she had been going to write, or for her for that matter. He had said in the truck that she would be 'Okay', meaning of course that he had seen to the formalities of getting her back home, but he wouldn't have shed any tears about being free to go on without her.

Claire gulped. That wasn't how *she* felt at all. She turned her tear-blurred gaze to the window and tried to concentrate on the view. She didn't move it when the door opened. It was probably the woman coming in again to do some more polishing. Slender pyjama-clad shoulders slumped against the pillows, she blinked at the curled tiled rooftops and grey stonework of the houses. Only when a maroon-sweatered figure moved into her vision did the mist in her eyes turn to stars.

'Greg!' She let her heart gloat over the sight of the big frame, relaxed and smiling at the foot of the bed, and then sat up to stammer demurely, 'I . . . I thought you would have gone on without me.'

'There's a law against leaving things in Bulgaria that don't belong,' he said lazily. 'How do you feel?'

'As though it never happened,' Claire smiled, realising that at this moment she could have jumped over the rooftops. She touched herself and asked thoughtfully, 'By the way, what was the matter with me?'

Greg shrugged. 'I don't know any Bulgarian, and no one around here speaks English, but I gather it was some kind of reaction from the jabs you had before you came out here.'

'Is *that* all?' Claire laughed in relief, then tilting her chin, said, 'I told you I was as tough as you.' The blue eyes trailed over her, lying small against the pillows, and because she suddenly felt overwhelmingly shy Claire asked lightly, 'What have you been doing all the time I've been stuck here?'

'I spent two days filling up forms for us to stay here,' he replied with dry humour. 'The rest of the time I've been working on the truck.'

'When can we start out again?' she asked eagerly. 'I feel I could get up right now.'

He watched her fidget with the covers, and commented sceptically, 'You could use a little more colour in those cheeks.'

'That's only because I need fresh air,' Claire bounced. 'The kind you get,' she added succinctly, 'as a truck driver's mate.'

He grinned at her humour. 'Hungry?' he asked.

'Starving!' Clare smiled.

'I'll get you something sent up.' He moved towards the door, saying as he went, 'Give it another day to get your sea legs and then we'll move out. I've got some friends in Istanbul. I'll get the doctor there to give you a going over.'

In the bathroom, adjoining her room, Claire swung the taps full on, and though the water was only just warm she enjoyed a soak. She dressed and strolled around, cursing her wobbly legs, but knowing she couldn't expect anything else after four days in bed. Though she vaguely recalled being plied with drinks and snacks, the feather lightness she felt could be due to a slight loss of weight.

The meal, when it arrived, was partly Bulgarian, a kind of concocted salad with hot and cold vegetables, and partly what Greg must have gone out of his way to procure for her; strong tea, a boiled egg and brittle crusty rolls. She felt better when she had eaten, but not confident enough to try her legs outside her room. She contented herself by sitting in the one armchair and gazing out over the rooftops.

Later she wrote a letter to Mike. There was no telling when she would be able to post it, or when it would reach him, but she felt she owed him an apology for ignoring his well-meant phone call that night in London. When the envelope was sealed and addressed, she toyed with the idea of writing to Tom Gerard, the features editor, but decided against it. He would think she was happily scribbling her way over the roads to Tehran, so why disillusion him with the news that she was never going to be able to bring herself to put a word on paper about this trip? Time enough to get the sack when she got back.

She didn't see Greg any more that day. Probably he had other things to attend to. But at least he was here with her in Bulgaria, she hugged the knowledge to her, and she would be up there beside him in the truck again tomorrow.

To make sure that she was reasonably fit, she went to bed before it was dark and stayed there until a breakfast tray was brought in to her at eight o'clock the next morning. She ate as much as she could, washed and dressed and packed her things into her case. A dour porter came to collect it and take it down, and after all the effort of the last half hour she sank on to the bed in anorak and jeans, and waited for a sign to leave. She was tempted to rest her head on the pillow for a second and had almost got there when the door opened and Greg, big in the suede driving coat, was moving in to ask, 'All set?'

Claire nodded, taking care to sit up straight. She was just planning to push to her feet when the dark head came down, and she was swung up into muscular arms. As they moved towards the door she looked up towards the lean jaw and laughed lightly,

'Really, Greg, I can walk!'

'I've just finished filling out forms for us to leave,' he said with a dry smile. 'I wouldn't want anything to go wrong now.'

Leaning against him, Claire didn't feel inclined to argue. She was taken down an iron-railed staircase and out on to a cobbled courtyard. The truck was rumbling in readiness a few yards away and Greg made his way towards it. The wind was unbelievably cold after the indoors, so cold that it snatched her breath away, but with her cheek occasionally brushing a lean hard one, Claire told herself she didn't particularly need any at the moment. Who wanted to talk at a time like this?

The cab was blissfully warm. She was just settling happily in when the big figure came up the other side and into the driving seat to say lazily, 'Maybe you'd better get back to the bunk.'

'Oh, Greg!' Claire turned entreatingly. 'I'm not an invalid. I'm a crew mate, remember?'

'Okay,' he grinned, 'you're a crew mate.' The blue gaze lingered on her for a second, then he was pushing his foot on the starter to state with energetic cheerfulness, 'So what are we waiting for, Dave? Let's get going!'

Claire watched him take the truck forward and out of the courtyard, then turned her gaze outside. She would always be just 'Dave' to him, but, as she had told herself before, you couldn't have everything.

They passed some old-looking wood and brick buildings, then the truck swung off on a road that alternated between smooth cobbles and asphalt.

'Where abouts are we?' Claire asked, watching the road climb between snow-capped hills.

'We've got Plovdiv coming up,' Greg said, settling down to a steady speed. 'After that nothing much until we reach the Turkish border.'

'Is it very far to Istanbul?' Claire asked with mounting excitement.

'About two hundred and sixty miles,' Greg estimated, swinging the truck smoothly away from a lorry crashing by on the other side.

'We could get there by tonight,' Claire pointed out.

'We could, but we won't.' The blue gaze stayed with the road. 'We'll take it easy today and pull into Istanbul some time tomorrow morning.'

He was thinking of her, of course, stepping straight out of bed into the truck. She pulled on her lower lip and sent him a guilty look to murmur,

'We're not making very good time, are we?'

As soon as the words were out she realised it was a pathetic understatement, but Greg just lifted his shoulders and remarked easily,

'These things happen.'

There were no chores for Claire that day. She found it rather pleasant to be helped up and down from the cab and guided into warm interiors and comfortable seats. At Edirne, just over the border, in a tiny café with an iron stove in the middle, she sampled her first Turkish meal; shish-kebab served with rice, cake soaked in syrup and Turkish coffee. Delicious!

It seemed colder in Edirne than anywhere they had gone through so far, but the scenery more than made up for it. Pencil-shaped minarets rose up from high-domed mosques and the carved stonework of ancient buildings. The whole outline, arranged picturesquely against the pale orange glow of a winter's sky, kept Claire on the edge of her seat.

'Isn't it fantastic!' she murmured half to herself, and then turning to the suede-coated figure lazily swinging the wheel, she demanded with impatient humour, 'How can you just *sit* there?'

'I did my leaping around about fifteen years ago,' Greg said drily.

Claire looked at him with a wry smile to comment, 'It must be awful to be old!'

'I wouldn't know,' he tossed her a metallic twinkle, 'I'm only middle-aged myself.'

She laughed softly, thinking he looked far from it with his lean jaw and hard white smile. Before she became too engrossed in the chiselled profile she turned her attention back to the view.

It was a leisurely ride down to Silivri on the coast. The Sea of Marmara was a pale grey strip in the evening light. They ate and drank tea from tiny bulbous cups in a roadhouse restaurant, then strolled along a path skirting the shore.

Claire thought they would have spent the night in the truck, where it was parked now a little way off the road, but Greg said, guiding her towards the town, 'We'll walk, if you feel up to it, until we come to a decent hotel and then get an early night.'

She nodded, taking a deep breath and gazing happily around. She was all for walking. What better way to absorb your surroundings, and what surroundings! Well on the way to becoming enthralled at the Turkish scene, she caught a faintly mocking light in the blue eyes turned down her way, and pulling herself up from going poetic, she laughed, 'All right, I won't say one word! But...' she turned a gaze towards the grey sheen of water stretching back under a starlit sky, 'you've got to admit the Sea of Marmara is a romantic-sounding name.'

'Okay,' Greg grinned, draping an arm about her shoulders. 'It's a romantic-sounding name.'

As she smiled, happy to have won her point, the arm about her tightened. She had this peculiar urge to stop walking, and Greg's steps were slowing to a halt too. She felt his fingers sink into the silk of her anorak, then they were gripping so tight she almost winced as he said briskly, 'Where's the driving coat? This thing's no good against the cold.'

Claire looked up, surprised at his words. Especially as it had been far colder coming down from Edirne than it was now.

'It's in the truck,' she replied. 'Where else?'

'A lot of good it's going to do there,' he clipped, striding back towards it. As Claire climbed into the cab on her side and meekly went to change coats, she heard Greg moving things around on the dashboard shelf. When she came out he turned to state laconically, 'And by the way, look what I found when I was turning out the cab the other day.'

Claire frowned away from the peaked cap in his hand. 'Oh, not that again!'

'Put it on.' He tossed it across to her. 'It's more in keeping with your role as truck driver's mate.'

She pulled down the corners of her smile to murmur, 'We don't have to take it that far, do we?'

'You're darned right we do!' he snapped, and as she went to sidle the cap back under the other items on the shelf he added menacingly, 'And while you're in this truck, you'll do as I say. Understand?'

Claire twisted her hair up under her cap and gazed at her reflection in her window. Back to the urchin look, she thought with an inward sigh, but she knew better than to ignore Greg's orders. As he pushed his foot on the starter, she said, slightly amazed, 'I thought we were walking?'

He swung the truck out on to the road and with glinting blue eyes following the headlights he clipped, 'It's quicker to ride.'

They ended up in a motel. It was the first thing to show up along the road, and Greg didn't seem inclined to cruise on looking for anything else. He booked in, changing traveller's cheques, and bade her goodnight almost as soon as she arrived at the door of her room. Claire didn't really mind. She was tired after her first full day up out of bed, and knew an early night was the wisest thing for her.

It was late when they set out the next morning. She had overslept and Greg had told her to take her time with her breakfast, while he went over the tyres of the truck. Around eleven o'clock she climbed up into the cab, small in the driving coat and cap, but spruce and smiling.

Greg had little to say. He kept his attention on the thick line of traffic being sucked in towards Istanbul and edged the truck along into the swell. At the sight of domes and minarets rising above ancient walls Claire sat forward in eager anticipation. They passed the Topkapi gate where the road cut into the walls of the city, then followed a thunderous stretch into the centre. Here things were somewhat chaotic, and it was here too that Claire dropped back into her seat, slightly deflated at the scene.

A grey pall of smoke hung over dull-looking mosques and streets glistening with mud and grease. Taxis flew like mad things in and out of the writhing traffic, and in the crowds porters were bent double under colossal loads. She had already learned that Istanbul was built on seven hills astride two continents. The fast-flowing water of the Bosphorus separated Europe from Asia and widened into the Sea of Marmara. Cutting into the European side was an inlet called the Golden Horn, and with a name like that one would have expected to see something a little different from an English canal, Claire decided gloomily as the truck came up to the bridge crossing it. When they had shunted their way over amidst noise and bustle and the nerve-racking hoots of the ferry sirens Greg flickered her a half grin and drawled,

'It takes time to get to know the real Istanbul.'

Watching him weaving in and out of the traffic, she wondered if *he* knew the city. He had mentioned that he had friends here, so probably he did. Claire had an idea too that they were going there now, for he turned off the road that would have taken them to the car ferry, and chose one that led away from the water. A few minutes later they were passing the British Consulate, a big neat building set in the thick of a teeming thoroughfare. Surprisingly it was here that Greg slackened the speed of the truck. He didn't quite stop, but cruised on around the side of the building to the back where one could see that the gardens and lawns and courtyards were an oasis of peace in a busy world. Claire could imagine the whole area being a blaze of colour in the summer, but now the lawns looked plain among sparse neatly clipped shrubs and bushes.

The truck had come to a halt in the main courtyard and she was aware that Greg was reaching up to the cupboard set above the seats. Seconds later he was swinging a crate of carefully packed wines down on to the ground beside him. Since he had said nothing to the effect that she should stay in her seat, Claire climbed down too. She was just closing the door behind her when a light call across the lawns made her turn. An angular tweed-suited woman was hurrying from a sprawling house, hardly noticeable off the side, under a belt of trees. She arrived at the truck breathless but smiling with 'Greg! What a lovely surprise! We didn't expect you on this trip.'

Greg, who had been draped against the mudguard totting up some figures on an invoice, stepped up smiling. He took the woman's hand, who in turn pulled herself nearer to drop an affectionate kiss on his cheek. Claire was aware of the blue eyes turning her way, then Greg was saying pleasantly, 'Dave, meet Mrs. Wentworth. Her husband, Doctor Wentworth, looks out for the staff around here.'

The woman tossed a friendly nod in Claire's direction, then swung her glance back to rivet it on the smooth girlish features, beneath the peaked cap. A twinkling gaze lowered over the small shoulders beneath the heavy driving coat and slim jean-clad legs, and she was turning back to say with the tilt of a sandy eyebrow, 'A girl in a truck?'

'She's making the trip out to her fiancé in Tehran,' Greg said briefly, and flicking a glance over Claire's peaked features he added, 'And not coming off too well. Better get inside out of the cold.'

'Of course, my dear. Do come along.' Mrs. Wentworth took her arm in friendly concern. 'You are looking a little drawn. I hope the journey isn't proving too much for you?'

Shaking her head shyly, Claire allowed herself to be led over to the house. Turning a glance back, she saw that Greg had swung up the crate and was striding towards the rear of the Consulate.

From the lawns she was led into a long room of English decor and design, comfortably furnished, but looking opulent, after days of seeing nothing but the interior of the truck cab and austere motels. There were big sprawling armchairs, polished wood cabinets and tables, and deep pile carpets as pale as the wash of the walls.

Feeling the warmth of central heating, Claire pulled off her coat and placing the cap with it, sank down on to a huge settee. She hadn't realised how much her legs needed to be relieved of her weight, but unhampered now in light sweater and jeans, her hair cascading about her shoulders, she felt considerably better ... until she looked out of the french windows running the length of the room. There was quite a commotion going on up on the terraces near the Consulate. Greg was surrounded by a number of people who must have come out of the nearby maisonettes and offices. She watched him shake hands with the men in the group, and smile that white smile of his over the girls. Judging by the way one or two of the latter turned their lips up for his to brush them, she would say that Greg knew Istanbul very well indeed! Struggling not to let her smile pull in sourly, Claire remarked lightly to Mrs. Wentworth, who was standing nodding over the scene, 'Greg seems to be quite well known around here.'

'Oh, he is!' The older woman's sandy eyebrows shot up over her smile as though she thought everyone ought to know that. 'He was attached to the Consulate out here for some time, you know, before he left the Army. Some of the girls have grown up knowing him. That's Sarah Littlewood.' She pointed to a golden-haired girl who was smiling up at Greg. 'Her father works for the First Secretary. And the two dark girls, they're the Murray sisters. Their parents have just

111

left for a spell at the Embassy in Ankara. And I believe that's little Miss ... is it? ...' Mrs. Wentworth rubbed her chin doubtfully and then threw up her hands with a chuckle. 'Oh, Greg knows them all, and of course he always looks in when he's out this way.'

'Of course.' Claire tried to sound matter-of-fact while the big suede-coated figure laughed deeply with a vision in blue, then she dragged her gaze away to the courtyard. She noticed that a car had pulled up, not far from the truck, and as an elderly man stepped out Mrs. Wentworth turned away with, 'Here comes my husband now. Would you excuse me, my dear? I'll just see how lunch is progressing.'

Claire lay back and closed her eyes. This was much more restful than gazing at the view out there. Her eyelids were just beginning to feel weighty when she heard footsteps outside, and Greg strolled into the room accompanied by the man she had seen stepping out of the car. He was thick-set with greying hair and a leisurely gait, and this he directed straight up to the settee to smile,

'Now then, young lady, what's all this? Greg tells me you haven't been too well.'

'Doctor Wentworth,' Greg drawled, and Claire stammered shyly,

'Oh ... it wasn't anything much.'

She looked up to where the doctor was standing, knowing that nothing of her pale features and shadowed eyes could possibly escape that penetrating gaze. He nodded over her for a moment and then said cheerfully,

'Pop along to my surgery. It's the door on the right as you go up the hall. We'll see if we can find out what's been the trouble.'

With Greg looking on, Claire had no choice but to obey meekly. She went out of the room wondering what all the fuss was about. True, her legs didn't hold her as well as they used to, but apart from that, she felt fine.

She found the door and sat down in the surgery to wait. After a while the doctor came in and with a jovial but authoritative, 'Now then, let's have a look at you,' he got down to the business of a routine examination.

It was very thorough, Claire felt, but not over-long. The silence was punctuated by the click of the stethoscope, and

Doctor Wentworth's satisfied mumbles, then he was rising and dumping his instruments back in the bag to say with a smile, 'There's nothing wrong with you that rest and good wholesome food won't put right. I don't hold with handing out tonics. Eat well and sleep well and you'll be fine.'

He turned at the door to back his smile up with a fatherly nod and went out.

Claire pulled into her sweater with a contented intake of breath. It was nice to know you were all in working order. She straightened her hair in the mirror over the wash basin, ran an interested gaze over the medical books and diplomas around the walls and went out along the hall to the room that she had sat in on her arrival. There was no one about, and no sound of anyone in the near vicinity. Her coat and cap were still where she had dropped them, and deciding that there was no point in hanging around a strange household, she donned them and went out to the truck. That seemed to be deserted too, but she decided the cab would be as good as any place to wait for Greg.

She was surprised to find him opening the door just as she had been about to climb up. As he jumped down, she twinkled, 'Have you heard the news? I'm well on my way to complete recovery!'

He nodded and turned back to the cab, and watching him, Claire said lightly, 'That's my suitcase you've got there.'

'I know it is,' he replied evenly.

She smiled, puzzled, as he dropped it at her feet and looked up to stammer, 'But Doctor Wentworth says all I need is ...'

'Rest and regular meals,' Greg put in, turning back to the cab. 'And you won't get either roughing it in a truck.'

'But ... but ...' She was all for collapsing behind a rush of despair until she saw Greg's holdall come down alongside her case.

'We'll hang on here for a week,' he drawled. 'You should be fit to move on by then.'

'A week!' Claire didn't know whether to laugh or cry. A prolonged stay in Istanbul couldn't be bad, but there was all that feminine attraction across the way. Watching him, she asked quickly, 'What about your schedule?'

'It's no good trying to go by the book on this trip,' he said with a taut smile, and then as the blue eyes flickered over her he added lazily, 'Sorry about the fiancé, but he'll keep. And if you were my girl I'd expect to have you delivered in good shape.'

Claire digested this as he swung up the cases and they moved back to the house. When they were almost there, Mrs. Wentworth rushed out to turn an arm around Claire's shoulder with motherly concern.

'My dear, why didn't you say you'd been ill? Charles has been telling me all about it, and I've decided to personally take you under my wing. I'm going to see to it that you get all the rest and quiet you need. I've got a beautifully secluded room upstairs, and you shall have your meals brought up to you on a tray.'

Before Claire could open her mouth to comment, kindly Mrs. Wentworth had swooped, picked her up and carried her off. In a dream she found herself being led up a curving staircase and along a carpeted corridor to a door set apart from the rest.

'You'll be quite undisturbed here, my dear. I'll get the houseboy to bring up your case. Now do go inside and make yourself comfortable.'

As Mrs. Wentworth turned and moved off, Claire went into the room and closed the door, turning the corners of her smile downwards. She wasn't so sure she cared for this kind of a rest cure, but Greg hadn't followed with her case to comment, so obviously he went along with the idea.

Trying not to feel too gloomy, she toured the room. It was spacious and comfortable like the one downstairs. There was a wide double bed elegantly draped in green satin and matching curtains hanging at the long line of windows. She had a fair view from here of the gardens and lawns, and though the terraces flanking the Consular buildings were deserted again now, she could still see the gay scene that had taken place on Greg's arrival. Turning away quickly, Claire told herself that she was too interested in the interior of her room to care what had gone on beyond it, but though she examined every cupboard and corner and picture on the wall, she couldn't take her mind off the man who had driven her across five countries. She had known little about him at the beginning, but she felt she knew him very well now.

He had left the Army to start up a business and he wasn't the type to ease up until he made it pay. Well, it was paying now. He had a fleet of trucks and men to drive them, and there was nothing to prevent him relaxing a little on his own trips, if he felt so inclined. He could probably afford to break the journey altogether when it suited him. And by the look of it Istanbul suited him very well.

So—Claire pulled in a breath and went to flop down on the bed—she needn't flatter herself that he was hanging about on her account. His only reasons for stopping off here were about half a dozen slender pretty ones, housed somewhere in the Consulate building.

A pale shaft of sunlight was streaming on to the coverlet, but Claire didn't see it. To her the world outside looked a dull overall grey.

It was Mrs. Wentworth who brightened it up for her over the next few days. Happy to have what she considered a real live invalid on her hands, she enjoyed fussing, and nothing she did for Claire was too much trouble. She was always trotting up with some special dish she had cooked, or a fresh spray of flowers to brighten the room. She got her friends to pass on their English magazines and would stay for long chats when she brought them. Claire never tired of the stories she heard about Istanbul, she just wished a little wistfully that she had been able to see some of it herself.

Sometimes when the sun shone, she and Mrs. Wentworth would stroll in the garden. There was never anyone about on these occasions, but Claire didn't need a deserted household to tell her that Greg was making the most of his stay. She had seen him from her window, guiding one girl or another across the courtyard. Her heart had spun in circles at the sight of him, immaculate in expensively cut lounge suits, which he probably left at the Wentworths for these occasions.

As the week drew on she consoled herself with the fact that at least that big red truck out there would have to be moving on to Tehran one day, and when it did, it would be she who would be up there alongside Greg.

When she wasn't gazing out of the window, she was marvelling at the difference in herself and her reflection in the mirror. She had to admit that the rest had done her good. The sparkle had come back to her eyes and there was an attractive blush of colour on her cheeks. She brushed her hair after the luxury of a shampoo until it shone and waltzed about the room feeling strangely keyed-up and restless.

One evening she was inspired to go feminine, and tossed aside her sweater and jeans for a deep kingfisher blue dress with a wide belted waist and full flouncing skirt. The colour made her hair flame and she tweaked the stand-up collar about her throat with twinkling satisfaction. After amusing herself applying a light touch of make-up, she wondered how to while away the rest of the time until bed. No one had ever forbidden her to go downstairs, but after the first couple of days she had grown attached to the idea of staying aloof in her room. Still, she could always be wildly adventurous tonight and go down for a book. There had been some colourful jackets around the ones she had seen on the bookshelf that first day in the big front lounge, and she knew her way there without touching on the other parts of the house.

Intrigued at the idea of a good wholesome novel as opposed to the light reading in magazines, she opened the door of her room and went quietly along the hall and down the curving staircase. Everywhere was tastefully lit, but there was no one about.

She hurried to the bookshelf in the lounge and ran her eyes quickly over the titles. It shouldn't be more than a five-minute job to select one which would keep her occupied for the next couple of hours. If she chose a slim one she might even finish it before she went to sleep. Smiling to herself, she reached up to the top shelf. There was nothing more satisfying than reading a book from cover to cover in one go.

The only trouble at the moment was that she couldn't get to the one she wanted. Pulling in her lower lip wryly, she wondered whether to settle for something on the lower shelves or to see if there was anything around to stand on. It must have been in her moment of indecision that the figure came into the room, for as she turned, Greg was just reaching down to a low table for his cigarette lighter gleaming there. He looked up at the rustle of her dress and stretched lazily to his full height to take her in. Lowering her arm, Claire was glad she had the bookshelf to rest against. The

116

sight of the big figure, crisp in evening dress, made her go weak at the knees. And it had nothing to do with her recent illness.

Greg didn't move from where he stood, but she thought the hooded blue eyes darkened slightly as they lowered over her. He took his time lighting up a cigarette, then asked evenly,

'How's the patient?'

Claire didn't know why she should suddenly feel screwed up inside. Perhaps it had something to do with his polished appearance and the thought that he had gone to all that trouble for a girl at the Consulate.

Try as she might to reply light-heartedly the words seemed to twist up tartly before they came out,

'Patiently waiting to move on. You *do* run a trucking business, don't you?'

He sloped a taut smile. 'Don't you like Istanbul?'

'I can't say I've seen anything of it,' Claire replied coolly, turning back to her book. She could only lift her chin and stare at the title, but then a brilliant white cuff in a dark sleeve reached up over her and Greg was saying mildly,

'Is this the one you want?'

Claire was too intent on moving a pace away to reply. Looking up, she saw the blue eyes roaming her face and used the movement to take in at close quarters the clean-shaven jaw and dark gleaming hair.

It was Greg who broke the silence. He said with a slight nod, 'You're looking better for the break.'

'And you're looking better for the way you've been passing *your* time too.' Claire returned waspishly.

Giving her a searching look, Greg twisted a smile to ask, 'Why the acid? Getting itchy feet for Tehran?'

Claire wasn't sure herself. She just knew it gave her immense satisfaction to snatch the book from his hand and toss him a stormy gaze.

The blue eyes narrowed at her action, then he was slackening his frame to sneer slowly, 'Don't worry. You'll be falling into your fiancé's arms any day now.'

'And believe me,' Claire thrust her chin up, 'I can't wait for that moment!'

Before the choking sensation in her throat could make

117

itself heard, she spun away and hurried blindly out of the room.

CHAPTER SEVEN

VALIANTLY for the rest of the evening she persevered with the book, but though she stared at the print and turned the pages mechanically, the only pictures she saw were Greg, ruggedly attractive in formal wear, escorting some chiffon-gowned female through the bright lights of the town.

She was glad of a bright sunny day when she awoke the next morning. It didn't do much for her lagging spirits, but it did give her an excuse to choose something really special to wear and perhaps walk with Mrs. Wentworth if she was going shopping. The older woman had often chatted on about how she preferred to do her own bargaining in the markets, and Claire had decided that anything would be better than mooning about her room, and watching when and with whom Greg left the house.

Bearing in mind that it would be cool, even though the sun shone, she slipped into a suit of smooth leather. It was a pale coffee shade with gold buttons, and a matching buckle on the skirt, and Claire felt that it did a lot for her colouring now that the healthy glow was back in her cheeks. With a cream fleecy jumper under the jacket she felt ready for any keen wind that might sneak up. Satisfied with a dab of powder and a brush of lipstick, she picked up the handbag she had searched out of her case and went downstairs to look for Mrs. Wentworth. She heard her talking lengthily to one of the houseboys, and deciding to wait, strolled outside to see what the day was like.

Surprisingly it was as warm as a spring day in England, but as she had heard, the temperature was just as liable to fluctuate here as it was back home. Still, this was one of the good days, Claire told herself, and with a bit of luck she might enjoy some of it, even if it was only walking along the road and back.

Musing her way over the lawn, she heard a movement near

118

the house and thinking that the footsteps coming up behind were Mrs. Wentworth's, she spun round smiling and came face to face with Greg. It was unnerving to come across him so quickly after last night. She could do nothing but stand and feel her smile sliding away. She wondered if he had come to tell her that they were leaving today, but soon discounted the idea. A grey lightly checked lounge suit, and silk shirt and tie, were hardly the clothes he would choose to drive the truck.

He did have some news for her, though. Dropping an appraising glance over her, he said with something of the twisted smile she had seen last night, 'I thought you'd like to know. We're pulling out tomorrow.'

And he was just dropping the news in passing, Claire thought gloomily. It was obvious he was all ready to go off again. When she didn't reply he added with harsh sarcasm, 'Sorry I can't make it today. If the document I'm waiting for comes up any quicker, don't worry, I'll let you know.'

'Tomorrow will do fine for me,' Claire replied coolly, and unable to resist a slight carping, she tacked on, 'What's one more day anyway?'

'That's right. What *is* one more day?' he came back with abruptly. As she moved off, he fell into step with her, and after a long silence he said casually, 'Thing is, how to use the spare time.'

Claire stopped walking and swung a knowing gaze up to him to reply sweetly, 'You've never been short of ideas up to now.' She saw the flicker of a white smile as he looked across the gardens to the building beyond, before thrusting his hands into his pockets to drawl, 'Maybe I haven't run out yet. I thought you wanted to see something of Istanbul?'

'Well, I do.' Claire watched him. 'I mean ... I always wanted to, but ...'

'Okay, then,' he shrugged, 'let's go.'

As he took her arm Claire found the nerve to ask, 'What about your ... your friends?'

'They don't need a guide,' he grinned, deliberately misinterpreting her question. 'They know the place inside out.'

She saw that they were heading towards the courtyard and stopped to say, 'I'd better tell Mrs. Wentworth I'm going out.'

'She knows,' Greg kept hold of her arm. 'I told her we wouldn't be back until tonight while I was phoning for a taxi.'

'Nothing like being sure of yourself, is there?' Claire said airily, though inwardly she was glowing.

The taxi arrived in the courtyard almost at the same time as they did, and though she wanted to appear aloof and uncaring at Greg's last-minute offer to show her around she couldn't contain herself when he rattled off something in Turkish to the driver. When they had turned out on to the road, she asked eagerly, 'Where are we going?'

'To the old town for a start,' Greg said lazily, lighting up a cigarette. 'When you've had enough of that we'll take a trip up the Bosphorus.'

She swung a happy gaze over jumbled houses and laughed, 'I can't really believe I'm going to see something of Istanbul after all!'

'It's a city like any other,' Greg said drily, pulling on his cigarette.

'I bet you didn't think so when you first came here,' she spun to face him, 'and I bet secretly you don't think that now!'

He held on to her gaze, as she laughingly challenged him, then he was tossing the barely smoked cigarette out of the window to say with a tight smile, 'Let's keep what I think out of it, shall we?'

Claire was too concerned with the view to take the conversation any further. They were coming up to the Galata Bridge with its teeming traffic and racing pedestrians. On all sides the water was crowded with vessels; ships with flags flying, crescent-shaped caiques and of course the fat hooting ferries. In the hazy distance she could see a mosque rising like a plump rounded mountain above all the others, and minarets unbelievably slender. Later, over the bridge, there were tall ungainly buildings scored with dozens of long thin windows, all looking as though being squashed together had made them stretch upwards instead of across.

They were in the thick of the noise and clamour now. The taxi moved at little more than walking pace through a crowded labyrinth of narrow streets, where the cobbles veered uphill in all directions to rickety wooden houses, and dated tenements three and four stories high. Washing lines cascaded from rooftops annd balconies, and ill-looking cats roamed among the refuse. As Claire gazed out on the melee of dark-eyed women and children and flat-capped men, Greg came up to look out over her shoulder. He dropped her a grin to say deeply, 'Old Stamboul.'

With the dark head a shade too close to hers, Claire asked lightly, 'Is it all like this?'

'No.' He gave a humorous glint at her small sigh of relief. 'But you might as well see all sides of it.'

Towards the end of the afternoon Claire considered happily that she had done just that. With Greg holding her arm she had walked the winding hilly streets of a beautiful section of the old town, visited the Sultan Ahmet Mosque—or the Blue Mosque as it was called, because of the blue tiles in the interior giving the effect of a glowing blue cave—and strolled in the grounds of the Topkapi Palace.

As it was not yet spring there was not much colour about, but in the bright sunshine and with the sound of the birds, one could imagine the rose gardens and tulip beds of summer. Inside the palace Claire had gazed on Persian and Italian embroidery and a breathtaking collection of jewellery that belonged to the Sultans. The harem building would have climbing roses up its yellow walls in the summer, she decided. She admired the pretty rooms and courtyards, but there was a coldness and a darkness in the passages that she was glad to leave behind.

Greg chose a restaurant in the market place for lunch, and judging by the elegant clientele and marvellous food it was quite a famous place. Nearby was the Grand Bazaar, a maze of streets and alleys covered over, and wider ones spreading out in heavy columned arcades. There was far too much to see in one afternoon, so as Greg lazily suggested, they concentrated on the heart of the bazaar, where there were displays of trinkets and filigree jewellery, silver and copper ware, and the famous Bursa silk.

The warmth of the sun was being sucked away by the late afternoon breeze as Claire sipped samovar coffee now in a wharfside restaurant, or *lokanta*, as she had learned to call them. Strident Turkish music was coming from a small wall radio, and across from her, Greg sat back, pulling on a cigarette and watching the passers-by. Looking at him, Claire wondered if he had forgotten about his proposal to sail up the Bosphorus. He must have had an idea of her thoughts, for as she rose he came up to tower over her, and glanced quizzically at his watch to comment, 'I don't know whether to risk the ferry trip. We're just about to hit the rush-hour traffic.'

'I don't mind the crowds, really!' Claire said quickly. With Greg at her side she had drifted through the day in a rosy-hued dream. The thoughts of it not continuing were unbearable. As they came out on to the pavement, she saw the blue eyes thoughtfully scanning the crowds. Looking up to him she begged,

'Oh, please! I'd like to go!'

He swung his eyes down to hers and sloped her a white smile to say slowly, 'Okay, if that's what you want. But you'd better stick close to me.'

'Oh, I will!' Claire laughed. As though anything could keep her away!

As it turned out it was the other way around. Greg dropped an arm about her shoulders and drew her close to his side as he forged a way through the crowding pedestrians and hostile traffic towards the Galata bridge and the ferry. People rushing for water transport home swept all before them across the bridge and the *hamels*—porters carrying everything from wardrobes to pianos on their backs—got a slightly assisted passage. Once their tickets were purchased, Claire felt herself being carried along too, but Greg chose his own pace, and close against him, she could smile at the scene. It wasn't quite so amusing, though, trying to find a foothold on the gangplank with dozens of maddened Turks all trying to do the same. But with the grey-suited arm steadying her, she managed it.

When she next came up for air they were near a window at the rear of the ferry and people were fast filling up the space behind. At least here there was room to move around, and shyly turning out of the arm that held her, Claire looked up to see if she was all in one piece.

'Phew! The London rush hour has nothing on this!' she gasped laughingly.

'Wishing we'd gone back to the Wentworths?' Greg asked

sloping her a grin.

The sight of him, big and dishevelled, with one lock of hair falling over his brow and the silk tie slightly off centre, made her heart roll over and over. She wanted to reach up and straighten the tie, and had to steel herself against doing so, until his own hands came up and casually set it in place, when she replied lightly,

'I certainly am not! I wouldn't have missed this for anything.'

'Even though we might have to stand for most of the way?'

'Doesn't worry me in the least.' Claire tilted her chin smilingly around her little space. She considered she had come off quite lucky; or perhaps it was due to Greg's manoeuvring. Anyway she was in a corner with a full view from the window before her, and a wall to lean against at her side if she needed it. The people crowding in at the back didn't bother her apart from one individual who insisted on breathing down her neck. Turning, she saw Greg drop an icy gaze over the dark-eyed young man who was eagerly smiling at her, then he was stretching his arm negligently behind her shoulders to lean against the wall.

That was how Claire made the trip up the Bosphorus, shut out from the world behind by Greg's bulk, and entranced by the scenes beyond the windows that he pointed out to her. As the ferry moved off with a melodious hoot, she saw the bridge become a criss-crossed silhouette against the paling sun. The mosques and minarets were etched against a pearl-sheen sky, and the trees in the palace gardens looked black against the walls and domes. Moving over to Uskudar on the Asian shores, she saw Leander's Tower rising from a rock and named, as Greg told her, after the legendary lover who was drowned swimming across the stretch of water to his lady-love.

After Uskudar, the Bosphorus really began, with its palaces and gardens and *yalis* or summer villas. She saw the Dolma Bahce Palace sprawling white and magnificent on the European shore and further up on the Asian shore the Beylerbey palace sparkled like icing sugar in the fading light. All along the water's edge buildings overhung enchantingly and among the mosques and *gazinos* there were green lawns and clouds of bushes, suggesting that everything would be a blaze of colour in the summer. The ferry stops were frequent, and when they had travelled a fair stretch Greg guided her ashore to a *lokanta*. They dined overlooking the water and listened to music from a *saz*, a stringed instrument sounding something like a mandolin.

Going back, the ferry had few passengers and there were plenty of seats for the choosing, but Claire found she preferred her place at the window, open now that there was no breeze. Greg lazily stepped up to take his place beside her, and stealing a glance at him, she wondered if he was bored with the trip that he must have done many times during his stay in Istanbul. Apart from pointing out the places of interest he had said very little, but once or twice when she had turned a smile to comment on something that delighted her, she found the blue eyes resting on her with a gaze she couldn't fathom.

She was sorry in a way that there would be nothing for him to draw her attention to on the way back, for that meant there would be no conversation at all, but as though to compensate for this, he turned an arm about her and drew her back to rest against him.

Though Claire had decided the Bosphorus was lovely by day, she found it infinitely more beautiful at night, when the lights of the ferries were added to those of the fishing boats and the golden lamplight shining from the houses on both shores. Some of the ferries had powerful searchlights which apart from raking the water in front of them, sometimes spilled over into the hills, among the trees and houses. Occasionally the shaft of white light trailed over the surrounding ferries, picking out people talking and gesticulating like animated dolls. The Turks didn't seem to mind being spotlit in this way, there was always a ripple of amusement among those who found themselves caught in the beam. When it swept blindingly over Claire standing close against Greg, she laughed up at him, wondering if it would ever move on. In the moment before it trailed away she saw the gleam of his white smile and felt his fingers brip her shoulders slightly.

The ferry berthed back at Galata bridge in comparative calm. There was no mad scramble to disembark, and strolling ashore, Claire had time to gaze on the wharfside stalls piled with fruit and cakes and sweet sticky biscuits. Now that her day with Greg was at an end, she wanted to hang on to every moment while it lasted. There was only the taxi ride to the Wentworths', and then it would be back to reality.

Much to her happy surprise things didn't turn out quite like that. Greg hailed a taxi as she expected he would, and conversed with the driver in Turkish, but instead of making for the residential area over the bridge, they turned towards the old town then took a road that climbed up and away from the lights of the city. Claire had no idea where they were going, and she didn't dare ask. One word from her and Greg might think that she preferred to go straight back to the Wentworths'. She kept her gaze towards the window and watched the lamps and houses give way to fields and hills and a world grey-black in the darkness of night.

She didn't expect the car to stop at the height of this nothingness, but stop it did, and moved off again when Greg had helped her out. She stared after the receding red light and asked, mildly amazed, 'Are you just going to let him go off like that?'

'He'll be back when we want him,' Greg said, taking her arm and guiding her away from the road to a grassy plat-form that hung suspended in the darkness.

She saw at once the reason for the trip, for the whole of the city was spread out below like a carpet of shimmering jewels. She could see the palely-lit mosques, the subdued glow of the bazaars and souks, and the Bosphorus, a wide glistening strip, studded with moving yellow lights. As she continued to gaze on the scene in delight Greg said drily, 'You wanted to see Istanbul!'

'I've really seen it, haven't I?' Claire murmured happily when she could drag her gaze away.

Turning to Greg, she felt she ought to offer some kind of thanks for the trouble he had gone to for her today, but somehow in that moment she couldn't speak. He was stood only an arm-stretch away and with his eyes on her it was difficult to think of words. It seemed in her mind an eter-nity that he stayed there etched motionless against the night, then as the wind rustled around her throat inducing a shiver in her, he moved up to ask in deep tones, 'Cold?'

'A little,' she smiled, hugging her arms about her.

As his arms came up to take their place he eased her back to rest against him and drawled, 'We're lucky to have made the trip up here at this time of year.'

'I'm glad we did,' Claire breathed, keeping her gaze to the front. There seemed to be so many things to be glad about just now; Greg's nearness, the feeling that his lips were close to her hair. When she could concentrate on the view again she vowed lightly, 'I'm going to come back to Istanbul one day.'

'That's what you said about Austria,' Greg pointed out humorously.

'And what if I did?' Claire turned in his arms, her happiness bubbling up into soft laughter. 'What's wrong with being in love with the world?'

'Not a thing.' There was a long palpitating moment when his gaze rested on her upturned mouth. She felt his arms slowly tightening about her like a steel band, then with an abruptness that left her swaying on her feet, the steel band snapped and he was moving away to reiterate sourly, 'Not a *damned* thing!'

For a long time Claire stood gazing at the view and listening to pacing footsteps over the grass. When there was a lull in the pacing, and a lighter flared under a cigarette she asked tentatively, 'Shall we be going down soon?'

'As soon as I've decided what to do with you.'

Claire blinked at Greg's bulk in the dark and asked with a half smile, 'What's that supposed to mean?'

'It means I'm not taking you with me to Tehran. That's what it means.'

The harsh words struck Claire like a blow. In a daze she moved up to him to ask querulously, 'Wh ... when did you decide that?'

'About five minutes ago.' With a slight curl to his lips he looked down at her, then flinging a hand up through his hair he growled, 'Look. The worst of the trip is still to come. The route across the Anatolian plateau can be hell at this time of year. It will be snow and ice all the way, tough going even for the best of us.'

'But I'm fit. You know I am!' Claire turned big eyes pleading to him.

'I said I'm not taking you and that's exactly what I

126

meant,' Greg bit out, swinging away and starting to pace again.

Seeing him walking out of her life, Claire asked shakily, 'How ... am I going to get there?'

'You can take a plane.'

His abrupt manner and the way he was neatly disposing of her brought the tears to her eyes. To hide her hurt she retorted angrily, 'You know I haven't any money.'

'I can supply the air fare.'

'Oh yes!' She tossed him a brittle laugh. 'On top of the two years' wages I owe you for what you've done for me already.'

'You can consider this trip on me, the air fare included,' he stated.

Anything to get rid of her, Claire gulped miserably. When she could find a steady voice she replied acidly, 'Which would make me indebted to you for life. No, thanks!'

'Suit yourself.' He stopped pacing and came to stand over her to drawl, 'I just thought you were keen to get to the fiancé.'

'Oh, I am!' Claire wailed, terrified that she was letting a slender chance slip through her fingers. 'I'm longing to see Robin again.'

'Okay, you take the plane,' Greg said flatly.

That seemed to be the end of the matter until Claire thought to start up again with, 'And what about my job?' She knew she could say goodbye to that, but at the moment she felt desperate enough to grab at anything. 'I have to make some kind of feature out of this trip, you know,' she said coldly, 'and how can I do that if I don't see it through to Tehran?'

'With a wedding coming up you won't need to worry about your job,' Greg sneered. 'A fact you were probably aware of when you wangled this trip.'

For a moment she was knocked off balance. He actually thought that she had never intended anything but a one-way trip! Her incredulity and anger made her retort hotly, 'Well, that's all *you* know! Surprising as it may seem to you, I like to see a job through, and I will too!' Hardly caring what she was saying or doing any more, she turned blindly towards the road with the words, 'If you won't take me to Tehran I'll find a truck that will!'

Greg was beside her in two strides. He grabbed her wrist to say roughly, 'Now listen!'

'I thought you'd said all you wanted to say,' Claire tried to shake herself loose, 'or are you worried I might easily get another truck?'

'Too damned easily for your own good,' he snapped, pulling her against him with a force that knocked the breath from her. When she could speak again she said, suddenly finding that she was enjoying the moment, 'I've noticed the Turkish drivers are friendlier than most.'

'And how far do you think you're going to get in one of their trucks?' A tiny muscle flexed furiously in his jaw as he held her.

Meeting the blazing blue eyes, Claire said evenly, 'That won't be your problem, will it?'

He gripped her so tight she thought she would snap in two, then slowly his whole frame relaxed, and he said, heaving the words out, 'Okay. You want a lift to Tehran. So you've got one.'

Claire gazed up in misty-eyed wonder. 'You mean ... you're going to take me with you after all?'

He let out a sigh to mutter through clenched teeth, 'I was fool enough to fall for that doe-eyed look, back in Holland. I reckon I deserve to be saddled with it all the way to Tehran.' He held her against him for a while, then flung her away to curse softly, 'Where's that damned taxi?'

As though he had rubbed a magic lamp, the taxi headlights came up over the hill and within seconds it was shuddering to a stop at their side. Claire made sure she climbed in unaided, and sat dejectedly against her own window. She might have won her battle to stay with him until Tehran but it was no use fooling herself that Greg wanted her along.

CHAPTER EIGHT

EARLY the next morning Claire dressed dutifully in the shapeless corduroy slacks, thick woollies, and Mike's driving

128

coat. Still obeying the clipped instructions she had received last night, she pulled on the peaked cap and slanted it defiantly over her brow. Greg had taken a dislike to her, and it hurt all the more because she didn't dislike him at all, but she could jolly well pretend to if that was the way he wanted it! Tumbling the rest of her things into her case, she swung it up aggressively and went downstairs. Doctor Wentworth had been called away, but Mrs. Wentworth was there to bid them goodbye. She tilted a twinkling gaze over Claire and said, smiling,

'Now I know why Greg calls you Dave!'

Feeling like a barrow-boy against the other woman's trim-suited appearance, Claire shot a foul glance towards the suede-coated figure in the doorway, but stretched a hand out to say pleasantly, 'Goodbye, Mrs. Wentworth. I'm very grateful to have been able to stay.'

'I hope you'll come back and see us again one day, my dear.' The older woman dropped a kiss on her cheek. 'And bring that young man of yours along!'

'It's time we were on the road,' Greg clipped irritably, turning through the door. He turned back to swing Claire's case up out of her grasp and strode out towards the truck.

Following with Claire, Mrs. Wentworth twinkled, 'I thought it was only Charles who was grumpy in the mornings!'

She stood to one side, folding her arms against the wind as Greg opened the truck door. Hardly caring that they had an audience, Claire shook away his helping hand to say coolly,

'I can manage very well, thank you.'

She saw his twisted smile as she struggled up. When she had gained her seat he slung the door to behind her and strode round to his side to push the luggage in. Seconds later he was kicking the engine into life. As the truck crawled round towards the entrance to the courtyard, Claire waved through the window. It seemed to her as Mrs. Wentworth waved back that the woman's gaze rested rather thoughtfully on Greg.

They made their way towards the car ferry in stony silence, and sailing over the Bosphorus, Claire cast her mind

129

back wistfully to last night, Was it only a few hours ago that she had sailed these waters with Greg, and the world had been a tinselled gold and silver? It seemed like a dream now, with the water rushing by cold and grey, and the buildings dull in the morning light.

It should have been a thrill to land in the East on the Anatolian shore, but she found herself gazing indifferently over trams and pedestrians and lorries all mingling in oriental confusion. The truck climbed away from the noise and chaos and took the road that led to Ismit. As Claire reached absently towards the dashboard, Greg said testily, 'You can forget the map. There'll be so many detours we'll be lucky to get through at all.'

She dropped back and smiled thinly towards the wheel to carp, 'My, we *are* a bundle of fun this morning, aren't we?'

He gave her a look that said if he hadn't been fully engaged with the wheel, he might have replied in actions, not in words, but she thought she saw a flicker of icy humour in the blue eyes. After soaking up the sight of the lean features, Claire turned her gaze airily back to the view. There wasn't much to see, just the road and a lot of dull-looking buildings and the occasional stretch of open country. Had there been anything out of the ordinary, Claire doubted whether it would have held her attention. Her senses were highly tuned to the atmosphere inside the cab and she couldn't for the life of her feel for anything other than that. Every swing of the wheel that Greg took, each quick intake of breath as a child or animal fled across the road, she was aware of. Even when there was barely an inflection of his wrists she knew it, for her pulses jumped along as bumpily as the truck.

Thankfully this suspended state didn't last, for once they were on the main highway, there was little to do but lie back, and with her eyes closed she found the area of calm she had been looking for. When she opened her eyes later, the scene had changed and turning her attention to the string of pretty villages trailing by, she found she could ignore the bulk in the driving seat completely. Well, almost.

Izmit, which in Claire's calculations was about sixty miles out from Istanbul, was a large town trailing down the slopes of a hill, and overlooked by the ruins of an acropolis. The sight of the sombre shapes painted against a wintry sky rekindled all the old excitements within her and in spite of her vows to sit poker-faced, she couldn't help but exude at the fascination of travel, though she was careful to keep her exclamations to herself. Out of Izmit the road crossed a river and by-passed several villages, and then the terrain became barren and mountainous. Snow was thick on the higher slopes, dusting out to frosty stretches over tawny fields and plains. The traffic had thinned out, and only an occasional lorry rumbled by in the opposite direction, the drivers leaning out from their wheels with comradely waves and black-toothed smiles.

Just before the road started to twist upwards, Greg stopped the truck and wordlessly went about the task of fixing the wheel chains. Claire soon saw why. The surface was packed hard with windblown snow and shingle. Even without this hazard it was a miracle that anything could stay on the steep incline. She thought the climb would never end. The truck's progress was about ten miles an hour, and it seemed to her that they would still be clawing up the road at nightfall. Once or twice she saw Greg lean out alongside his window and frown at the instrument panel. Perhaps he wasn't pleased with the truck's performance, for when they finally came out on to a bleak plateau he pulled up off the road and pushed his door open to jump down. He came round to her side of the engine and lifted the bonnet, and seeing that they were going to be there for a while Claire opened her door. The wind smote her as she climbed down, pushing her back against the truck.

Greg looked up from where he was bending and bit out, 'What are you doing out here? You'll freeze to death. Get back inside and make with the coffee.'

With him and the wind against her, Claire didn't waste time arguing, but before she had turned round, Greg added crisply, 'Come to think of it, make that a meal. I don't intend hanging around the *lokantas*. We're pushing straight on for Ankara.'

With an attempt at friendly conversation Claire asked pleasantly,

'Is it far?'

'Far enough,' he barked, giving her the benefit of a steely

131

glare. 'Now get back inside.'

'*All right!*' She swung away from him irritably. 'No need to bite my head off!'

Angry and hurt at the rebuff, she lunged for the door and missed her footing. Before she had time to stumble Greg was behind her turning a steadying arm around her waist. She shook herself free of him to snap, 'For heaven's sake take your hands off me! I'm not an old woman.'

'You can say that again,' he glinted, swinging away.

Up in the compartment behind the cab she breathed away her bad temper, and set to work to prepare a meal. The cupboard had been re-stocked—a task that Greg had attended to no doubt, during their stay in Istanbul—so there was plenty to chose from. When everything was piping hot, she called abruptly, through the window, 'It's ready!'

Greg nodded, screwing on a cap, 'Put mine in the cab.'

She might have known! Slapping the dishes on a tray, she shrilled, 'You'd better come now if you want it hot!'

When there was no response she dropped the tray on the table top that pulled out from the dashboard and jutted her head out of the window pointedly.

He looked up from the spanner he was turning and said icily, 'One thing I *don't* want is a crew mate that sounds like a nagging female. I'll come when I'm through.'

Well, jolly well please yourself, Claire thought, fuming her way back to her own solitary meal.

There was no conversation for the rest of the run before dark, and Claire told herself she couldn't care less. Who wanted to fraternise with a hunk of rock anyway?

She had found out from the map that Ankara was less than three hundred miles from Istanbul, a distance not too far to cover by nightfall in normal circumstances. But there was something very un-normal about the truck's behaviour. As they chugged along, Greg frowned out over the wheel and finally pulled in at a fuel station some thirty or forty miles out from the city. His temper was little improved by the fact that the doors were locked and the building without any signs of life. Claire thought he would simply swing back to the wheel and drive on to the next garage, but either this was the last one before Ankara or he didn't want to take the truck further without attention. Whatever the reason, and

132

she certainly wasn't going to ask, he turned the truck up alongside the building and took it on for several hundred yards to an open stretch of camp site.

Back to the nomad existence, she thought, climbing down and staring at the desolate waste of ground and tall swaying trees. With the fuel station closed and locked up for the night, there probably wasn't another human being within miles of here. Thankfully dim lights had been left burning in the nearby facilities, and exploring Claire found a neat washroom and oh, bliss! warm water and towels. Washed and refreshed, she went back to the truck to see about a meal. She was surprised to find that Greg had built a fire, some way off at the side. As he bent to drop more wood on, the dancing flames picked out terse craggy features and an over-hanging lock of dark hair. Claire carried on to the truck. Much as she would have liked to move up into the golden glow, the reception there didn't look too promising.

It was while she was swinging her way up into the dimly lit cab that something stopped her halfway up and held her there, stock still. At first she thought it was a large black button lying on the seat, until long hairy legs heaved the disc upwards and carried it further along. As it came nearer she stared at it more in fascination than in horror. For one thing she had never seen a spider this size in her life before, and another, this one had great pronounced claws that swivelled busily as it moved. It certainly was an odd-looking creature, Claire twinkled absently, watching it gangle towards the edge of the seat. Maybe she ought to scoop it up and drop it in Greg's lap. That ought to get a smile out of him.

It all seemed mildly amusing until the long hairy legs came probing for their next steps some two or three inches from her throat. She realised then, with sudden revulsion, that if she didn't move the thing would surely drop on her. It occurred to her at the same time that she couldn't jump back, for the step behind her was too high. The only thing for it was to carry on up and sidle her way along the front of the seat somehow.

The legs clawed frantically in space. As she edged herself up she kept a sharp watch on them and the fat furry body wobbling precariously on the edge of the seat. It looked as though she was going to have to pull herself in uncomfortably close to get a foothold up into the cab.

Concentrating on what she was about, she didn't pay much attention to the footstep behind and the sudden sharp intake of breath. The force with which she was grabbed almost stunned her. In the split second that the spider teetered over the edge, she felt herself being whirled away and down to the ground with heartstopping suddenness, then Greg was snarling, 'Don't take the independence *too* far!'

The lightning speed with which he stilled the scuttling shape made Claire ask faintly, 'Wh . . . what is it?'

'Latrodectus.'

He didn't enlarge, but as far as she was concerned he didn't have to. Even the name sounded deadly. And to think she had almost picked it up! The thought drained the colour from her face. She gazed down at the inanimate black ball, feeling a distinct urge to collapse into tears, then Greg was pulling her close against him to murmur gently, 'You're all right now. They're pretty rare at this time of year.'

Wondering how she could have been fool enough to treat the thing so lightly, she quavered, 'How do you suppose it got into the truck?'

'Probably left one warm spot for another somewhere along the way.' Well, she was all in favour of that, Claire told herself, nestling against the wide chest and feeling the muscular arms about her; providing it didn't concern spiders, of course.

The grip tightened as Greg said sternly close to her ear, 'Any more incidents like that, and you yell your head off, understand?'

She nodded against him, prolonging the moment. It was funny to think it had taken an ugly, hairy-legged creature to set the world on its feet again. When she could bring herself to, she drew away and moving towards the cab again managed a light-hearted, 'Well, here we go! If there's anything else up there, I won't bother to use the steps.'

Greg dropped her a grin as he swung her lightly up and then he went back to stoke the fire. They ate later, beside its crackling warmth, Claire curled on a wad of folded blankets, Greg leaning back against the truck, coffee cup in hand. Claire couldn't remember when she had ever felt so at peace

134

with herself. Out there the night might be dark and cold and disturbed, but here the leaping flames gave the little plot an aura of comfort and serenity. She couldn't stir herself to clear away the supper things, but dropped back instead to gaze at the sky frosted with stars and a pale wash of cloud. Greg stayed where he was against the truck.

A long time after when the fire was a deep red glow he came to sit down on the other side of it and lit up a cigarette. Once the lighter flame had died under it, Claire only knew he was there by the pinpoint of red light and his outline black against the night.

Pondering over the day's events it occurred to her to ask after a while, 'What's wrong with the truck?'

'Nothing that a new attachment won't put right,' he said easily. 'If this place opens at a decent hour, we should be in Ankara early in the morning.'

'Do we stop there?' she asked.

'Only to make a delivery at the Embassy and then it's straight through.' He pulled deeply on his cigarette before adding, 'From then on, we'll have to take it as it comes.'

'I won't mind if it's all like this,' Claire smiled, propping her head on her elbow to gaze into the fire.

After a pause Greg asked casually, 'Looking forward to Tehran?'

'Very much,' she replied, taken unawares. And then, making herself look squarely at the reason why she was going, she added meditatively, 'It's almost a year since I've seen Robin.'

'What made him take a job out here?' the question came out of the darkness.

'I don't know,' Claire shrugged. 'Restless, I suppose. Those last few weeks before he left he seemed on edge. I think he wanted to try something new.'

'Known him long?' Greg asked.

'Since I was eighteen,' she smiled reminiscently. 'He and Mike have roamed around together quite a bit, then they met again one night in a club in the West End. Mike brought him back to the flat and . . .'

As she trailed off, sardonic tones beyond the fire tacked on, 'And you keeled clean over at the sight of him.'

'Not exactly,' she tilted her head humorously, 'but it was difficult not to with Robin. I'd never met anyone like him.

135

He was such marvellous fun to be with he took my breath away.' She laughed softly. 'Before I got it back he had bought an engagement ring!'

'And from then on the sun shone every day.' The sardonic tones lapsed faintly sarcastic.

'More or less,' Claire finished lightly, considering the subject closed. She thought it was until after a long moment, Greg asked lazily,

'Don't tell me there were problems?'

'Of course not,' she came back with staunchly. 'Just a minor disagreement. It soon cleared itself up.'

'About money?'

'Robin never gave it a thought,' she smiled absently, thinking of her own often empty purse.

'I take it it was he who was doing the disagreeing?' Greg drawled.

Keeping the light tones, Claire returned, 'I've told you, we sorted it out.'

She saw the cigarette flare and then Greg was asking, 'Sorted what out?'

Put as bluntly as that, there was no skating round the question. She said awkwardly into the fire, 'It was nothing really. Neither of us wanted to rush into marriage and yet ...'

'And yet?'

'Oh, you know... Some men think when they've bought an engagement ring that it's all right to ... that everything's ... you know....' She floundered around, wondering how she had let herself get on to this tack and wishing to heaven she could get off it. She tried to, desperately with, 'Well, Robin just got the wrong idea about me, that's all.'

'You mean after he had given you the ring he considered he was entitled to other things?' Greg's tones were coldly matter-of-fact.

Even so, Claire felt her cheeks flame in embarrassment at his words. Thankful for the darkness, she struggled to find a lighter note and breathed, 'I wish you'd stop playing the heavy aunt!'

'At eighteen I'd say you were in need of one.'

Amused now at his harsh reply, she rose to her feet and putting her hands on her hips, leaned over into the darkness to say impishly, 'My dear Grandfather Millard, girls are married at sixteen these days.'

'And some of them without engagement rings,' he replied obliquely.

Claire didn't know how to take this last remark, but not wanting to spoil this kind of friendly estrangement that they had arrived at she said lightly, 'I'd better get on with the washing up.'

'Leave things as they are tonight,' Greg said, stirring the fire into life. 'It's time you were between the blankets.'

Claire had no arguments to offer on this score. The heat of the fire had made her sleepy. She drifted over to the truck, calling over her shoulder as she went, 'Goodnight, Greg.'

'Goodnight, Dave.'

She set her teeth at his reply. He called her that as a matter of course, yet every time she heard it she cursed the day she had named herself to him as Dave St. Claire.

Rising as soon as she awoke the next morning, she washed and dressed, and got down to the business of putting every-thing in order ready to move. There were no blankets or pillows in the cab, and it occurred to her that Greg must have spent the night by the fire. He wasn't around now, but the fuel station was clattering out sounds of life, so she gathered he had gone off to talk about the truck.

She washed the plastic crockery from last night's meal and tidied the small back compartment, and when everything was neat and shining again she felt justified in relaxing with a cup of coffee. She had just made it when footsteps sounded outside, and looking out she saw Greg strolling up with a garage mechanic. They lifted the bonnet of the truck and talked about its insides, and seeing they were going to be there for some time, Claire went out on the steps to offer, 'I've just made some coffee. Shall I bring it out?'

Greg flicked her a nod and came to take the steaming liquid from her when she reappeared. The mechanic lifted his head. She smiled to say, 'I'd better bring another cup.' She filled one and came back to the door to offer it to the Turk. He was a lightly built young man with black crew-cut hair and a scintillating set of white teeth, and these he flashed as he came to collect the cup. He went back to sip the contents against the front of the truck, and taking his grin from her, he turned it on to Greg to nod, vigorously approving, 'English truck driver got good job.'

Something in the tones made Claire aware for the first time of her jeans and soft sweater and cascading hair. As she met Greg's gaze, he heaved in a breath and jabbed under the bonnet of the truck to say succinctly, 'English truck driver *want* good job. See what you can do.'

Claire turned back inside feeling that her presence was not required. Some twenty minutes later she heard the bonnet being clamped down with finality and Greg was swinging up behind the wheel to start the engine. He must have found it satisfactory, for he went back to the fuel station with one arm across the shoulders of the Turk. When he returned she had donned cap and coat and woollen mittens. For once she didn't mind the heavy clothing, for the air was freezing.

On the road to Ankara she could have sworn that the heating wasn't working, but Greg assured her good-naturedly that it was. He also pointed out that it would be likely to get colder as the altitude got higher. Gazing out at the snow-dark sky and windswept steppe, Claire braced herself for the worst. Perhaps because she *had* done, Ankara came as a pleasant surprise, with its wide two-way boulevards, modern buildings and parks. The people were dressed as in any European city, and there was a distinctly westernised flavour about the theatres and shops.

Greg turned on one of the tree-lined boulevards that twisted its way up a hill away from the city. There were modern houses here, and then Ministries and Embassies and Legations. The British Embassy was situated on top of a hill and any one of its windows must show a marvellous panoramic view of Ankara, Claire decided. As the truck skirted the graceful white buildings she saw a paved courtyard and then formal gardens and crazy-pavemented walks.

Greg pulled up on a small tarmac stretch of road, and unloading a labelled crate strode off with it. Some time later when she was stretching her legs, Claire saw him talking to a beautiful dark-eyed girl in the courtyard. The seconds seemed to stretch into hours as she watched the white smile gleam above the lovely upturned face. Without knowing it, she found herself pacing to while away the years, then at last

Greg was taking one of the slim hands in his and shaking it cordially before swinging away.

When he arrived back at the truck, Claire said with a warped smile, 'What, no embrace? I thought you kissed *all* the girls and said goodbye!'

'I do normally,' he grinned down at her. 'Does it bother you?'

'Of course not,' Claire said airily. 'Why on earth should it?' As he gave her a lift up he said drily, 'That was the wife of a friend of mine.'

'I see,' Claire said primly, wishing she had never made the remark.

From the Embassy it was a winding route that brought them back on to the main highway, and along this they sped away from Ankara and out towards a bare landscape. So far, the roads had been swept of snow, but as they progressed there got to be little to distinguish between the way ahead and the rolling white plateau. Picking its way through, the truck was reduced to half its speed. Occasionally they passed through a huddled village of square almost window-less houses and Claire got her first glimpse of veiled women, and old men in caftans.

At midday Greg pulled off the road near one of these small communities and pushing on the brakes sat back with a deep intake of breath. Though they must have made very poor time, he seemed good-humoured, and after flicking his lighter under a cigarette he dropped her a grin to enquire,

'Not reduced to ice yet?'

Claire smiled back and shook her head. 'I think I'm getting acclimatised.'

She felt the blue gaze lingering on her and to give herself something to do she reached for the map and trailed her finger along the route. Perhaps Greg saw it waver after Ankara, for he leaned over to drop his hand next to hers.

'This is where we want to get to. Erzerum.' He pointed to a town in the north. 'From then on it's straight going to the Iranian border and Tehran. But it's this stretch in between that's the snag.'

She watched his finger trace over the space between Ankara and Erzerum and shrugged, 'It looks perfectly straightforward to me.'

139

'Oh, it is!' he murmured sardonically. 'Apart from earthquakes, avalanches, blizzards ...' As she turned a wide gaze to his he grinned, 'You name it, they've got it!'

Holding on to the glinting blue gaze, she said with a thoughtful smile, 'I know. You've kept telling me how terrible it is. Of course it could have been just to discourage me from coming.'

With his shoulders close to hers, Greg gave her a crooked smile and drawled, 'Let's hope you're right.'

All things being wonderful at the moment, Claire found herself wishing that the geography lesson would go on and on, but after a few seconds' silence, Greg pulled himself into his own seat and went back to drawing on his cigarette.

Claire put the map away and said brightly, 'Well, I suppose I'd better get busy with the tin opener.'

As she made to rise, Greg looked across and said, 'There's a good *lokanta* down the road if you want to sample the local food.'

'Do I?' Always eager to try anything new, Claire raised a sparkling gaze.

Greg hunched his shoulders over the wheel and throwing out his cigarette grinned, 'Okay, then, let's go.'

The *lokanta* looked as though it might be a popular stopping-off place in the summer. Though it was steeped in warmth now from a large central stove and tightly sealed windows, there was a wide area of garden surrounding it, and a shed at the side where tables and rolled umbrellas were stacked, probably waiting for better days. Claire decided to play safe and let Greg choose the meal for her as she had grown used to doing. It would be awful if she chose some quaintly titled dish that turned out to be uneatable. Happily the food was all decidedly eatable and exciting. It wasn't every day that one got to the heart of real Anatolian cooking.

And it wasn't every day either, Claire thought gaping along the road outside afterwards, that one saw a group of big brown bears strutting along upright. As they approached she saw that there were three of them on chains like dogs on leads. Two men holding the leads carried tambourines and bells, and dancing around excitedly was a knot of head-shorn village boys. Bringing up the rear was a couple of over-burdened donkeys.

'Gypsies about to do their act,' Greg said offhandedly, turning her in the direction of the truck.

'Oh, please!' Claire swung back. 'Can't we watch?'

Greg shrugged tolerantly and led her back along the road. The gypsies beamed at the obvious signs of interest, and promptly arranged a circle where each bear was given a stick and coaxed through the motions of getting some sound out of the instruments.

It was a sight for the eyes on that bleak day—three massive bears delicately tinkling bells and tapping drums. Claire was convinced she would never see anything like it again. One of the bears fixed his deep sad eyes on her and rested his head on his loose shaggy coat. She was tempted to put a hand out to touch the fur, but Greg had an arm about her shoulder and drawing her back he said drily, 'That paw can do more than tap a tambourine.'

At the end of the performance he dipped into his pocket and the gypsies went off openly delighted at the payment. Turning back up the road Greg said, sloping a smile, 'Shall we get back to the business of ambling to Tehran?'

Claire tossed him a sheepish look and murmured, 'I do slow you down, don't I?'

He drew her against him and casting a doubtful look around the sky, said vibrantly, 'It's not your kind of slowing down I'm worried about at the moment.'

The snow started to fall almost as soon as they had got back to the truck, but Claire didn't see anything to worry about. The white flakes floated down with a docile gentleness, and spread themselves evenly over the ground. It was true they impeded the truck's progress somewhat, but she gathered that Greg must be used to that by now.

It was late afternoon, when they were travelling along a narrow gorge, that she saw there was another side to the picturesque white cloak. Draped over the curving rolling landscape it only added beauty to the scene, but falling on the steep mountainous slopes it grew top heavy and eventually thundered down to the lowest level. To combat the menace of these snow-falls, engineers had built concrete tunnels at intervals along the route, but none of them had been able to stop the mountainous mass that Greg was pulling up in front of now. Slamming on the brakes, he tilted his gaze up

141

the great white wall and whistled piercingly between his teeth. Claire stared up too, wondering what happened next. There was no comfortable wayside inn to turn to, as there had been in Austria, in fact nothing as far as she could remember for miles, and the size of that snow-fall looked more than an overnight's job to clear.

Greg must have been thinking on similar lines, for he said on a long-drawn-out breath, 'Take 'em, a week to dig through that. We'll have to turn back and take another road.'

'Will it be much out of our way?' Claire asked, watching him swing the wheel.

When he had made the turn Greg shrugged grimly, 'Can't tell. This is the only hard surface road in these parts, so the going's likely to get tougher rather than smoother.'

Claire settled herself down for the detour, taking a philosophical view. It didn't really matter how rough it was, did it, so long as they got through. Once away from the gorge, progress across a barren sweep of land was bumpy but passable. They had a meal on the road and continued again. Claire thought they were getting on rather well until Greg said, frowning up ahead,

'We should have hit the main highway again by this time.' He carried on, hunched over the wheel, and manoeuvring the truck along rough tracks that only just qualified for the name roads. Claire saw one or two signposts, but she couldn't find the villages on the map. Happily a fair-sized settlement showed up in the distance not long afterwards.

When they arrived at what looked like the main square of the village, though in the fading light there appeared to be little signs of life, Greg opened his door, saying as he climbed down, 'I'll go and see what I can find out in the way of information.'

To the sound of yapping dogs in the distance, he strode off towards a rickety line of dimly lit shops and disappeared inside what looked like the local café. Alone in the cab, Claire gazed around with interest. The houses here were old style, with wide eaves, presumably for protection against the winter weather. No more than tiny boxes, they clustered together along the snow-ridged road and spread back among fields and bare clumps of trees. In the distance she could see black birds wheeling under the evening sky, and nearby a group of oxen were treading the snow miserably. It wasn't a scene to excite the interest, but Claire decided on the spur of the moment to investigate the area around the truck. It would be better than sitting here just waiting, and she might see something or meet someone that would make the effort worth while.

The wind whistled about her cheeks as she opened the door. Heaven knew what the altitude was now, but it certainly was colder than cold. Perhaps she wouldn't stay out long after all. Walking, she could hear the snow crunching under her shoes, a lonely sound. She saw a leaning sign that said 'Motorbus' in English, with the equivalent in Turkish written underneath. There was a contraption that looked like a cart, but it didn't have any wheels, so it must have been some kind of a sledge, and nearby was a carriage that resembled the open landaus that were used in English seaside towns. Across from the row of lighted shops where Greg had disappeared, there was another cluster of rickety buildings, and that was all.

It had taken her about two minutes to explore, and shivering, she resolved to be back inside the cab in half the time. Little did she know that it was going to be considerably longer before she sat in her seat again. Since stepping down from the truck she had paid little attention to the gathering crescendo of barking in the distance. Now as she turned, she wavered at the sight. A pack of yellow dogs, with powerful shoulders and bushy tails, came rushing and slithering round the side of a building and straight towards her. She watched them approach, telling herself shakily to stand her ground. It took some doing, but she managed it until they were within a yard of her, then she found herself splayed back against a wall in the midst of some horrible nightmare.

It wasn't because Greg had told her to sing out if she had problems, or that she immediately thought of crying for help. It was the sight of bared teeth and the hot breath on snapping jaws that drew from her a terrified scream.

From nowhere a man appeared, and began beating off the dogs with a stick, and just as suddenly there were figures and faces where there had been no one. Greg came loping across from the café and kicking his way through the thrashing animals, he flung a tense-faced gaze over her, then pulled her jerkily against him.

'You crazy little fool!' he growled. 'Why didn't you stay in the truck?'

'And why didn't you tell me I could get eaten alive if I came out?' she countered tearfully, clinging to him.

His arm tight about her, he cast a glance over the prowling shapes and muttered darkly, 'Village dogs! The bane of all travellers through Turkey!'

'You're not kidding!' Claire quivered, trying to effect a flippant note. It was either that or let the tears have their way, and that wouldn't look good just now, not with half the inhabitants of the village looking on. And what an odd shabbily dressed assortment they were! Overcoated, duffle-coated, pullovered, and robed; some had tattered scarves swathed around their heads, others wore the flat peaked caps that appeared to be the national headgear.

It occurred to Claire, as her heart finally stopped banging against Greg's chest, that there were no women present. What a topsy-turvy world! If this had been an English village, the females would have been the first to investigate the fuss.

While she was telling herself that it was time she tried standing on her own feet again, the man with the stick stepped up from the onlookers and started talking to Greg. Claire listened uncomprehendingly to the babble of words, then Greg was saying down to her, 'He wants to know if you'd like to take a glass of tea at his house? A kind of apology for the dogs.'

The man smiled at her and Claire sent a weak smile back, saying as she did so, 'I can't think of anything I'd rather do more.'

She turned her glance to the ground, searching for her cap that had come off in the fray. Spotting it, Greg picked it up, then with one arm about her he followed the man through the knot of dispersing villagers. His house was only yards away, which probably explained why he had been so quick on the scene. There was a small porch where he promptly slipped off his shoes, and looking to Greg for guidance, Claire followed suit. In stockinged feet she stepped through a door on to a carpet that looked as though it had been knitted out of rope fibre. The walls of the room were supported by

144

slender dark beams and the panels in between had been whitewashed. There was a heavily cushioned divan down one side, and at the back, running along the length of floor and wall, was a kind of continuous rolled pillow with covers on.

The room was warmed by a square iron stove in the middle, and enjoying the cosiness were five barefooted children, their ages ranging from probably five years down. The youngest, a plump baby, was lying on a cushion and kicking happily to himself.

Towering in the small room Greg cast a grin over the children and drawled down to Claire, 'Quite a family!'

The man with his flat cap, jet black eyebrows, and moustache, beamed proudly as though he had understood something of the remark, and reached for gleaming glasses that were lined up neatly on saucers on a small shelf.

As Claire unfastened her coat, Greg took it from her shoulders and draped it on the divan. She noticed for the first time that there was a mound of blanket on a cushion over by the far wall. When it moved, she realised with a slight shock that someone was sitting there, then it came to her why she had seen no women outside. This was the region where the veil was still worn, and the woman huddled there was probably hiding herself from Greg. The husband seemed to find nothing odd in this, and proceeded to pour a pale liquid from a brown enamelled pot on the stove. There were two stools which the men took, and Claire curled on the mat beside the children. The tea had a bitter tang, but it was pleasant and somehow satisfying. She sipped it with four pairs of wide black button eyes watching her every move, and to satisfy the gurgle on the cushion she let a plump fist fasten around her finger and hang on to it.

As the conversation was in Turkish, there was nothing she could say, but from the way he was pointing and nodding, it looked as though the man was giving directions for getting back on to the main highway.

As night dropped over the small window high up in the wall, the clear glass oil lamp fastened to one of the beams came into its own, casting a muted glow over the room and its contents. The huddled shape stirred, and Greg rose to say goodnaturedly to Claire, 'I'd better be getting out of here.'

145

He spoke to the man, and then coming back to Claire told her, 'We'll finish our conversation over the road in the café.'

She gently disconnected her finger from the tiny grasp and pushed herself up from the mat, but Greg was already laying a hand on her arm. She looked up, puzzled, to point out, 'I'm coming with you, aren't I, over to the café?'

'These Turks are no fools,' he smiled drily. 'They don't allow women in their places of relaxation.'

Claire stared and then shrugged a smile to carp, 'And I bet the women complain like mad!'

She watched him stoop his way out and turned back to the children. After a moment the blanket near the wall began to open. Little by little, without appearing to stare, she saw rounded cheeks, a slim straight nose, and beautifully fringed black eyes. As a shy smile radiated the dark features, Claire couldn't help thinking what a sheer waste of beauty, to keep it hidden away like this. She smiled shyly back and that was as far as they got. But the children had suddenly found their nerve, and began romping around noisily, only stopping to tighten up shyly if Claire happened to smile their way.

The mother, at ease now, padded around the room doing small chores and crooning occasionally over the baby. Claire picked him up while the other four children queued up to have their hands and faces sponged. Watching the impish line-up, she saw the little girl, the oldest, had patterned cotton trousers beneath her dress and cardigan. Her brother was similarly clad, and the two toddlers had all-round pinafores over thick woollen dresses. Claire noticed that none of these clothes came off as the children prepared for bed.

The baby struggled up manfully in her arms, and she was happily letting him find his feet on her knee, when Greg came in. He lowered a gaze over her and the gurgling bundle and said a little gruffly,

'We'll hang on in the village tonight. There's no such thing as hotel accommodation, I'm afraid, but Azim says you're welcome to stay here.'

After a conversation with the veiled form against the wall the smiling man nodded vigorously and then beamed over his son on her knee. As she wrestled with the baby's energetic jerks she looked at Greg to ask, 'What are *you* going to do?'

'I'll go back to the café with Azim,' he told her. 'It's reasonably comfortable, and it's only across the road from here. Think you'll be all right?' He lowered a finger to a small fist as she nodded and then turned away to say briskly, 'Sleep well, then. We'll try and get an early start.'

When the men had gone out, the shrouded form came to take the baby from her and started making signs that puzzled Claire. Finally it dawned on her that the mother was offering to take the communal pillow on the floor with the children, while she had the bed. Claire wouldn't hear of it, and smilingly but firmly declined the offer. When she saw the children flopping down with their heads on the rolled pillow and their feet towards the stove, she did the same, just to make sure there was no argument.

With a smile the mother gave up the battle and turning the lamp down to half its glow, she took the baby and ducked down inside her blanket on the bed, just as she had done on the cushion. For a while the children kicked and giggled restlessly, then there was just deep and steady breathing all along the line.

Listening to the peace, Claire raised herself on one elbow and gazed at the row of angelic faces. She dropped back on to the pillow with a twinkle. It certainly was a unique way to spend the night—fully dressed, no blankets, and a thick mat for a mattress. But primitive as it was, it was all spotlessly clean and comfortable and the air from the stove was as warm as any electric blanket. She stared drowsily at the patch of sky through the window, feeling her eyelids grow heavier with every wink of a star.

All was noise and activity before first light—the baby crying to be fed, the children wrestling energetically around the stove. Claire stirred sleepily and then dragged herself up. Greg had said he wanted an early start, and she couldn't have wished for a better alarm clock. She rocked the baby until his breakfast was ready, then smiling her thanks and goodbyes over the family she slipped on her coat and went to collect her shoes.

The snow was falling steadily as she stepped out into the road. Remembering the dogs, she shrank back hastily, but almost at the same time Greg came out of the café over the

147

road. It had only been a few hours since she had seen him, but to Claire it seemed a lifetime. As he strode towards her she soaked up the sight of him, big in the suede coat and dark slacks. The lean weathered features were clean-shaven, the dark hair gleaming and freshly combed. His spruce appearance only served to make Claire more conscious of her own tousled hair and sleep-misted eyes. She said quickly when he arrived, 'I was going to the truck to wash. I didn't want to be a nuisance here.'

Greg nodded and took her arm, keeping a sharp eye along the road as they walked. When they got to the truck he unlocked the door and helped her up, to state easily, 'Take your time. We won't start out until it's fully light. I'll come back in half an hour.'

He turned back along the road and Claire moved into the compartment behind the cab. Well, it was something not to have to rush, anyway. Indulging in the luxury of a kettle full of hot water, she sluiced down and dressed warmly in fresh slacks and sweater. With her hair brushed and her coat back on she felt good enough to spin the world on one finger.

There was another glass of tea at Azim's and a piece of flat wheaten bread, then the truck was being waved and barked on its way out of the village. Greg settled over the wheel and steered the truck cautiously along the snow-packed road. Listening to him whistling softly under his breath, Claire smiled, '*You* must have had a good night!'

'Passable,' he grinned, 'amidst the *raki* and *narghiles*—drink and smoke,' he enlightened her, 'I made out.'

Recalling her own cosy night, Claire stretched blissfully and sighed, 'I slept like a dream.'

'I know.' When she turned a questioning gaze his way, Greg drawled laconically, 'I looked in through the night. It was difficult to pick you out from the rest of the sleeping babes.'

Claire lowered her eyes quickly, feeling the shyness turn her cheeks pink. When a reasonable pause had elapsed she asked,

'Will we get far today, do you think?'

'I wouldn't count on it,' Greg said watching the flurry of snowflakes, 'but we'll do what we can.'

148

CHAPTER NINE

THOSE last twenty-four hours seemed to set the pattern for the days ahead. The snow-plagued truck furrowed its way across the Anatolian plateau, stopping at remote fuel stations and then rocking away again to cross another lonely stretch. Wherever they were, Greg always made a point of pulling in at a settlement or a village for the night, even if it was sometimes off the main route. When there wasn't an inn available, Claire could usually expect to find that he had arranged for her to be welcomed into a family. One night she slept in a mud-built house, another, in a room with nothing more than an iron bed and a rusted sewing machine. She was convinced they would have made better time if they had just pulled off the road and spent the night in the truck, as in the early days, but for some reason Greg was dead set against the idea.

Still, they were making reasonably steady progress, and despite the off-putting stories she had heard, she didn't find truck life in these parts bad at all—until the night of the blizzard.

It had been a day like many others, when the snow fluttered occasionally, or the wind whipped it from the ground and sent it spinning in tornadoes across the plains. Then, when the truck was heaving its way up a mountain road, the wind and falling snow suddenly got together, and gusted and hammered around the windscreen in a frightening way. The sky, the normal pale grey of dusk, dropped blue-black with the furore and within half an hour there were snowdrifts curving up in the beam of the headlights. As the truck began to strain noisily, Claire looked to Greg for assurance, but for once he wasn't offering any. She saw him shoot a scowl of concern at the instrument panel and kick an extra jerk of life from the engine; after that she found she preferred to stare straight ahead.

The drifts started sloping out from the side of the road and joining up with the ones across it and before long the inevitable happened. The truck met one more than a match for its strength and discreetly gave way. For a while Greg jerked at various levers and then clamping his jaw, turned to climb down.

'What are you going to do?' Claire asked worriedly.

'Dig us out,' he clipped. 'We can't risk getting stuck up here.'

Claire knew what he meant. Though the blizzard had blown itself out, the air was positively freezing even inside the truck. She said quickly, 'Let me dig too.' As he let an impatient breath go, she persisted, 'Really, I'd rather help than just sit here.'

He dropped a glance over the small pinched face lost in the cap and coat, and changing his mind nodded, 'It might be better for you to be moving about.'

She jumped down eagerly, telling herself that the drift didn't look too bad, and since the blizzard had been short-lived, it wasn't likely that there would be any more worse than this. She crunched her way down to the back of the truck where Greg was pulling two shovels out from a ledge under the body. Claire took hers, trying not to buckle under its weight. She trod the path that he dug up to the front wheels and then laid in, lifting one shovelful of snow for about every half dozen of his. It was warm work, but not warm enough to keep the raw ice-toothed wind from sawing through her clothes. An hour's digging saw them through the worst of the drift, and the way ahead in the headlights looked a fairly heartening sight. Claire felt quite cheered, but Greg kept his tense expression to the last shovelful.

When they were settled in the cab again she asked brightly, 'Aren't we all right now?'

'Not with a temperature of thirty below zero working on every movable part of the truck,' he said grimly. 'It's a question of what's frozen over while we've been stuck here.'

Claire watched as he tested the levers. The solid ungiving sound of a foot pedal made her pull in her lip uneasily. She waited, not daring to ask, and then Greg dropped back and muttered tautly. 'There had to be something. The brakes are out of action.'

'The brakes?' She flung her eyes wide, unable to imagine being without *them* on the descent. 'Well, good heavens! What can you do now?'

'I'll have to jack up the axles and free them,' he replied,

150

already on his way.

'I'm coming too,' Claire put in, hoping to be able to act as a useful crew mate. Whether she was any help or not, it kept her mind off the cold pretending she was. Handing various tools, she got her fingers oiled up and there were probably smudges on her face where she had flicked a wisp of hair back under her cap, but who could worry about looks at a time like this?

Greg dropped a lopsided grin over her as she worked beside him, but there was a drawn look about him that did nothing to curb her anxieties. He laboured for a long time with ungloved hands, gritting his teeth against the rawness of the night and then, flinging the tool down, he pushed a hand up through his hair and barked, 'We're not going to beat the cold at this rate. It will be into the tanks next.'

'You mean the fuel could freeze?' Claire looked aghast.

'It can and it will unless we get some fires going under the tanks and the engine. Not wood fires,' he corrected as Claire sent a puzzled gaze over the snow-laden terrain. 'A tin with a few rags soaked in diesel oil will keep the area heated.'

The gently flickering tins gave a camp-fire touch to the surroundings, but offered barely a pin-prick of warmth in the vast space of cold. Though she tried to keep moving, Claire found her limbs shaking non-stop. Battling with the brakes, Greg looked to be carved out of ice. Every now and again he went to re-soak the rags to keep the fires burning and then they would move on to another axle.

Claire had no idea how long the operation would have taken if Greg had had the assistance of a real crew mate, but she guessed, dejectedly, that it would have been a lot quicker than this. She wouldn't have blamed him if he had ranted on at her incompetence, but he just worked at the brakes, tight-lipped and silent. What his thoughts were she couldn't tell, but it didn't occur to her that they were fighting a losing battle until he went to tend the weakly flickering fires and returned almost at once. He pulled her up from where she was stooped under the truck prodding energetically, and said flatly, 'Forget it. There's nothing more we can do. We're stuck.'

'But we're almost finished,' Claire said exhaustedly. 'And the fires...'

'They're out. The diesel oil's like treacle. Too thick to syphon off.'

She looked dazed at his words, then said on a breath, 'What about the solid fuel for the stove?'

'I used most of it to get the fires going. We've only got a couple of blocks left. They wouldn't help.'

'So that's it, then?' She said the words, but it took her numbed senses some time to grasp their meaning. No fires! No comfort at all! And no hope of getting any for who could say how long? While there *had* been hope she had been able to fix her sights on it, to tell herself that it wouldn't be long before they were off this wretched mountain. Now Greg's words were the last blow to her morale. It was no use pretending any longer that she wasn't frozen to the bone.

As she began to shake uncontrollably Greg clipped, 'Inside. You won't solve any problems out here. Luckily we've kept the doors and windows closed in the cab, so what heat there is in there will stay for a while.'

The thought of a seat after hours of activity and struggle made Claire slump almost before she arrived at the door. Greg hoisted her up at the driving seat side, then swung himself up, closing the door quickly behind him.

If there was any heat in the cab it was a long time making itself felt. Vaguely aware that Greg had gone into the back compartment, she sat in a stupor waiting for something to happen to her numb fingertips and face. She wouldn't have believed it possible, but within minutes she was engulfed with an overwhelming desire to sleep. Just when her head was nodding blissfully, Greg came back into the cab with steaming coffee. She took one look at the cup he held for her and turned away to slump, 'Oh, I feel too worn out to....'

'Drink it,' he snapped, 'if you want to stay just worn out.'

He seemed to be getting testier by the minute and Claire found herself obeying meekly. She had to admit that the coffee went a little way towards thawing her out, but the effect was short-lived. There didn't seem to be anything to beat this kind of cold. Placing her empty cup down, she rose stiffly and moved towards the sliding door. The back compartment was like an ice box. She expected any minute to see the walls frosting over. Thinking about bed, she didn't see herself removing one item of her layer of clothing, or for that matter battling with her grubby appearance. Things would have to stay strictly as they were tonight.

Consoling herself that at least they had the truck for shelter against the howling wind, she went to pick up the tray from the cab and said through chattering teeth, 'Goodnight, Greg.'

He turned round and settled his glance on her, then lowering it to the cups he said briskly, 'Get rid of them and then get back in here.'

Muddleheaded, Claire did as she was told. Dropping into her seat afterwards, she asked pettishly,

'Are we going to sit up all night?'

'Not as far as I know,' Greg said matter-of-factly, pulling the sliding door closed and turning the step over to make a continuous padded seat. 'I could do with some sleep.'

'Well, so could I,' said Claire, staring mystified at his movements. 'But shouldn't I . . .?'

He followed her gaze towards the back compartment and snapped, 'To hell with convention tonight. It's more important to get through it.' Settling down, he dropped an arm about her shoulders and pulled her against him, adding flatly, 'And you won't do that unless you stick close to me.'

Well, who was arguing with that? Nuzzling her cheek into the suede-coated shoulder, Claire had only one small grumble to voice inwardly. It would have been nice if he could have held her a little less impersonally than, say, one of his delivery packages.

She must have dropped off to sleep with the wish firmly fixed in her mind, for it seemed in her dreams . . . or was it half waking? . . . that Greg's hold softened, and once or twice when she shivered from the cold, his arm tightened to draw her closer.

An excruciating stiffness finally awoke her. She stirred painfully and opened her eyes. There was a mist inside the windows and the cab had that vivid brightness that dazzles the vision when snow is all around. From the shoulder she was resting against she looked up and saw Greg looking down at her. There was the stubble of grey-black bristles on his chin and the blue eyes were creased and slightly bloodshot. He sloped her a worn grin to comment, 'Not exactly the Hilton for comfort, was it? But we got through.'

Claire forced a wan smile and sat forward to stretch wincingly. Every bone in her body seemed to creak at the effort. The reflection she caught of herself in a clear patch of her side window horrified her. She saw a streaked, drawn face with a washed-out paleness, and eyes dull and fatigue-smudged. The wisps of hair that sprouted from her cap gave her a Mrs. Mopp look, and if that wasn't bad enough, a thick smudge of oil was nicely imprinted down the front of her sweater. She grimaced away from the sight. Wasn't it just her luck to have Greg see her like this? Cursing and yet feeling too wretched to bother she asked glumly, 'What do we do now?'

'*You* don't do anything,' Greg said, straightening his tie and flicking back the lock of dark hair. 'I'll walk up the road and see if there are any signs of life.'

'Around here?' Claire slumped despondently as he jumped down. 'Who'd want to live up a mountain?'

He turned to glint at her warningly before shutting the door. 'Just don't get it into your head to go trying to find out. You stay put in that seat. Understand?'

'Don't worry,' Claire shuddered wryly at the sight of frost-spangled snow. 'Wild reindeers wouldn't drag me away!'

As he slammed the door she huddled down into her coat, trying not to think of all the luxuries that would have been on hand if there had been a nice big modern motel lurking just round the corner. She heard Greg crunch off up the road and settled down to doze, expecting him to be gone at least half an hour. When footsteps sounded again in a matter of minutes, she jerked up, wondering who could be striding along at this hour, and in these conditions. A rub at the windscreen showed Greg returning, and feeling that he must have some news, she opened the door and almost fell out, in her eagerness. He came up frowning, but allowing the ghost of a smile to show through.

'There's a road camp about two hundred yards from here. It's not the place I would have chosen'—he swung her down into his arms, to tack on—'for you, but it's better than what we've got here.'

Claire was in half a mind to tell him she could walk the distance, but he wouldn't have taken any notice anyway, and it was rather nice to have him carry her over the freezing cold snow. There was so much of it, about she realised that there must have been another fall through the night.

The camp, a cluster of corrugated huts, was just around the bend in the road and ironically just out of sight from where the truck had seized up last night. Obviously work was hampered by the freezing conditions for huge machines were standing idle and muffled men scuffed around blowing warm air into their hands. There was a glowing red brazier in the centre of the huts, and here other men, perhaps another shift, were sat on boxes drinking from tin mugs. Greg put her down when they came into view, and held on to her arm only when she needed it, as she stepped as best she could through the snow. He made towards the fire and spoke to one of the men, who in turn referred him, with a grubby finger, to another man who was standing in a group some distance away.

Greg went off and Claire crept up to the fiery embers, feeling the hot blast hit her like a solid blow after hours of knowing only bitter cold. Gradually her cheeks began to glow and her fingertips to throb achingly as they thawed out. Expanding in the warmth, she unbuttoned her coat and pulled off her cap. She saw the men around the fire eyeing her curiously and the feel of clean silken hair falling about her grimy oil-smeared appearance gave her back a little of her equanimity.

She didn't know that Greg had finished his conversation with the man across the clearing until he stepped up, and clapping the cap on her head, grabbed her by the arm and swung her roughly towards a nearby hut. She was inside before she could take a breath and then he was biting out, 'Can't you *look* what you're supposed to *be*, a truck driver's mate, just for once?'

At first Claire was too surprised to speak and then the anger at his fierce hold on her, coupled with the pent-up misery of all the discomforts of the past few hours, made her retort hotly, 'Just once? I like that? Since I've known *you* I've never been allowed to look like anything else. If you had your way I'd be smoking a pipe and wearing hob-nailed boots!'

She couldn't fathom the teeth-clamped look he gave her,

but it wasn't one of amusement. Perhaps it was her imagination, but it seemed to her that *his* mood had something to do with their night-long stay in the cab of the truck too. He paced thunderously, then spun round to snap, 'There are thirty-odd men marooned up here in this camp. How do you think they're going to feel with you swishing your perfumed hair under their noses?'

Claire felt her cheeks go pink, but she tossed her head to say coldly, 'My mind doesn't work like yours.'

'Well, it had better start,' he growled. 'You're a long way from home.'

There was a long raging silence in which Claire made an airy pretence of examining the interior of the hut and Greg stayed granite-faced near the door, then the ramrod frame slackened and lumping together certain personal effects that were scattered about he said in tones a fraction less harsh, 'The foreman has allocated you his hut. I'll bring your case and some blankets up later. He said something about hot soup. Want some?'

Feeling completely drained after this sudden and unexpected eruption, Claire nodded wordlessly. As he turned at the door she said quickly,

'Greg, do you think we'll be here long?'

'I hope not.' He followed her gaze over the cold comforts of a workman's hut; a bunk, a bare trestle table with a tin bowl, and a bar of soap on it, and a small set of steel drawers. 'We'll just have to sit tight and wait for the thaw. When it comes we'll be rolling in no time.'

But when was it going to come? That was what Claire asked herself every frost-crackling morning. She longed for a good hot bath and something to eat a little different from the road workers' diet. Though there was food enough in the truck, the men had rallied around so wonderfully when they had heard of its plight, Claire gathered that Greg wouldn't want to risk offending them by refusing what they offered.

Ever since Istanbul she had never ceased to be amazed at the change in the dour unsmiling Turks once they got to know you, and the road workers proved to be no exception to the rule. After an uncertain beginning she found the men generous, gentle-hearted, and quite full of fun, and there was

156

much hilarity round the fire when she tried to get them to say a word of English.

Greg was the only one who was dour and unsmiling these days. In fact, he seemed to tighten up a little bit more each time she saw him. He made several daily treks to work on the truck and Claire was expected to go along too, though she did nothing but stand around when she got there. She began to resent being dragged away from the comfort of the fire and the friendliness of the men, and one afternoon when she saw him striding towards her, she decided to stay firmly where she was in her seat. As usual he gave her that authoritative flick of the head that told her to get up and follow him. Trying to ignore it, she looked up crossly to say, 'Why do *I* have to go every time?'

'Because where I go, you go.' He took her arm, pulled her up, and pushed her ahead of him. Angrily Claire spun round to snap,

'Look, I know I've been nothing but a nuisance to you ever since we started this trip, but that doesn't give you the right to push me around!'

'Doesn't it?' Menacingly he dropped his hands on her shoulders and jerked her forward.

Claire shook away from him again to retort, 'No, it doesn't!'

The men, who had no idea what was going on, watched the exchanges with puzzled delight. Quaking a little now, but lifting her chin spiritedly, Claire stood her ground to say, 'And I'll have you know that I don't intend to move from here!'

'Oh, you don't!'

A murmured hush rippled round the fire as Greg moved in. He stopped for a moment to tower over her, then before she could anticipate his move, he swung her up roughly into his arms. As he strode off, with her kicking frantically to be released, a roar of throaty applause went up from the men. Catching sight of them nudging one another knowingly, Claire felt her cheeks blaze a brighter red than the glowing embers of the fire.

The heat didn't subside until Greg dropped her unceremoniously beside the truck. When she could contain her temper enough to speak, she sneered shakily, 'I suppose you think you're very clever? Well, let me just say that I ....'

'You can cut out the acid remarks,' Greg clipped, looking over the truck, and then nodding towards the back compartment, 'See if you can still remember how to make coffee.'

'I see,' Claire fumed from a heaving bosom, '*I* can cut out the acid remarks, but it's all right for *you* to keep the sarcasm. But then you've probably got special privileges!'

'I have,' he smiled down at her annoyingly, '*I'm* the boss.'

Claire flung herself away and went to make the coffee. Some time later when her natural demeanour had returned she couldn't help viewing her recent antagonism with Greg with a certain wistful unhappiness. She knew what was wrong with him, of course. They were coming to the end of their journey, and he must be cursing every day that he was stranded with her here.

Claire wanted to be moving to, but for different reasons. She longed to be back on the old footing with Greg. When she could talk and laugh a little with him, and he wouldn't be too impatient to explain the things she found interesting. That time seemed to be ever out of reach until one morning, five days after the truck had got stuck, the dawn sky was warmed by pale fingers of sunshine, and the sparkling ice-encrusted snow began to drip and trickle in a chatter of busy activity. It wasn't long before the road machines were rolling, and without bothering to check up on the truck's performance, Greg was swinging up the bags and nodding his farewells around the men. He shook hands with the foreman and drew Claire forward to do the same. She just had time to wave around before she was hustled off down the road.

To hear the truck start up the first time it was almost impossible to believe it had been frozen to a standstill for so long. It rumbled forward, swishing the slush from its wheels, and gradually picked up speed. Greg sounded the horn as they went past the camp and a flurry of road implements shot up in salute. Then they began the climb that would take them the rest of the way up the mountain road and down somewhere near Erzerum.

As though he wanted no more hindrances, Greg kept up a stiff speed and they arrived in the garrison town while it was still early in the morning. It had taken them two weeks and one day to travel the six hundred and thirty odd miles from Ankara.

Claire saw an ancient citadel with a leaning tower and thick ugly walls and then a main street with food stalls and taxis and several multi-storied buildings. She rather hoped that they might take advantage of this brush with civilization to sample some of its luxuries, but a brush with it was all she got, for Greg kept going. Soon there were only the peculiar village houses with humped haystacks on their flat roofs looking like fair straggling wigs, and then they were back on to a narrow mountainous route. Mid-morning they stopped to sample the refreshment facilities of a fuel station and later pulled in at a *lokanta*, but the accent was definitely on travel today and the truck wheels never stopped spinning for long. Claire didn't need the map now to tell her that they were heading for the Iranian border. Erzerum was the last reasonably sized town in Turkey, and that was well behind them.

Even as she thought of it the Turkish and Iranian Customs signs loomed up along the road. She gazed ahead eagerly, wondering if there would be any change in the scenery, and Greg, looking sufficiently mellowed now after his burst of action, nodded to her left and drawled,

'Mount Ararat.'

Claire considered she had had a surfeit of mountains these last few days, but the gleaming white peak and massive shoulders of Ararat were a sight to take the breath away. She also nursed a tiny glow of pleasure that Greg had thought to point it out to her. She hoped it was a sign that he could stand the sight of her again.

Watching as he chivvied the truck forward in short spurts up the Customs queue, she had plenty of time to study the lean face and its mood. Relaxed and smiling with the Customs men, he seemed his usual self. A little travel-worn, perhaps. The lines on his face were deeper etched these days, the white smile somewhat tight at the edges.

But then ... Claire gazed down at her own appearance. What must she look like after living rougher than rough for five days? Ten times worse, probably. Oh, for the luxuries of a hot bath and a shampoo and the feel of smooth sheets again!

She kept this dream uppermost in her mind, but nothing

159

materialised and the truck sped on into Iran and to the outskirts of Tabriz, the last big town before Tehran.

It was pitch dark when they arrived and Claire saw nothing, but she was past looking anyway. The only thing that interested her were the lights of a ramshackle motel and its rooms spreading back from the road. As it was past eleven, Greg wasted no time in swinging the bags down and ten minutes later Claire was freshening up as best she could in a small room with limited facilities and pulling wearily into pyjamas. It wasn't until later, lying in bed, that she allowed herself to think fleetingly on the fact that tomorrow they would be in Tehran. But only fleetingly. It wasn't here yet. was it? And after all, it was something like four hundred miles away. Perhaps Greg might spin it out to two days.

She blinked up into the darkness, knowing that she was fooling herself there. Something about the businesslike set of those shoulders, the determined grip on the wheel, told her that Greg would make it Tehran tomorrow or bust.

CHAPTER TEN

As though to confirm her last waking thoughts he was knocking on her door at first light the next morning. Claire rose and washed and pulled into her truck clothes, actually experiencing a pang of regret at wearing the accursed driving coat and cap for the last time. Taking her seat in the truck, she didn't let her gaze hang too long on the figure over the wheel. Just long enough to catch the blue glance trailing over her, with a light there that she couldn't fathom, and his taut smile.

The sky was arranging itself into patterns of blue and gold as they drove towards the city. For once the greenery of orchards, vineyards, and groves was not clouded with snow. There were remnants of it at the side of the road and on the outlying hills, but the air had that sharp sweet sparkle of spring about it. Claire felt slightly effervescent herself. It was a beautiful day and Greg had smiled and she still had a little time left with him. Could she help it if she wanted to hang on to every minute of it?

The truck seemed to sing along with her mood, the world outside wax more colourful with every second. She saw slender minarets again and blue-domed mosques. Along mud-walled streets, veiled women were doing their early morning wash in the gutters, and outside the carpet shops, turbanned bearded men were beginning to haggle over the day's business.

Awakening to the real feel of the East, Claire asked musingly, and with a hint of regret, 'I wonder why they dropped a beautiful name like Persia for "plain Jane" Iran?'

'Who can say?' Greg shrugged good-naturedly. 'Maybe Iran sounds just as beautiful to them.'

'Maybe.' Claire pondered for a while, then bounced to the edge of her seat to state, 'Well, I shall still call it Persia. The name conjures up all the ... well, you know....' She stared fascinated at a man in a red fez and balloon flapping trousers, and Greg grinned.

'In a Persian market place ... and all that?'

Persia or Iran, it was to Claire's mind the loveliest country so far. At first there was only the usual roadside nothingness, but later in the day she sat dazzled at the sight of mosaic palaces and shrines and lace-like minarets.

She half suspected that Greg had digressed a little from the normal route to take these in, for when it grew dark he turned the truck away from the sights and they spent the time after that, speeding along a wide busy strip that could only be the main highway for Tehran. Now she had nothing to do but to keep the thoughts of their arrival locked in the back of her mind.

It gave her a peculiar jolt to see the name of the city with the diminishing number of miles rising up at the roadside every now and again. To her, Tehran had always been some mythical place that need only be talked about. Now here it was looming up on the horizon. Of course she ought to be feeling a wild thrill of accomplishment at actually having completed the trip, but strangely enough, there was nothing like that inside her. All she was aware of was a heavy heart-dragging sadness, and the wish that Tehran would stay forever mythical in the distance.

The road zipped by behind them and the buildings started

to rise up in the darkness. As the truck wheels spun nearer and nearer their goal, Claire knew that the city was all too real and she would soon have to be saying her goodbyes to Greg. He had done her a favour in bringing her all this way, but that was all it had been—a favour. Once they reached their destination his obligations were finished.

When they were pressing on into the city she wondered how she would get through the parting. Should she offer a hand and shake his politely, or should she reach up and drop a light kiss on his cheek?

She could feel the letter with Robin's address on it crackling in her pocket, and any minute now she would be stepping down from her seat in the cab for the last time. She hadn't really thought of how she would get to where Robin lived, but perhaps a taxi, with a promise to pay at the other end, might be in order.

In the darkness she couldn't tell where Greg was taking the truck. He swung and turned through a succession of dimly lit streets, then it seemed to her that he was backing alongside a warehouse similar to his own in London. There was the shutting off of the engine, the securing of the brakes, and in the silence he was reaching for the luggage. Trembling madly, Claire climbed down her side and went round to collect her case.

Greg already had it in his hand. He slammed and locked the doors, then swinging up his holdall in his other hand he said, moving off,

'We've got quite a walk, but I doubt whether we'll get a taxi in this area.'

Her insides catapulting with anti-climax, Claire stepped up to him and jerked through a strained laugh, 'I thought this was where we parted company?'

'It is,' he said testily. 'But I can hardly drop you into your fiancé's lap in the middle of the night. We'd better wait until morning.'

He lifted an arm, instructing her with a flick of his head to slot hers through. Claire did so musingly. It was late, but not that late. Still, who was she to argue?

Stumbling over strange ground in the dark with Greg's arm for support she was reminded suddenly and blindingly of those other nights. The one in Germany when he had

162

guided her through the inky blackness to the motel set back from the road. And the time when he had carried her wrapped in blankets through the courtyard in Bulgaria. How far away it all seemed now, and yet somehow incredibly close. It was crazy, but she believed she would give anything to be back at the beginning again.

Up towards the brighter lights Greg hailed a taxi and a short while later they were pulling up in front of a huge impressive-looking hotel. At first Claire thought there must be some mistake, that they would probably walk on to something down one of the side streets, but the driver was already hurrying across the pavement, a bag in each hand, and taking her arm, Greg led her towards the gleaming glass doors. In the beautiful muted glow of pink tinted lights she saw marble floors stretching endlessly in the distance towards arched alcoves and more soft lights. A huge Persion carpet was spread in the centre of the vast space of the foyer and dotted around, dark-eyed, olive-skinned attendants stood arms folded, each one resplendent in mustard and gold uniform and wine-red fez.

Greg seemed to be well known, judging by the salutes and smiles he got on the way to the desk. He went through the usual formalities of booking in and came away with two keys and the tail end of a white smile after his conversation with the receptionist.

Standing alone and small in the fantastic size of the place, Claire felt blazingly conscious of her dusty truck clothes and travel-worn appearance, but Greg came up and guided her through the gold and white interior, past sequin-gowned ladies and dinner-jacketed men, without flicking an eyelid. A lift attendant dressed similar to the ones in the foyer took them up to the third floor, then they were whispering over deep pile carpets past lounging settees, glass-topped tables and ornate pitchers holding tall feathery fronds.

Greg stopped at a door about half way along the hall and turning the key led the way inside. He waited for the porter to drop the bags, thrusting his hand into his pocket for a tip, and Claire turned around, taking in the size of the room and its lush comfort. There were pastel-shaded armchairs and stools, mirror-polished lamp-lit dressing tables and a huge satin-draped bed. She couldn't bear to stay clumsily dressed any longer in such surroundings, and quickly pulled out of her coat and cap. Feeling a little like someone in soft fleecy sweater and jeans, she tossed her hair loose and went to finger a bowl of waxen blossoms.

Greg hadn't moved from where he had stopped near the bags. Turning to him, she thought they might have dropped into an easy conversation now that the porter had gone, but he stayed silent, his gaze on her. Meeting his eyes in that peculiar stillness, Claire found herself suddenly knotted up with an excruciating shyness. All this was so vastly different from the unfeeling, impersonal inside of a truck cab. Though she had sat next to him in its small confines, she felt overwhelmingly, shatteringly closer to him now, even though he was at the other side of the room. Her heart buckling, she dived for something to say and came up with a high-pitched, 'I've got Robin's address in my pocket. Do you think I ought to try and get in touch with him?'

Greg seemed to slacken his frame gradually. He bent to pick up his bag and turning to the door, said curtly, 'I'll see you in the morning. We'll take it from there.'

She heard him turn the key in the door next to hers, listened as it closed with a quiet click behind him, then fell into a glorious whirl of returning to femininity with a perfumed bath, shampoo, and hand and face cream massage. Swishing around in soft mules, lacy nightdress, and negligée, she enjoyed pottering over small insignificant little tasks, and finding herself unable to decide what to wear tomorrow, she hung everything but jeans and sweaters in the wardrobe so that whatever she chose, it was bound to be crease-free. It was very late when she finally climbed into bed, but she spent several minutes luxuriating in the feel of nylon sheets and pillow slips, before dropping off into a dreamless sleep.

Her awakening was nowhere near as tranquil. Flickering her eyelids at the sound of honking traffic and the feel of bright sunlight, she shot up and flung an alarmed glance at her watch. Good heavens, look at the time! She was almost out of bed before she realised that there was no truck schedule to keep today, and Greg wouldn't be waiting leaning over the wheel for her to join him. A heavy depression settled over her at the thought. It had been fun sloughing her crew mate's image last night, but now there didn't seem to be anything to take its place. She scuffed off to get washed, wondering when the excitement at seeing Robin again was going to bubble up. She tried to dress with him in mind, but somehow all she could think of was how a certain pair of glinting blue eyes would see her in pale primrose suit, sheer nylons and slim-heeled shoes.

Silken hair swinging, she ventured out of the door and into the hall. It was quiet out here, so quiet she could hear her own heart beating erratically. Why, she didn't know. There wasn't a sign of anyone. She was just about to shoot back into her own room when the door next to hers suddenly swung open and Greg stood there. He trailed a glance over her and then turning it briskly to the watch on his wrist he commented drily, 'Good job we had no tight driving to do today.'

'That's what I thought when I woke up and saw the time,' Claire laughed, half sheepish, half keyed up with shyness again. When she could bring herself to lift her gaze from the carpet she said a little breathlessly, 'Well, I suppose I'd better be on my way to see Robin?'

Greg closed both doors and took her arm to say on a slightly sour note, 'I think he'll keep until we've had breakfast.'

Downstairs Claire was led into a french-windowed dining room, where white-clothed tables flanked green gardens and stubby palms. White-coated waiters moved smartly about and Greg ordered suavely for two, as though he was well aware of her likes and dislikes by this time.

Watching him across the table, her heart almost overbalanced. Rugged as she had come to know him in hardwearing slacks, polo-necked sweaters and the big suede driving coat, there was no denying the fact that dressed as he was this morning in expensive lightweight suit, crisp shirt and tie, he went well with these surroundings.

It was a leisurely meal and one that Claire felt herself to be achingly in tune with. The soft tinkle of silver and glassware around the tables, the gentle whisper of patron's requests, and the murmured strains of music coming faintly from all sides; it was as though everything was striving for perfection for this her last morning with Greg. There was no conversation at their table. Had there been it might have spoiled things. Even though they were rising before Greg spoke, it had that effect. As he held her chair for her he asked brusquely, 'Got the fiancé's address?'

'It's upstairs in my handbag,' Claire said, putting on a smile. 'I've got to collect my luggage anyway.'

He nodded and led the way out. Back upstairs he stood around while she folded everything into her suitcase and then handed her her briefcase and documents to go on top. When she was finished and ready to go he dropped a glance over her lightly clad figure and commented, 'You might need a little more on against the cold. Have you got a light coat or something?'

'I've got a mac.' She looked up for his approval and opened her case. He took the stone-coloured silk from her and held it open for her to slip into. As it came around her shoulders she felt it trap her hair down, but before she could reach up to flick it out, Greg had the tresses in his hands and was spreading them over her collar. There was a moment when he came close enough for her to lean against him. She even thought she could feel his breath in her hair, and then he was saying roughly,

'Well, what are we waiting for? Let's get going.'

CHAPTER ELEVEN

AN added disappointment to the many that Claire was experiencing at the moment was her first sight of Tehran in the daylight. With tall modern buildings and wide main streets it looked no different from any other big city. It was only when she saw the breathtaking view of snow-ridged mountains dropping down to the very street ends, and the people, a strange mixture of East and West, that her interest perked up. She stepped forward, eager to see what there was to see, but Greg was already drawing her to a halt and hailing a taxi.

Not bothering to hide her disappointment this time, Claire pleaded, 'Oh, can't we walk a little?'

'No, we can't walk a little,' he returned testily.

The mask-like expression that she had turned to find after being helped on with her coat was still there—a clear sign, Claire told herself miserably, that Greg was becoming impatient to be rid of his last delivery. As the taxi sped on its way she sat meekly in her seat, feeling like a child being delivered home by an austere uncle.

The address that Robin had scrawled on the top of his last letter to her was a house over-arched by tall trees, on the outskirts of town. Walking along the path and up the steps leading to the alcoved doorway, she felt her knees getting weaker and weaker, not so much for what was up ahead as for what was being left behind. Her suitcase was at her feet, the bell had been rung, the taxi was ticking over in the road. The stage was set for Greg to step out of her life for ever.

She heard the bell jingle again distantly through the house and a dark-eyed servant appeared. Greg stepped up. She stood behind the big frame ready to be ushered inside. Ready, yet hanging on as though her heart would never let go of the sight of a lean, worn profile, the dark slightly curling hair.

The conversation was going on. She heard Robin's name being passed backwards and forwards. Ashamed of her own lack of interest in the name and jolted into a sudden mood of concern, she pushed forward to say quickly. 'What's wrong? Where's Robin?'

Greg turned and ordered, 'Get back into the cab and wait.'

Terrified that she was going to hear some awful news when she hadn't even been giving it a thought, she said chokingly, 'But I want to know. Something's happened to Robin, hasn't it?'

Greg dropped an arm about her shoulders and drooped a worn smile to say gently, 'Take it easy. Nothing's happened. It's just that your fiancé hasn't been living at this address for some time.'

'You mean,' she blinked up, 'he's moved?'

'That would appear to be the case,' Greg replied, the harsh tones returning.

'But where?' Claire directed her question past him, but the servant could only shrug and lift his hands apologetically. Greg nodded his thanks, picked up the case, and led the way back down the path. Hurrying alongside, Claire asked worriedly, 'What can I do now?'

'Have you got the name and address of his firm?' Greg clipped.

'Well, yes, I have,' she looked up dubiously, 'but I don't think he would want me to involve them in ...'

Greg threw her case in the back of the taxi with such force she feared for its safety. 'You've travelled three thousand miles to be with him,' he bit out. '*Someone* should get involved!'

Miserable at his mood, she huddled in her corner, until they arrived back at the hotel. He strode off with her case and her coat, led her through into the lounge where a cup of coffee was waiting for her on a crystal-topped table, and went off to phone Robin's firm. Ten minutes later he was back, nodding for another cup of coffee. Watching her, he draped down in his seat to drawl, 'Brace yourself. The boyfriend has been dismissed from the job he had in Tehran.'

Claire jerked forward, wide-eyed. 'But that's not possible.... Surely he would have told me?'

Greg pushed a slip of paper towards her. 'I got on to a friend of his. He's given us one or two addresses to follow up in the city where he thinks he might be.'

Claire dropped back in relief. 'Well, thank heavens he hasn't left Tehran anyway.'

'Thank heavens.' Greg twisted a smile down at his coffee. When he had finished he rose to say matter-of-factly over the slip of paper, 'Looks like you're going to get your walk after all. Most of these addresses are down streets too narrow for a taxi.'

Claire was soon finding that out for herself, and she wasn't sure she cared for the dark overhanging alleyways, only a stone's throw from the main busy thoroughfare. The first house they tried looked reasonable enough, but after that the people answering the doors seemed to get more shifty-eyed, the neighbourhood more sinister. She told herself it was only because the sun couldn't get down to brighten up the place. Just the same she was glad when Greg decided to take a break and go back to the hotel for a meal.

It was late afternoon when they set out again. The spring sunshine was fading to leave a cool greyness over everything. Shivering slightly, Claire felt Greg's hand grip her arm tighter as they walked. She looked up to say dejectedly, 'I can't keep on taking your time like this. You've probably got things to do.' When he didn't reply she asked, 'Shouldn't you be with the truck?'

'I was up there this morning,' he stated evenly. 'They don't need me while they're unloading.'

'What will you take back?' she asked, trying not to think of him going on the return trip.

'Carpets mainly.'

There was a silence while he reached for the list of addresses in his pocket, then they were making their way once again through a maze of alleys. Listening to their echoing footsteps in the silence, Claire couldn't help thinking that either Robin had had a lot of peculiar addresses, or his friend had been rather over-zealous in trying to be helpful.

The building of the door that Greg was knocking on now looked like some kind of tenement block. As there was no answer he pushed his way into a stone passage. There was a flight of chipped iron-railed steps at the end, and grim-faced, he led her up them. A shadowy figure hovered at the top, probably waiting to come down. When they were alongside the robed shape, Greg stopped to say something in the local language. Whether he was asking directions for the room number or not, Claire couldn't say, but she had seen it on the slip of paper and she could see it now, along the corridor on her left about four doors down. She was already moving towards it. To her mind there seemed little point in hanging around when all it needed was a few steps to learn that they had drawn another blank. That's what it would be again undoubtedly. Robin wouldn't be in a place like this, she was convinced of it. So convinced that when she got to the door, finding it off its catch she pushed inside without thinking.

The size of the room was considerable. The few good pieces of furniture were swamped in Eastern bric-à-brac. Persian rugs overlapped each other on the floor and facing the door long windows looked out over crowded rooftops. It was perhaps because the couch was set immediately against the afternoon light that Claire didn't see it until she was but a few feet away. Then she stopped as though the ground had suddenly dropped away in front of her.

Robin was draped on the couch and alongside him was a

slim, lovely creature of perhaps no more than sixteen. The way he was turning his kiss over the full upturned lips made Claire want to sink out of sight in embarrassment. Her one thought was to escape quickly, but her shocked intake of breath was like a cymbal clash on the silence. Robin raised his head, and the girl sprang up and went to lean back coyly against the window frame.

Several seconds elapsed in which the long lithe figure on the couch turned negligently to a sitting position, then the voice that she had almost forgotten was asking in thin annoyance, 'Did nobody ever tell you to knock before coming into a room?'

'I ... I'm sorry ... I just wasn't thinking,' Claire jerked hysterically.

Here she was facing him after a journey across seven countries and he was talking as though she had just popped in from next door. Seeing that there was to be no form of greeting she babbled on foolishly, 'I made the trip out from London in a truck. You wouldn't believe it, but it's taken us about six weeks to get here. The weather's been awful and we got stuck several times and ... well, anyway, this is Greg Millard, the man who brought me.'

She waved her arm back to where Greg was leaning just inside the door. She wasn't sure how much he had seen, but since he had moved up swiftly behind her when she had left his side in the corridor, it was fairly certain that little had escaped his notice.

Robin was going through the motions of lighting up a cigarette with a disinterested frown. The girl over by the window had a vacant look, as though she didn't understand English. Since nobody was saying anything Claire struggled on. 'We've had quite a time finding you. You moved from the address I used to write to, and then I found you'd lost your job with the export firm.'

At her look of questioning concern, Robin blew his cigarette smoke in the air and breathed off-handedly, 'I'm doing all right.'

'I'm glad,' Claire smiled, relieved to hear him saying something at last. She was only just getting over the shock of his changed appearance. The classic good looks were still there in the thick fair hair waving about his ears and the

170

finely shaped features, but there was a fleshiness about the face now, and a slackness about the mouth that dispensed with much of the youth of his twenty-five years.

She took a step forward to say pleasantly, 'It's been such a long time since I heard from you, I was beginning to wonder.' Afraid that he was going to close up again, she said softly, 'It has been a long time, hasn't it, Robin?'

He stretched his long legs indolently and gazing at the tip of his cigarette, twisted his mouth over it to say, 'I thought you'd get the message when I didn't write.'

'Message?' Claire blinked. 'I don't think I understand.'

'You always were a bit dim in some things.'

'I didn't think I was,' Claire said slowly, watching him swing his gaze around the ceiling, 'but if you're trying to say . . .?'

'Me?' Robin's face suddenly took on an innocent look. Shooting a glance across the room, he seemed to be seeing Greg for the first time. He rose to say slowly, swaying on his feet, '*I'm* not saying anything. I don't have to, do I? Not with the line you're trying to hand me.' At Claire's blank stare he went on sneeringly, 'No bloke in his right senses would take his girl back after she's travelled the way you've travelled.'

Claire couldn't believe her ears. When she could find her voice she gasped, 'You mean . . . you want to call everything off, just because I . . .?'

She couldn't finish. It was all too fantastic. She had Robin's ring on her finger, but it meant nothing at all to him. He had bought it simply to try to acquire her along with the rest of his playthings. Being Mike's sister had made her a little different from his usual pastimes, but there was no doubt that he had always intended to discard her, as he did anything he grew tired of, when it suited him.

She knew all this now, and the knowledge didn't touch her. What did hurt was the barefaced way he was trying to turn the tables. Rapidly blinking back the tears, she was hardly aware that Greg had stepped up to her side. She heard him drawl evenly,

'A guy doesn't necessarily have to fall in love with a girl just because he's ridden three thousand miles in a truck with her.'

171

'No, but I bet...'

As Robin slid his glance suggestively from the big figure to Claire, Greg strolled up to within a foot of him to say crisply, 'You bet what?'

For a second baby brown eyes met piercing blue ones, then Robin was dropping back to smile lopsidedly towards Claire, 'I can hardly put it into words just now, can I? Let's just say if anybody should be marrying the kid to save her good name, it's you, not me.'

Much of the colour seemed to drain from Greg's taut features. His voice dropped down to a menacing low note as he pointed out, 'She's got your ring on her finger, Melville, and as far as I know I came here to hand her over to you.'

Robin swayed back on his heels with apparent unconcern. He took his time thrusting his hands into his trouser pockets, then holding Greg's gaze, he said, pulling a smile, 'Sorry, old man. Second-hand goods are not my line.'

Hearing the swift intake of breath, Claire sprang forward and choked, 'Please, Greg! I want to go.' Trembling, she twisted the ring from her finger and placed it down carefully on a table. As she moved across the room, the girl drifted away from her place near the window, and as she draped herself down on the couch again Robin twisted a grin to murmur, 'Close the door when you go out. It's getting a bit draughty in here.'

How Claire got down the stairs and outside, she never clearly remembered. All she knew was that Greg was beside her matching his steps to hers as she stumbled along the alley and up to the main thoroughfare. Back at the hotel he guided her silently through the foyer to the lift and out at the third floor to her room. She waited white-faced until he opened the door and then drifted inside. As she stood around trance-like, Greg thrust his hands into his pockets and said deeply,

'Shall I get you a meal sent up?'

Claire shook her head. 'No, I don't want anything, thank you.'

He stood for some time longer, then, nodding, 'Okay,' turned and went out. As the door clicked behind him Claire slumped down feeling the full force of humiliation and embarrassment wash over her. The cheap things that Robin had implied were bad enough, but to have him throw her at Greg's head like that—That was something that she was never going to be able to live down.

She paced the evening hours away, reliving every awful moment as it had happened. When it was very late she undressed mechanically and climbed into bed. Her heart weighted her down as it went over that sentence of Greg's with her.

'*A guy doesn't necessarily have to fall in love with a girl just because he's ridden three thousand miles in a truck with her.*'

No, he doesn't. She blinked back the hot tears. It was she who had done the loving. From about Frankfurt on, hadn't it been? She could admit it now. Admit that she loved Greg more than anything else in the world. That was what made it so terrible. Before the tears could spill over she turned her face into the pillow and gulped her way through the night.

She was dry-eyed and calm when Greg looked in the next morning. He dropped a glance over the pale features and neat dress and drawled, 'Want any visitors?'

Claire shrugged over the comb she was fiddling with at the dressing table. After a long pause she heard him say some what harshly, 'Well, if you can't do anything else you can eat.'

Minutes after he had gone a tray appeared, and they continued to appear at regular intervals throughout the day. At eight o'clock, washed out and too weary to care any more, Claire crawled into bed and fell fast asleep.

The sun was streaming in at the chiffon-draped windows when Greg stepped in the next morning. He dropped an approving glance over an almost cleared breakfast tray and to where Claire was looking less of a ghost. Big in tailored slacks and smooth sweater, he clipped, 'Got a coat? It's too good a day to hang around indoors.'

Uncomplainingly Claire slipped on the jacket to her coffee-leather suit and picked up her handbag. He held the door wide as she passed through and closed it softly behind him.

It certainly was a beautiful day. Claire couldn't deny that. As they walked down Shah Reza avenue, the sky was the

173

deepest turquoise blue she had ever seen, the mountains overhanging the city near enough to touch in the clearness of the air. Greg couldn't have been more considerate. With his hand on her arm he guided her around most of the beautiful sights of the city. She saw the Rose Garden Palace and the King's Mosque and shady courtyards over-looked by glittering minarets. They had a lunch of local dishes at a native restaurant, and strolled the afternoon hours away in the City Park. The air was warm and embracing everywhere a blaze of flowers.

A Persian spring! Claire's heart swelled at the mere thought of just being here. Swelled and contracted despondently. If only things were different. If only Greg wasn't doing all this because he felt he had to. Because Robin had made him feel obliged to.

It was dusk when they got back to the hotel. Greg said off-handedly when they were going in,

'Put a dress on tonight. We might go down for a dance later.'

Claire pondered around her room nursing a mixture of excitement and misery. A dress...! And a dance with Greg! How could she say no to that? Before she could stop herself she was taking the tissue paper away from a soft pink lace dress with full skirt and low scalloped neckline, and laying it lovingly on the bed.

She enjoyed lingering over her bath and touching herself with a light perfume. There was flimsy nylon underwear to go with the dress and later a touch of soft make-up and pale lipstick. In pastel slim-heeled shoes, and her hair gleaming in her shoulders, she was ashamed of the pleasure she got from her reflection in the mirror. As she picked up a small beaded handbag, Greg stepped in, devastatingly immaculate in smooth lounge suit and brilliant white shirt. The blue gaze seemed to darken slightly as he looked at her. She wanted to go on taking the sight of him in, but wouldn't let herself.

As her gaze trailed over the carpet he said deeply,

'Shall we go?'

There were smart Europeans, beautifully dressed dark-eyed women, and attractive, smiling Persian officers at the tables around the dance floor in the hotel. The orchestra was set back in a red and gold alcove, and the polished floor sent up the dim reflections of couples moving to the music. Claire sipped at the wine that Greg had ordered, watching the dancers. When she was halfway through it he took her hand and led her on to the dance floor. A sharp physical pain of pleasure shot through her as he drew her close. She knew she ought to be firmer with herself, but there was nothing sweeter at this moment than knowing Greg's nearness.

They swayed for a long time under the dim lights before she could bring herself to face up to things as they really were—herself let down and bewildered, with an ex-fiancé on her hands, and Greg trying to make it up to her in some way. She finished the dance leaden and without feeling. Greg's arm was still around her waist. Instead of going back to the table he guided her ahead of him past laughing couples and groups towards open doors and a terrace. Perhaps Claire's apathy gave her an unconscious poise. As she walked she caught the appraising glances from dark-eyed men. Greg drew her suavely forward and out into the night. With the music faint in the distance now, and only the starlight above he said after a long moment, 'You've grown up, Claire.'

Claire lifted her shoulders, her heart rending at the sound of her name on his lips at last. 'I feel ancient!' She tried to force a laugh.

'Because of Melville? You'll get over him.' He was close to her before she knew it. As his arms came up to pull her against him, she heard him say vibrantly, 'I might be able to help a little there.'

His kiss was like the crashing climax to an achingly beautiful piece of music. Music that she had heard playing distantly in her heart ever since that February day in London when she had seen him standing outside his office. She drowned in the ecstasy of it, of the hard mouth on hers, the muscular arms straining her close. His lips trailed jerkily along her throat and through her hair and because she wanted it so much she could almost believe that he wanted it too.

But what was it really? Just the age-old chivalry that some men had in them to do the right thing. The hurt made her push away suddenly and stammer up with tear-starred eyes, 'Please, Greg!'

He stepped away from her. She saw his hands shaking as

175

he reached for a cigarette. He lit one up and pulled on it deeply, then he was blowing the smoke out slowly and evenly into the night.

A long time later when she could find her voice she said brightly, 'I suppose you'll be taking the truck back any day now?'

'Tomorrow.' The dark head nodded. 'I'm leaving for the warehouse tonight to check over everything.'

So soon! She had to catch the gasp back. He turned to say levelly,

'Your seat's there if you want it.'

There he was, trying to be nice again! She pulled in a breath to say firmly, 'No, thanks.'

Greg took a long tug at his cigarette and sneered, 'Are you staying on in the hope that Melville will change his ways or his mind?'

Claire made no reply. As far as she was concerned the Robin Melville episode was over and done with. She just wanted to earn her own fare back to England and then get a job out of London. Far, far away from the Euranian Transport company.

She didn't know that Greg was watching her until he flung his cigarette away and grabbed her roughly by the shoulders to blaze, 'And just what do you think you're going to do here on your own? You crazy little....' As she lifted her gaze to meet his, he clamped his mouth over a long sigh.

'I'll think of something,' she said quietly.

'Sure you will. And land yourself in some kind of spot at the first step,' he snapppd. 'Don't be fooled by the modern buildings and the bright lights around here. You're in Iran, and European girls need constant protection.' As his fingers gripped her she lowered her gaze to the level of his tie and kept it firmly fixed there. Letting out another breath, he dropped his hands and said violently, 'Okay. You don't have to spell it out.' He flicked his head for her to lead the way inside. 'Let's get going. I've got things to do.'

Back upstairs in her room, Claire tried to concentrate on the pictures of a glossy magazine. Her door, like Greg's, was open. She could hear him moving around—packing, probably. She heard the zip of his holdall being pulled. He went downstairs a couple of times and around ten o'clock came to her door. She lifted her head trying to affect unconcern at the sight of him standing there. Something about the way he was looking at her made her heart tumble down a step, then he was striding in to say,

'Your room's booked up to tomorrow night. If you want it any longer, just mention my name at the desk.'

'I won't.' Claire rose from her seat.

Granite-faced, he lifted the flap of his suede coat, and thrusting a hand into his pocket drawled,

'You've still got crew mate's wages to come, so....'

As he pulled out a roll of Iranian notes Claire flung herself away to choke, 'Oh, Greg!'

She heard his resigned intake of breath as he pushed the money back into his pocket and then he was moving towards the door. As he reached it to go out Claire hurried up to blurt, 'Will ... will I see you before you go?'

'You might. If you're up at dawn,' he clipped. 'I have to stop off at the Embassy just down the road from here.' He took hold of the knob of her door and pulled it behind him. When only her face was showing, he said abruptly, 'Goodnight.'

'Good ... goodnight,' Claire stammered through the crack. This couldn't be the end, could it? The door closed with a firm click. She dropped against it trying to close her heart and her ears to the sound of his footsteps striding away.

CHAPTER TWELVE

It was a long night. She got through it dozing fitfully and staring every few minutes at her watch. Terrified of sleeping in, she rose while the stars were still bright in the sky, and washed and dressed. Dawn was just silvering the heavens when she slipped on her coat and turned the knob of her door.

The hotel was like some vast empty palace as she trod

softly along the corridors and down three flights of stairs. A cleaner looked up to give her a curious stare. The night duty staff followed her with their eyes as she walked across the foyer. The dawn air was cold and biting. She looked out and waited, small in the huge portals of the hotel entrance.

The streets were empty. Only the rustle of the breeze and the faint chirpings of the birds disturbed the new day. She knew where the Embassy was. She kept her gaze fixed in that direction, listening to the stillness of the world and her own thudding heart.

And then she heard it. That other sound. A slow steady rumble in the distance. The rumble increased and became the hum of an engine that she knew so well. She saw the big red truck turn the corner and come lumbering its way through the sleeping city.

She waited, faint with anticipation, for it to draw level. The engine throbbed to its very loudest, then she was gazing up to suede-coated shoulders and familiar lean lined features over the wheel. With aching heart she started to lift her hand to wave, but the dark head didn't turn. As the cab passed by, the blue eyes stayed intent on the road ahead. In the dust and grey light of morning the truck rumbled on its way. It grew smaller and smaller in the distance and turned out of sight at the end of the avenue.

Claire watched it disappear through a dazzle of tears. And he hadn't even waved!

But why should he? He had done and said all the right things. Now he was free to go on his way without a backward glance.

Staring straight ahead as she walked back through the foyer, she didn't care who knew that she was fighting a losing battle with the tears. Back in her room it was some time before she could bring herself to start doing some constructive thinking. She had no money and nowhere to go, and she knew no one. She had to get a job to earn enough money to get back to England, but she had no idea where to start, and the thought of leaving the sanctuary of the hotel was abhorrent to her.

Engulfed in a wave of cowardice, she spun out the time, packing her things and lingering over her lunch tray. But towards mid-afternoon she knew she couldn't keep putting off the thoughts of leaving. After a re-cap on her previous thinking she came up with something. There *was* someone she knew in Tehran. Robin. Much as she detested turning to him, he was the one person who could tell her how to go about applying for a job. He might even be able to get her one. He had lived in Tehran for a long time. He must know lots of people.

Relieved at last to be moving, she picked out the aquamarine dress, slim-heeled shoes, and light coat. She would want to look her best in case any interviews came up. Everything packed, she turned and went out, shooting a misty-eyed glance through the open door of the vacant room next to hers. Downstairs she handed in the key and left her case to be collected later, then walked bravely out into the afternoon. There was nothing so terrible about it. People were strolling in the sunshine. The traffic was swinging by and the shops and cafés were crowded and friendly-looking.

After five minutes Claire began to feel quite worldly. When she got to the labyrinth of narrow alleys with their straggle of robed pedestrians she was stepping along as though she had been walking here all her life. She was fairly certain she remembered the route that Greg had taken her on to Robin's, but every now and again she stopped just to make sure she was taking the right turnings.

It was on one of those stops that her crown of jaunty confidence began to slip a little. That man pretending to look at oddments in a dusty doorway. Hadn't she seen him on the last turning? And the one before that? After a moment's consideration she shrugged off the uneasiness, and carried on with a wry smile. Just when she had been telling herself how well she was doing, she had to go and get the jitters. She mustn't let her imagination run away with her, just because Greg had said...

What was that? Hurrying down a lonely alley she could hear her own footsteps echoing out hollowly. But there was something else—the shuffle of subdued ones coming up behind. She swung her glance back. He was there again, the same man that she had seen almost at the start of her walk. He was black-eyed and olive-skinned, and she was sure now that he was following her.

She started to quicken her steps even more. When she

turned a corner she would run on ahead, but each time she looked back he was there. The way he kept his black eyes on her made her skin go cold. She began to take any turning as it showed itself now, losing all sense of direction. What did it matter where she ended up, just so long as she got rid of him.

The alleys were dark, the late afternoon sky just a strip above. The doors she passed were thick with dust and looked as though they hadn't been opened for years. There seemed to be no escape. There *was* no escape!

Giving her panic full rein now, she ran, ran like the wind and faster when she heard the footsteps hanging on behind. Her breath caught in her throat. She knew she couldn't keep up the pace. And if she didn't. . . .

The lighted window up ahead was like a helping hand reaching out to her from the shadows. She fell on the door and knocked frantically on the glass, 'Let me in! *Please* let me in!'

There were one or two people sitting at tables. Nobody paid the slightest attention to her and then a rounded woman, who was counting money at one of the tables, pursed a slack lip under her cigarette and nodded to a man near the door. He rose indolently, flipped the catch and dropped down in his chair again.

Claire rushed in, too terrified to look behind her. As the plump woman seemed to be the only one remotely interested, she stumbled over to her and gulped, 'There was a man. He was following me!' She saw a double chin rise under the cigarette. A pair of deep-set eyes narrowed against the cloud of smoke and the woman was shrugging to say offhandedly in accented English, 'It happens.'

Claire stared out into the alley. It was too dark to see anything now even if he *was* still there. She said quickly, 'May . . . may I sit down?'

The rounded shoulders lifted towards a chair opposite. Claire thought the narrowed smoke-filled eyes had gone back to counting the money, but when she dragged her gaze away from the door she saw them wandering over her thoughtfully.

As Claire's eyes swung round, the pursed lips fell into a slack smile. The woman, her thinning hair dyed to a dusty black, asked, nodding slowly, 'You walk down here. Lost way, mmm?'

'Oh no!' Claire replied, regaining a little of her composure. 'I'm not lost really. I'm on my way to a friend's. He lives round here somewhere.'

The woman watched her for a while and went back to thumbing through the dirty notes piled on the table. She seemed to be concentrating on counting, yet every now and again she lifted the smoke-narrowed gaze to drop it over Claire. After several seconds had elapsed she asked, 'You live in Tehran also?'

'No,' Claire smiled, relieved to be able to pour her story out to someone. 'I've only been here a few days. Now I've got to think about finding a job to earn my fare back to England. That's why I'm going to see Robin.'

The cigarette drooped and swivelled as it was drawn upon. 'You go to work for this Robin?'

'No.' Claire felt to be constantly shaking her head. 'But I've got nowhere to stay and no idea how to go about finding employment. I'm hoping he will give me some advice.'

The woman traced a nicotine-stained finger over the pictures on the notes. 'I say advice. Get good job with much money. Get fare to home quick soon, hah!'

'Well, that's what I want,' Claire smiled eagerly, then shrugged, deflated, 'But I don't suppose it will be that easy.'

She turned her gaze towards the door. It should be all right to go now, although heaven knew how she was going to find her way out of the maze of alleys.

Just as she was about to rise, a pudgy hand came down on her arm. The cigarette was pushed to one side by a wet tongue as the woman said softly, 'You want job. I haf job.'

Claire looked across the table. 'But I'm English. I'm afraid I wouldn't understand a word of . . .'

The plump shoulders curved round into a shrug again. 'I haf girls from the four corners of the earths working in my night club.'

Night club! Claire stared down the long dingy room with its bare tables and garish decor. There was a line of curtained alcoves down one side and at the end, a wide rickety flight of stairs curving round out of sight.

'Well, what would I have to do?' she asked uncertainly. A job was a job, and without a penny to her name in a strange country, she couldn't afford to be too hasty.

'Serve drinks. Be ... how you say? ... pleasantly with the customers ... you soon learn.' The woman was slowly scooping the money up into a thick wad. Claire hesitated. It wasn't the kind of job she had had in mind. The trouble was, if she turned this offer down she might not get anything at all. Even if she could remember where Robin lived now he wasn't forced to be able to help her or even to want to.

The woman's great bulk spread over the table as she leaned forward to murmur, 'With job I gif room. So you work and haf somewhere to stay also in Tehran.'

Claire brightened. Well, that did put a different complexion on things. Living in while she earned her fare would solve a lot of problems. It was really better than she could have hoped for, having a job handed to her out of the blue like this. She ought to be counting her blessings, and yet ... well, she just wished the place was a bit more cheerful.

Still, who could be choosy at a time like this? She needed the money to pay her fare back home, and if it was only for a short time.... Before she could dither any longer Claire said quickly,

'Thank you. I'll take the job. As soon as I find out where to get the necessary permits I'll ...'

The hand came down on her arm again. 'Forms, work permits—who can wait weeks? You want start work tonight, so I fix all myself.'

'Well, if it will save time,' Claire smiled. She thought for a while. 'I'll have to go and collect my case from the hotel, of course, and then I'll ...'

The hand pressed her arm. 'You come see room. Rest before work begin. I send boy for case tomorrow.'

'That's very kind of you,' Claire said gratefully. She wouldn't have liked the idea of struggling with her case down these dark alleys anyway.

The woman rose and shuffled towards the staircase, then wheezed her way up. Round the curve Claire saw a long line of doors set close together like the alcoves downstairs. The woman opened one of the doors and tapped at the sign painted on it pointedly.

'This is your room, remember. You work for me from eight night to five morning. After that ...' the shoulders lifted, 'your time is own.'

Shrinking from the sight of the dowdy bed and cigarette-burned chest of drawers, Claire said hurriedly, 'Do you think I'll be able to earn my fare quite quickly?'

The light in the narrowed eyes sharpened to something that Claire couldn't quite define. As it slid over her the woman tilted her head to shrug, 'I think maybe we be lucky.' She sucked up the wet cigarette from her lip and turned to go, saying 'Come down to Sophie's night club at eight o'clock.'

There was no telling what nationality Sophie was, but she could put her tongue to half a dozen languages to get her orders across. The proprietress stood behind the bar now, a fresh cigarette dangling above a dusty black-beaded dress, ringed fingers handling the money as the girls drifted in for drinks and change.

Among the tube dresses, spindly heels, and high-piled hairdo's, Claire felt miserably out of place in her silk full-skirted dress and shoulder-length hair. But it wasn't just the girls. It was everything about the room. Smoke-filled and full of brooding men, it was getting to be less and less her idea of a job.

She had mastered the different names for the drinks, but that didn't help. Nor did the fact that several times she had been stopped by one or another of the men, who came to mutter something to her in their own tongue. Each time she was aware of Sophie's tilted head, and the man who had let Claire in this afternoon drifted up and said something, then the customer would shrug off back to his table.

Claire was wondering how she would get through the night, when she saw a man looking at her over by the bar. He was middle-aged and bearded and, unlike the average class of customer in the club, quite expensively dressed. He had come in about five minutes ago and all of that time he had spent in close conversation with the proprietress. Now he was nodding and Sophie was slanting that cigarette-jerking smile of hers in Claire's direction.

183

The two of them came over, the proprietress snapping her fingers impatiently for wine to be brought. But not at Claire. She was guided into one of the curtained booths and Sophie was saying smoothly, 'You will entertain our guest, hah? He needs a little company.'

A tray with bottles and glasses on was placed on the table, the thick-set man stepped inside, then the plump bangled arms were reaching up to draw the curtains closed in one quick jerk. Claire sat at the table, not knowing where to turn her gaze. The man had placed himself opposite and was beaming over her and the wine on the tray. He poured himself a huge drink and one for her. Not wishing to offend, she took a tiny sip and then pushed it discreetly to one side. He began to talk after his second drink, smiling and shrugging and apparently caring not at all that Claire didn't understand a word. Occasionally he would try out a few words of English, but his speech was slurred and she wasn't really interested anyway. She didn't care for that face with its gold-toothed smile and black hair frizzing around it. She hoped the man would hurry up and go. Though it was something of an ordeal serving around the tables out there, it was infinitely preferable to this.

The man threw the rest of his drink back, but instead of replenishing his glass he pushed it to one side and smiled across at her. Claire tried to smile back. If he was leaving now, that was the least she could do. She half expected him to rise, but instead he stretched a hand across the table. Her skin prickled cold as the stubby fingers stroked through her hair. When they came trailing down the length of her arm, she jerked up from her seat and pushed blindly through the curtains. She had always felt this job wasn't for her, now she was a hundred per cent certain.

There could be no rushing outside into the alley at this hour, but at least she could lock herself into her room until daylight. After that, all the money in the world for fares home wouldn't keep her here.

Without lifting her eyes she made straight for the flight of stairs. She was almost on to the landing when a heavy creaking made her look round. Her heart started to thud hollowly in her throat. The bearded figure complete with gold-toothed smile was coming up the stairs behind her. The sight made

184

her strength ebb from her limbs. She stumbled up the last remaining stairs and on to her door. Even as her fingers trembled around the knob, a hand with a heavy gold watch on the wrist splayed out on the wood above her and the door was pushed open.

Summoning every ounce of courage, Claire pulled herself up and said icily, 'If you don't mind, this is *my* room and...'

She turned quickly inside and tried to put her weight against the door, but already the thick-set frame was in the gap. Faintly she backed up into the room as the gold-toothed smile advanced. When there was only the wall at the back of her she looked around wildly for something to throw. With a slightly puzzled quiver of a black eyebrow the neat-suited figure pressed in. On a wine-soaked breath she heard the murmured words, 'There was this one favour you can do for me.'

'Like what?'

In the same split second that the voice whipped into the room, the door was kicked back on its hinges and Greg stood there.

Through the mist of a spinning world, Claire saw the blue eyes glinting in pale taut features and then he was saying in razor-edged tones, 'Get your things—we're getting out of here!'

As she whipped up her coat, he flung it over her shoulders and swept her out of the room. His arm around her, she was compelled to run to match his strides, as they took the landing and the stairs. Walking the length of the room below, no one turned a head. Over at the bar, Sophie swivelled the cigarette around her mouth and went on pouring drinks.

The night air to Claire was like breathing new life. She could only take gulps of it at first as she was thrust along the alleys. Then coming up to the lights of the city, the rapid strides slackened and she had time to pause for a moment to inhale deeply and shakily.

She wasn't sure how she came to be in Greg's arms. It seemed that one moment the blue eyes were blazing down at her and the next she was being pulled roughly against him, his words lost in her hair. 'Of all the...'

Claire didn't care about his anger. Only one clear sweet

185

note rang out in her heart. Clinging to the wide chest she glowed,

'You came back!'

'I didn't go anywhere,' he said drily.

'But you did!' She stared up at him. 'I saw you go in the truck this morning.'

'Only as far as the airport,' he drawled. 'I put a call through to London last night to have another driver flown out. As soon as the plane came in I handed over the truck and came back.' The blue eyes were suddenly roaming her face. 'Don't tell me you missed me?'

'Oh, Greg!' Half laughing, half blinking back the tears, she dropped her head on his shoulder. After gazing down at her for a long moment he said briskly, 'Let's go somewhere where we can talk.'

It must have been only a five minutes' walk back to the hotel, but he stopped a taxi and they were there within seconds. He dropped her coat at the desk and led her through to where they had danced last night. The orchestra was strumming and the couples were swaying under the dim lights, but Greg guided her on towards the doors of the terrace.

The world shut out behind them and only the stars above, he drew her close and with a lop-sided grin drawled, 'First things first.'

His kiss was long and lingering and faintly enquiring, but as Claire gave herself completely, the hard lips grew more demanding. After an endless moment he raised his head to say shakily,

'I came back to try and talk some sense into Melville—but maybe I don't have to?' Watching her shake her head, he said searchingly, 'But you wanted to stay on?'

'I thought you were just being nice to me because'—she pulled in a breath to finish, 'because of what, Robin said.'

His eyes narrowed. 'So that was it!' He pulled her against him and dropped his mouth on hers. When she had to push away for air he said smoulderingly, 'You think differently now?'

'Mmhmm!' she smiled dreamily.

Strolling down into the gardens, Claire thought for a moment of where she had been half an hour ago. Suppressing a shiver, she asked, 'How did you know where to find me?'

Greg drew her close to counter vibrantly, 'First of all you tell me how you got yourself into that sordid little mess?'

'I was just walking down the alleys,' she explained, 'and then I noticed a man following me. I didn't worry at first and then it got to be just him and me, so I did worry quite a lot,' she smiled wryly. 'I ran until I got to ... that place. It seemed heaven after the dark outside. Then the woman offered me a job and ... well, I wanted to earn my fare back home. ...'

Greg tossed a look to the sky and let a low breath go through clenched teeth.

Realising her foolishness all too clearly, she blurted, 'Well, what could I do with that loathsome man following me?'

Greg looked grim. 'I'll have a word with Omar. My instructions were to keep an eye on you, not scare you half to death.'

'You mean,' Claire blinked, 'you know him?'

'I expected to be at the airport the best part of the day,' Greg pointed out. 'I wanted someone here to look out for you.'

She nodded dawningly. 'So that's how you knew where to come tonight!'

'The only useful thing your escort did was report back to me when he didn't see you come out of the place,' Greg said. 'I took it from there.'

'How did you know where to find me?' She looked up, 'Inside, I mean.'

The blue eyes glinted metallically. 'I told them I'd tear the place apart if they didn't hand you over.'

She leaned against him. 'It's like a horrible dream!'

'Forget it.' He stroked her hair, adding tightly, 'Though I don't intend to with Omar.'

'Don't blame him.' She turned her face up to him. 'It was me. I just went completely to pieces.'

'In that neighbourhood I'm not surprised.' He gripped her. 'What made you go down there anyway?'

'Well, I remembered Robin lived around there somewhere, and I thought he might help me to get back to England.'

'Melville again!' Greg slanted a look at her. 'And come to

187

think of it, you were pretty keen to get out here.'

'Before you came along to complicate things,' she twinkled. 'When I thought Mike would be driving the truck, I was simply paying a flying visit to say hello.' She traced her fingers over tight lips. 'I realised some time ago that that was all Robin would ever be to me. Someone to say hello and goodbye to.'

Greg's frame slackened. He asked, glinting down at her, '*How* long ago?'

'Oh, as far back as Frankfurt,' she said softly. 'Maybe earlier.' As his lips trailed through her hair she asked jerkily, 'What about you?'

'That first day you walked across the depot yard.'

She looked up at him wide-eyed. 'You mean you actually saw me?'

'I saw you,' he grinned. 'But a guy has to keep his mind on his work.'

Turning her arms around his neck, she asked innocently, 'Did I take yours off it?'

'You've been doing nothing else for the past six weeks.' The blue eyes glowed darkly.

Gazing up into them, Claire twinkled, 'Oh, I don't know! You've had your little sidelines along the way. Very pretty ones.'

'That was just to take my mind off you,' he grinned, and then drawing her close, 'Things are different now.' As she turned her lips up to his, he brushed them with his own, then held her away from him to breathe, 'First thing tomorrow morning we see about making those two rooms upstairs one room upstairs. That's if you don't mind getting married in Tehran?'

'Mind?' Claire gazed up at him with shining eyes.

'We'll honeymoon here for a couple of weeks,' he drawled, 'and then I think there was somewhere else you wanted to see.'

Watching him, she asked glowingly, 'You mean we can go to all those places again? Istanbul and Austria?'

'It's on the way home,' he shrugged, smiling down at her. 'And I'm in no hurry.'

'What about transport?' she asked quickly.

Guiding her back to the terrace, he said drily, 'I can think of better ways to travel with my wife than in a truck.'

On a happy sigh she murmured, 'We will do it again, though, some day, won't we?'

'Some day,' he nodded, dropping an arm about her waist. 'With maybe a couple of small additions to the crew.'

With her head on his shoulder Claire listened to the music drifting out into the night. It was no sweeter than the rhapsody playing in her heart.

HARLEQUIN ROMANCES

If you enjoyed

reading this novel,

watch your newsstands

for new releases

every month.

Have You Missed Any of These
Best Selling
HARLEQUIN ROMANCES?

All books are 50c each. If you cannot obtain these titles at your local book seller, use the handy order coupon below.

Here are other

HARLEQUIN ROMANCES
you will enjoy